WHEN THE SPELL BLOWS

Grimoires of a Middle-aged Witch Book 3

RENEE GEORGE

Barkside of the Moon Press

When The Spell Blows

Grimoires of a Middle-aged Witch Book 3

Publisher: Barkside of the Moon Press

Print ISBN: 978-1-947177-44-4

PRAISE FOR RENEE GEORGE

"Grimoires of a Middle Aged Witch is my new favorite series! I want a gnome named Linda of my own. Trust me. Read the series. You will not regret a single delightfully hilarious and heartwarming moment.

- Robyn Peterman, NYT and USA Today Bestselling Author of Good to the Last Death series.

"I love Renee's books, and recommend any of her series! They catch me right up and keep me turning those pages."

-Yasmine Galenorn, New York Times Bestselling Author

"Renee George has crafted a fantastic start to this magical midlife adventure. Pick up Earth Spells Are Easy today! You won't be disappointed."

-Dakota Cassidy, USA Today Bestselling Author

"I'm loving the Paranormal Women's Fiction genre! Renee George's humor shines when a woman of a certain age sniffs out the bad guy and saves her bestie. Funny, strong female friendships rule!"

-- *Michelle M. Pillow, NYT & USAT Bestselling Author*

For Layla Bea
Welcome to the world

ACKNOWLEDGMENTS

I have to thank the usual people for helping me get to the end of this book.

First, Robyn Peterman, Michele Freeman, and Robbin Clubb, my critique partners, who know just when to kick my ass when I need it! Thank you, Lindas! Once again they have saved my flippin' ass.

Second, to the readers and my Rebels, without you all, what would be the point? I am so happy and blessed to have you guys in my corner!

Forth, but not least, coffee. Thank you strong black coffee, for giving me the energy to bring this baby home. You are the miracle in my life.

Being a forty-something, newly divorced, single mom can have its ups and downs, but discovering that I possess elemental witch magic has turned the downs deadly.

Most days, I'm just trying to raise my kid and not die. So, when a troupe of randy pixies gather in my garden, demanding I protect them, *I'm like, bitch, I can barely protect myself.* On top of that, I have to worry about monster attacks from enemies new and old.

My grimoire keeps talking in riddles. No help there. Linda the Gnome is more surly than usual. Even less help. Thank heavens for my hottie druid boyfriend, who has my back, front, and side, and a fat cat named Bob, who calms me better than a prescription mood stabilizer.

Tru-craft has been nature's midlife gift that keeps on trying to kill me.

Earth nearly turned me to dust.

Fire almost extinguished my flame.

If I don't master this new element, Air is going to blow me into the next life.

Literally.

CHAPTER 1

I BLINKED SWEAT FROM MY EYES, CURSING AS I RAN across my boyfriend's backyard like I had a tornado chasing my ass. Mainly because a tornado was chasing my ass.

"Knock it down," Keir Quinn, my soon-to-be-ex-boyfriend, yelled unhelpfully.

"If I could knock it down, I wouldn't be running away," I shouted back. Luckily, the tornado was small, only about six feet high, but I'd been tossed around like those flying cows in the movie *Twister* enough to know that I didn't want to take another hit. "Do something!"

Keir ran in my direction and fell in step next to me. "You created it," he said. "Only you can dismantle it."

Again, not helpful. Two weeks earlier, while telling my son about tru-craft and what it meant for him and our family, I'd accidentally activated aero-craft, aka air magic, by blowing on my family's grimoire, and I'd been trying to figure it out ever since. It turned out that learning magic had two basic outcomes, you either became one with the element, or it killed you. I was partial to living, so finding balance with the element was the only option I was willing to entertain.

Keir Quinn, my soul's companion who had been born two hours before me, had told me about tru-craft. He'd also told me that he'd felt my birth the instant I drew air. He'd been born into a druidic family, and he'd devoted most of his adult years to preparing himself to walk life's path with me. His words, not mine. We'd become intimate after I'd taken on a fire god name Volres and smote his ass, and our magical bond had strengthened as a result.

"Just collapse it," Keir told me as if I hadn't been trying to collapse the damn thing for fifteen minutes.

I sent up a prayer of gratitude for my sister Rose, whose cross-fit training had given me some stamina, and another prayer of thanks for my terra-craft for making me hard to kill, thanks to a protec-tion spell that had made my skin as tough as ironbark.

"Just concentrate, Iris," he instructed. "You have the power."

"I'm not She-Ra, princess of power. I'm just a girl, running from a tornado, asking it to stop!" I came to a halt, turned around and flung my hands up. "Stop!" I yelled at the treacherous swirling wind. "Just sto—"

The tornado picked me up off the ground and threw me into Keir's waterfall. "Son of a bitch," I sputtered. The wet, icy chill made my ovaries shrink. "Not cool, dude."

Keir high-stepped his way across the small pool of water and helped me to my feet. The corner of his mouth lifted in a half-smile.

"I will cut you," I told him.

"Sorry," he said. "You're really cute right now."

I quirked a brow at him. "You like the drowned rat look?"

"On you? Yes." He chuckled, then twirled his finger. "We better get this wrapped up if we want to make Michael's game tonight."

It was early afternoon, and the football game didn't start until seven. It was Michael's first game of the season, and since it was his senior year, it was his last first game. This year would be a series of last firsts, and it made my heart squeeze. My kid was nearly grown, and in less than a year, he'd be off to college.

My ex-husband Evan Callahan and his partner Adam Hauser had recently moved to St. Louis. Adam, who used to be Michael's coach, had taken a job at a private high school. The happy couple was still settling into their new house, so Evan had dropped the bomb earlier in the week that he wasn't going to be able to make it down for Michael's game. Michael didn't say a thing, but I could tell it hurt that his dad wouldn't be there. Evan had never missed a game before.

Which meant I couldn't miss it. Come hell or high wind, I would be there tonight to cheer him and the team on.

I looked at Keir. "I'm open to suggestions."

Keir shrugged. "Try to stay out of the water."

"Har har." I thought about how funny it would be if Keir was the one getting dunked by the tornado.

That's when the base of the cone shifted its target away from me and barreled itself into the smirking druid.

It proceeded to knock him down, and he fell into the water with a great splash.

The look of pure shock and disbelief as he sputtered to the surface tickled me to my core, so I laughed. And laughed and laughed.

Until the foul wind, once again, turned on me.

"Plug your nose," Keir shouted.

I screamed as he lunged at me and dragged us both under the water. I held my breath, eyes wide and fighting the urge to struggle.

Keir blinked at me, then pointed up.

The tornado circled above us, looking for a target. Its deadly swirls slowed, and it started to shrink.

The water around us began to swirl. Bubbles trickled out my nose as my eyes widened. The tornado had breached the surface and was creating a whirlpool.

I damn near drowned when I tried to scream as the watery vortex of death yanked me from Keir's grasp and threw me out of the pool and onto the grass.

Coughing and wheezing, I rolled onto my hands and knees. The freaking tornado spanked my ass, knocking me face down into a puddle.

"Enough!" I ordered the ill-wind.

The ill wind ignored me and smacked me in the shoulder, sending me spinning.

"Iris!" Keir shouted. "Look out!"

I loved the fact—not—that he thought I wasn't doing my very best to avoid getting pummeled. "Trying to," I yelled as I spat out a clump of grass, got to my feet, and took off in a sprint with the tornado on my heels. "This thing won't stop."

"You have to relax," he instructed.

"When should I relax? When I'm getting knocked to the ground? Or when I'm getting tossed like a rag doll?" I was huffing and puffing now. I couldn't believe I'd conjured my own demise. "This thing isn't going to stop until it kills me."

"Not on my watch," Keir said. His scary black eyes peered at me as he used superhuman speed to swoop me off my feet to outrace the swirling death.

Don't get me wrong. Keir was fast. Really fast. Unfortunately, the tornado was faster.

"Oh, shit," he growled out as we both went flying.

I grunted as Keir turned us so that I landed on top of him. Partially transformed into a pooka, his hips were bonier, so it wasn't a soft touchdown. Still better than having him land on top of me.

He groaned. "This isn't how I thought I would die," he said.

"Preaching to the choir," I told him. The tornado had circled around for another run at me. "Son of a bitch." I wrapped my arms around Keir, buried my face into his chest, and braced for the next blow...

...that never came.

There was a sharp "*I-eeeeeee-yaaaa*," followed by a "*Scheisse*!"

I opened my eyes in time to see Linda the Gnome shoot up from the ground and through the tornado's eye. "Fire," she demanded. "Hit it with heat, *Kleinkind*!"

I'd been around Linda long enough to know that she usually knew what she was talking about, so I rolled off Keir and got up on one knee. Since my encounter with the fire creature Volres, I'd had the ability to call fire whenever I wanted without casting a spell. I could pull the flames from my blood at a whim. It had frightened me at first, but now I embraced the magic as if I were Johnny Storm, the Human Torch, going up against Doctor Doom.

I held my hands out at the oncoming cyclone and yelled, "Flame on!" Fire flowed from my palms and off my fingers, creating a massive wave of heat that burned so bright it sucked the oxygen from the air.

The tornado evaporated.

I shook the flames creeping up my arms and was thankful my shirt was wet, or I'd have turned the sleeves to ash. "Ta-dah," I said with zero enthusiasm. I glanced over at Linda.

The stern gnome had her arms crossed over her chest. "Stupid, *Kleinkind*," she muttered. "Whose bright idea was it to make *der Tornado*?"

Keir's eyes had reverted to their normal gray color. "I didn't exactly ask her to—"

I raised a brow at him. "Are you really going to throw me under the bus?"

Keir grinned at me. "It was one hundred percent my fault."

Linda rewarded his honesty by pelting him in the head with a rock.

"Ow." He rubbed his forehead. "How did you know the heat would work?"

"Oh, I know," I said. "Because fire eats air, right?" A rock nailed me above my left eye. I gave the sadistic gnome a dirty look. "That freaking hurts, Linda."

"That's how you know it's working." She pointed her tiny, pudgy finger at me. "You shouldn't play with things until you understand them." She frowned. "*Der Tornado* is made when cold air collides with warm air, but if you warm the cold air up, warm air and warm air...." She flattened her palms. "Poof."

"No tornado," I said.

"*Ja*." She nodded. "*Korrekt*."

"Thank you for your timely arrival," Keir said. "It was getting pretty dire."

I snapped him a look of betrayal but then softened my expression. He wasn't wrong. I just hated admitting that I'd almost killed us with my terrible grasp of aero-craft.

"Iris needs to be rescued a lot. I am used to it." She tapped her winklepickers on the grass. "I think you should study wind patterns, cyclones, hurricanes, and how they are created before you try any more air magic. Next time, you might take out a house. Or the town."

That's why I'd decided to practice at the top of the mountain. "Did you just show up to nag me?" I asked.

"I showed up to save your life." She raised her hands, palms up. "I thought we established that already."

Keir chuckled.

"Are you sure you want to go there?" I asked him, my brow arched high.

He shook his head, but he couldn't quite get rid of his smirk.

Linda tsked. "If you would only consult your grimoire, it will help guide you in your aero-craft."

She meant its cryptic, scary messages in the form of bad, rhyming poetry. On top of that, the damn thing kept changing me in frightening ways that were going to get me killed. "Nope," I told her. "Aero-craft is the last element I'm dealing with. I'm not touching that grimoire ever again."

After the grimoire had activated air magic in me, I'd wrapped the leather-bound albatross in a newspaper, tied it up with twine, and used my earth magic to turn the bindings to steel before tossing it as far into the attic crawlspace as I could. Good riddance. As far as I was concerned, I was done with all the tru-craft elements trapping me in dangerous situations, not only putting myself in harm's way but also my family. Not touching it, looking at it, or breathing in its direction was the only way I could see to prevent any more tru-craft trouble. Still, I'd spent a couple weeks playing with aero-craft, and while I hadn't quite mastered it, like at all, nothing horrible had happened. Maybe my bad luck was over.

"That is a mistake, *Kleinkind*," she cautioned. "Your grim is your guide."

Hah! More like the bane of my existence. However, I wasn't going to get sucked into this argument again. The gnome might throw more rocks to make her points. "Thank you, Linda, for your intervention." I pressed my hands together and gave the gnome a bow. "I appreciate the assist, but I think I've got it from here."

She scoffed. "I've seen nothing so far that gives me confidence that you've got anything."

"You can go home," I told her. "Don't you have a bench to stare at?" Linda, when in her stone form, liked to position herself facing the garden bench. It used to creep me out. Still did a little bit, if I was being honest.

"Can't go home," she said. "My home is gone."

"What?" I couldn't keep the alarm out of my voice as my mind went to all the dark places. "Did something happen to my house?"

"Your home is fine. It's mine that's been demolished."

"The garden?"

Linda nodded. "It's too horrible, Iris."

Oh, God. She used my given name. That was never a good sign. "Pestilence?"

"Of a magical variety," she said.

I gasped. "Supernatural aphids? Is that a thing?"

Linda harrumphed. "Not aphids."

"You're killing me, Smalls," I told her. "Just tell me what we're dealing with, so we can fix it."

"There is no fixing this, stupid *Kleinkind*," she snapped. "Once they infest your garden, there is no getting rid of them."

A horrifying thought jumped into my head. "Snakes?" I resisted the urge to crawl up Keir to get off the ground. "Please tell me it's not paranormal snakes."

"Not snakes," Linda said blandly.

"Spiders?" Keir asked.

"Don't even joke about that." I rubbed my arms to get rid of the goosebumps. "I would relocate to the top of Mount Everest if magical spiders moved in."

"Stop guessing," Linda ordered.

"Then spit it out already." I was wet, windblown, exhausted, and in no mood for whatever Linda was pussyfooting around.

"*Heimchen*," she said without any fanfare.

Keir made a grunt of surprise.

"I don't understand," I said.

"Pixies," Linda explained. "A troupe of them."

"Wow." Keir winced. "A whole troupe?"

Linda nodded. "They have taken over the entire garden."

"And why is this bad?" Pixies didn't sound dangerous. "Aren't they just tiny little fairies with wings?"

"There are hundreds of them. All violent." Linda gave me a piteous stare. "So, if you like your blood on the inside, I wouldn't call them that to their faces."

"They aren't generally a warring species," Keir disagreed. "But they do hate being compared to fairies. They're small, but the two races have little else in common."

"Got it. Pixies are assholes, not fairies." I rubbed my lower lip nervously. "So, why do you think they're here, and how do we get rid of them?"

"You're the reason they are here, *Kleinkind*," Linda

accused. "And the only way to get rid of them is to destroy them down to the last one."

"Whoa." The idea of destroying a pack of tiny pixies, however brutal they might be, seemed extreme and a bit too much like genocide. We needed a less mass-murder-y plan. I shook my head. "Harsh, Linda. Way harsh. What's option number two?"

CHAPTER 2

Fair Konig, the leader of the pixies, had requested an audience with me. Alone. He swore on his first-born son that I would be safe. Keir, who had watched his own father, a druid bard, negotiate terms with many species during his childhood, had told me that the pixie wouldn't go back on his word. Still, it had agitated him that he couldn't come with me.

I swatted at a dozen pixies that swarmed me as I exited the kitchen door to the garden.

"Stay back," I rasped. "Or I will torch the lot of you." I waved a flaming finger around until they all flew to a safe distance.

Pixies, it turned out, were six inches of pure chaos. They wore leaves and flower petals in strategic positions on their bodies as clothing. With razor-sharp wings, skin a deep green like the color of blue-grass, glossy black hair, and tempers that rivaled

Linda's, I was beginning to think they were just as dangerous as the gnome had suggested.

The pixies' chattering sounded like a series of deranged clicks and squeaks as they escorted me to the bench in my garden. There, sitting on top of the backrest, was a pixie with hair that was tied back in a ponytail with a flower stem. He had a thick black beard and what appeared to be a permanent scowl.

I stopped just short of the bench, crossed my arms over my chest—mostly to hide my shaking hands—and waited for the tiny bastard to speak. This was his show, after all.

We stared at each other for a few minutes. I was about to say screw it and walk away when he finally said, "So, you're Iris Everlee." His accent was Germanic, much like Linda's. It made me wonder if her grudge or vendetta against the troupe was even more personal than them taking over her garden.

Was there a history between her and the pixie leader that she hadn't told me about?

"I am," I told him. "Why are you here?"

"Because you are the one responsible for our awakening." He held up his hands as if surrendering. "So now you and your tribe must act as our *der Beschützer*."

"Your what?"

"Our protector."

I shook my head. "Nope. You're barking up the wrong witch."

"Your power carried the summoned *die Fruchtbarkeitsriten*." He gestured around the garden. "Now, my troupe and I are at the mercy *auf Staub Jäger*. This will be our refuge until it is completed."

A series of clicks and squeaks from his family grew louder as they zipped around my late-blooming flowers I grew near the fence, the zinnias and lilies.

I cleared my throat to quiet them. "No offense to you and your people, but there's a gnome who has already claimed this garden. And she isn't fond of sharing."

He narrowed his dark, beady eyes at me. "Then she'll have to leave. You have ignited our quickening with your power before we could make arrangements for our protection."

"It's not my fault." But I felt a twinge of guilt. My aero-craft had been chaotic and unpredictable. Maybe whatever was happening to the pixies was my doing, even if it had been inadvertently. "But even if I did trigger your fruit bats to write, poor planning on your part doesn't constitute an emergency on mine," I said, using a quote my mother liked to use when any of us kids would come to her in a panic because we'd left an important school assignment to the last minute.

Fair Konig's frown deepened. "You have incited the *die Fruchtbarkeitsrite* eight-hundred years early. If not for you, we would have made other plans. Now, you must protect us until the rite is complete."

RENEE GEORGE

Well, shit. "Uhm, I can barely protect myself."
Not altogether true, but I didn't have space in my life
to add hundreds of pixies. "You'll have to fruit-bite
somewhere else, pal."

Before he could counter, we were interrupted by
unnatural squeals and shrieks of fear. I whipped
around in time to see a giant orange and white tabby
with no tail jumping into the air, trying really hard to
catch pixies between his paws.

"Bob," I scolded my familiar as he managed to
grab ahold of one. "Put that pixie down."

"Annibish!" Fair Konig shrieked. His wings jutted
out from his back, and he flew into the air, his movements darting like that of a hummingbird. He zipped
back and forth, slashing at Bob with a tiny sword.

Bob, who thought it was a game, let go of his
captive, flipped onto his back, and started swatting at
the angry pixie every time he buzzed by.

"Stop," I demanded as Fair Konig drew first blood
by nicking Bob's ear. I stepped in and grabbed Bob,
hauling his fat butt into my arms to shield him from
the onslaught of miniature psychos and took a few
cuts to my arms in the process. "Don't hurt him."

Bob, for all his flaws—and there weren't many—
was my cuddle monkey. Having him around was like
taking Xanax with an edible. In other words, he was
Zen personified, and I'd be damned if I was going to
let any creature damage my Zen.

Fair Konig's ponytail was frayed, and loose hair

floated out from his head. "I told you to come alone, Iris Everlee." He pointed his sword at me. "You've broken our agreement by bringing this imp along."

"I did come alone." This dude was giving me a serious case of the ass. "Bob came after. Agreement still intact."

The crotchety pixie looked disappointed as he shook his head. "It might be to the letter, but it violates the spirit."

I pursed my lips and shook my head. "Does not."

He zipped into the air until he reached my eye level. The wind from his beating wings blew on my face. "Does so," he angrily declared. "Does so, does so, does so!"

Wow. My first thought was that Fair Konig was having a meltdown to rival any toddler. My second thought, am I really arguing with a six-inch dude? And is this my life now? My need to flick him like a bug was intense. I tamped back the urge, seeing as how that probably wouldn't end well for either of us.

Instead, I held Bob tight and walked past the pixie leader, ignoring his cries of outrage.

When I got to the kitchen door, I told him, "When you're ready to talk to me like an adult, we'll try this again. Until then, you can have your temper tantrum without me."

I hurried inside, then slammed the door behind me. I exhaled noisily as I sagged against the door. "What a shitshow."

"Now can we eliminate them," Linda said, giving me I-told-you-so eyes.

"Definitely not." I touched the scratches Fair Konig had left on my arm and shivered. "They weren't trying to kill me."

"Those aren't love bites." Keir frowned. "The pixies have broken the terms of their agreement."

"*Pish*." I waved off his concern. "They're just a little excitable. A lot like children, actually," I mused. "I've put Fair Konig into a timeout."

"You've done what?" Linda sputtered. Then she began to cackle like a maniacal villain. "I can't wait to tell my kin. It will be most entertaining."

"I'm glad you're amused." I rolled my eyes. "What are we going to do about these winged nuisances?"

"I've already offered the solution," Linda said.

I shook my head. "We're not killing them."

Linda spat. "*Luftdämonen.*" When I gave her a confused stare, she added, "Air demons. They bring nothing but trouble. It is too dangerous to allow them to stay."

"That seems about right." I was more convinced than ever that she wasn't telling me everything about her past with the pixies. "Still. Killing them wrong."

"When you realize I am right about them, I expect a full and complete apology," Linda declared.

"This is a little far from where pixies usually live," Keir said. "Did they tell you why they came?"

"They said they came for me." I sighed. "Something about barking fruit baskets."

"That doesn't sound right," Keir said.

"They said I had to protect them against some stabbers who liked Jagermeister."

"*Jager?*" Keir asked, and it sounded like the way Fair Konig had said it.

"Sounds more right," I answered. "And a lot less like an alcoholic beverage. What does it mean?"

Keir frowned. "Hunter."

"So, does the hunter part give you any hint about what the fruit basket rites are about?" I set Bob on the counter near the gnome. It seemed like she needed his good juju more than I did. "He said I had to protect him and the other pixies. What do you think he meant?"

Keir was a professor of supernatural and all things occult. In other words, he was an expert, so I fully expected him to know.

He shrugged. "I'm going to need more than a fruit basket."

So much for being an expert.

The more we talked about fruit, the more I wanted some. I grabbed a clementine from a bowl on the counter near the sink as I tried to remember how Fair Konig had said the foreign word. "It sounded a lot like fruit bark eye or ite. Yeah, like rite. Rite of Fruit-bark-ite." My voice had gone up an octave with my excitement.

Keir's brow dipped. "I'm going to have to do more research."

"Or I can ask the little dude after his chill pill kicks in."

"Oh, for zee love of sanity," Linda said before she let out a string of curses. "It's pronounced *Fruchtbarkeitsriten.*"

I snapped my fingers. "Yes, that's it!"

Keir groaned.

"I'm missing something, aren't I?"

Keir nodded. "You're not going to like it."

"I already don't like it."

"It's worse than you think," he said.

Linda composed herself and said, "It shouldn't be possible, but the flying demons are planning to procreate all over my garden."

"They're what?"

"I am speaking English, *Kleinkind*. Please follow along." She produced a rock and beaned me with it. "It is their fertility rites."

I glared at her. "Not funny, Linda. Unlike some people, I'm not made of stone. You're going to give me a concussion one day."

She pished at me. "Your head is tougher than you think."

Keir's expression was serious and sober. "*Staub jager*," he said. "Dust hunters."

"Dust hunters?" The way he said it made me shiver. "Give it to me straight," I told him. "I can take it. How bad is this?"

"Bad," he repeated. "If your magic started the pixies' mating cycle, they'll definitely need protection until it's over."

"What do they normally do to stay safe?"

Keir's mouth settled into a thin line. "They usually negotiate for safety from other groups strong enough to fend off creatures who would hunt them."

Oh, man. I had done this. I was responsible. This wasn't poor planning on their side. It was a wrecking ball on mine. "They said I awakened them eight hundred years early."

Keir nodded. "That would leave them with very few options."

I put my hand on Bob's belly to alleviate some of my trepidation. "How could my magic have really done this?"

"You've been playing with aero-craft without any guidance," Linda reminded me sharply. "You won't even consult your grimoire."

The grimoire liked to throw me into the deep end and tell me to sink or swim. That wasn't the kind of lesson I wanted. "It won't help me," I protested.

"It might have helped the pixies," she scolded. "Now their fertility has been awakened, and they are ready to mate."

"Great, hundreds of tiny horny creatures. How am I supposed to protect them? And from what? Themselves? Are they like praying mantises, biting off the heads of the males after sex? Or male bees, where their balls explode after doing the deed?"

Keir looked appalled. "Nothing like that. But there will be hunters searching for them now."

I waited for a moment for him to add more information, and when he didn't, I rolled my hand at him. "Why?"

"Pixie dust."

Again, he didn't elaborate. I narrowed my gaze at him. "I feel like you're stalling."

His gray eyes met mine. "Because I am."

"You're not usually this cagey," I stated. "Just rip the bandage off. Why is pixie dust bad?"

"Because it's concentrated magic." He held up his hands. "You know how there's all this stem cell research going on right now, and how doctors can take a stem cell that is a blank slate and turn it into a bone cell, or cartilage cells, or whatever?"

"I'm familiar with it. Are you trying to tell me that pixie dust is the magical equivalent to a stem cell?"

He nodded.

"So, anyone who had the know-how could take pixie dust and turn it into some other kind of magic."

Linda said, "Now, can't you see why we should exterminate them before zee screwing and dusting and the fighting and death that will surely follow."

I stared at the unusually blood-thirsty gnome.

"They just want to make babies, Linda. Surely, you don't hate babies."

She scoffed. "This isn't going to end well. You have other people in your life to think about. The rite takes place over three days, and it will act as a beacon for *sidhe* and other magical creatures. They will flock to your door in search of the dust."

Keir scratched his head and stared out the kitchen window. Pixies were doing constant flybys, creating a distraction. "It's as bad as it sounds," he told me.

I let out a noisy breath. "We have to figure something out. Maybe we can arrange for them to go somewhere else."

"They've already settled in this garden," Keir said. "They won't want to leave it until their offspring are born."

Panic welled inside me. "I'm going to be dealing with pixies for nine months?"

"Two days after the rites," Keir said. "But the dust will put off a magical signal until then."

Linda's eyes narrowed as she balled her fists at her sides. "A pixie *Fruchtbarkeitsriten* is a dangerous disaster in the making."

I'd seen Linda look angry, irritated, disappointed, relieved, and amused, but right then, she wore an expression I'd never seen on her cherubic bearded face. Fear. Linda was afraid.

Which meant it was much, much worse than I thought.

Crap on crackers. My son didn't have any powers yet. Although, Volres, the self-proclaimed fire god, had told me that Michael did possess tru-craft and would eventually spark. Would his DNA make him susceptible to the pixie dust, and even if he wasn't, I couldn't have him here if I was going to have to fight off supernatural dust collectors for the next three or four days? "Should I make Michael leave?"

"It couldn't hurt," Keir said. "At least until we see who or what shows up."

My stomach churned. "And you're sure this is going to happen? That the pixies are going to create this crazy hunt for magical stem cells?"

"Honestly, I'm not sure. I'm not a pixie expert, but from my studies, yes. There's no avoiding it, historically speaking." He put his arms around me, and I sagged against him.

"Great." The news didn't comfort me. I turned my head and glanced out the window. Fair Konig and his angry troupe were hovering just beyond the glass pane. I heaved a sigh. "I guess I better finish my friendly chat with the pests."

Keir kissed the top of my head. "I'm going with you this time. Let's see if we can persuade them to move to higher ground."

I looked up at him. "Your place."

He nodded. "I may not be a bard like my father

was, but I'm a decent mediator." Keir's dad was someone who could weave poems to influence the outcome of a conflict. Even without the bard magic, I trusted Keir. He'd mediated the situation between the fire giants and me when they'd wanted to sacrifice me to their god. Surely, he could handle a bunch of miniature amorous jerks. Unless.... "You don't think they want to sacrifice me to the fertility gods, do you?"

Keir made a face, his shoulders lifting slightly. "Probably not."

I took a step back from him. "Probably?"

He chuckled. "They would have to get through me to get to you, and that's not happening."

I glared out the window at the hovering pixies. Maybe Linda was right. Perhaps, I'd spoken too hastily earlier when she'd offered one simple solution. "Can we put slaughtering them back on the table?"

"Yes," Linda said quickly.

"No," Keir countered. "Your first instinct was right. I hope."

If he didn't stop qualifying all his responses, I was going to smack him. "I love you, but you're trying my nerves."

The corner of his mouth quirked up into a smile.

"Nuh-uh." I shook my head. "Wipe that pleased look from your face." It wasn't the first time I'd told him I loved him, but he perked up every time I said it. Even so, now wasn't the time for complacency. "This is bad."

"Potentially," he interjected.

He was asking to be slapped. "Let's fix this before potential becomes a certainty."

Keir nodded. "I'm on board."

I glanced at Linda to see where her head was at, and it was fixed and frozen in a stony expression of rage.

Why had she turned to stone? "Linda?"

The kitchen door swung open, and my sister Marigold hurried inside and slammed the door behind her. Her long, black hair was messy, and her tan skin was flushed. She held her hairpin in her right hand like a weapon.

"What in the flipping hell are those things?" She pointed out the window at the scattering pixies. "They attacked me!"

I grimaced. "Horny pixies," I said honestly.

My sister Marigold knew about the paranormal world. I'd told her after she'd confided in me that she had taken a DNA test and found out she had a biological half-sister who was ten years younger than her. So, I'd given her a confession for a confession, and I told her I was a witch. It had taken her a minute when I told her about my true nature, but she'd come around to support me completely. We'd both agreed to tell the rest of the family our secrets. Marigold kept her end of the bargain, telling our siblings and dad about the half-sister. They'd all been supportive, as I knew they would be. However, I was having a difficult time bringing myself to fulfill my end of the bargain.

Her eyes widened as more pixies frantically buzzed by the window. "You're living the most ridiculous life."

I smirked. "Tell me about it."

"Hey, Keir," Marigold said to my guy before turning back to me. "I guess I should've called first."

I gave her a quick hug. "You never have to call first." Of course, if paranormal dust collectors started hunting in my backyard, calling first might be a good idea. "Well, maybe for the next week or so. You know, just in case."

"In case of what?" She glanced outside to the garden. "Are they dangerous?"

"According to Linda," I replied, not wanting to get into too much detail.

Marigold studied the stone gnome. She poked her cheek. "She really talks?"

"Yep," I said. "And if you keep touching her like that, she's going to make me pay for it."

Marigold withdrew her hand. "Sorry. I still can't believe she's real."

"She is, but she can't animate in front of humans."

"You mean humans of the muggle variety," Marigold said, using the Harry Potter term for the non-magical.

"Yep." I gave her an apologetic smile. "Sorry."

She looked disappointed. "It's fine."

"What's up?" I adored my sister. She was my best friend and the only person in my family who knew everything about me. So, I didn't want to be rude, but I had a bit of a pest problem now. If what she wanted could wait, then it needed to wait.

"It's Dad," Marigold said.

"Is he okay?" I couldn't keep the alarm out of my voice. Dad had been forgetting things lately. His short-term memory was slipping. All of us kids had been taking turns checking on Dad and keeping him company where we could. He lived alone in our childhood home, and I worried about him all the time.

"He took a fall early this morning." Marigold put her hand on my shoulder as Keir picked up Bob and put him in my arms. "He's okay, but Rowan said he tried to call you several times earlier. I thought you were just ignoring our brother until I called and went straight to voicemail." She peered at me. "I know you'd never screen my calls."

"Never," I agreed.

She smiled. "That's when I decided to chance coming over. I thought you might be out in your garden practicing your hoodoo."

Marigold wasn't far off from the truth. I'd been at Keir's place all morning, practicing my aero-craft. He didn't have any cell phone reception. "Is he in the hospital?"

"Not anymore. His x-ray didn't show any broken bones, but his knee is banged up." She shook her head. "Dad was on the floor for a couple of hours. We're going to have to have a family meeting," she said.

"When?" I asked.

"Tomorrow afternoon. We'll all be at Michael's game tonight. Even Dad."

"But he's hurt."

"Dad said it would take more than a bruised knee and a bruised ego to keep him away from watching his oldest grandson do his thing."

That sounded exactly like our father. "Does he need a ride?"

"Rose is going to bring him," she assured me. "She's been hanging out with Dad since he got back from the hospital.

I tamped down the rising guilt. "I'm sorry I wasn't available." I stroked Bob's fur to calm myself.

"You look like you've had your hands full," Marigold said.

Keir gave me a meaningful look, then glanced out the window.

"After I deal with the pixies," I added.

"I'll see you tonight," Marigold said. "You only have a few hours before the game to settle whatever this is." She waved toward the garden. "Get your freaky-deeky shit under control, sis."

I chuckled. "I'm going to give it my best shot."

RENEE GEORGE

Marigold leaned in and kissed my cheek. "Love your guts."

Bob made me feel calm, but I still had to force a smile. "Love your guts back."

Marigold gave Keir a quick hug and a cheek peck. "When's Lu getting back?"

Lu was a badass warrior druidess, and she was also Keir's younger sister. She'd been called back to the Iron Grove, the ruling body of the North American druids, for a mission.

"I'm not sure," Keir replied. "Lu hasn't been able to tell me much."

I knew it bothered him that the Iron Grove hadn't trusted him enough to let him in on the mission. Keir told me that the Grove enforced laws for druid-kind and tru-craft witches since before the age of Merlin. That's when I'd found out Keir and Luanne's grandmother was the Archdruid, leader of the druid conclave. It had to bother him that his blood relative was keeping things from him, but if he took it personally, he never let it show.

"And Zev?" Marigold asked with nonchalance. "Is he, uhm, coming back? I mean to help you since you have all this going on." She gestured to the window.

Zev, the ifrit who had helped me tame the flames of my fire element, had been sent by the Grove to test my magic. He'd left Southill Village after my aero-craft sparked. I wasn't sure if it had been related to Luanne's departure or if he just had somewhere else to be. However, Zev had been flirtatious with Marigold while he'd been in town. I knew my sister had hoped more would develop between them, and she'd been disappointed when he'd left without saying goodbye.

"Zev does Zev." Keir shrugged. "Who can say with him?"

Marigold's expression was pinched, but she affected cheerfulness as she dipped down and kissed the gnome on the forehead. "Nice seeing you again, Linda. It's always a pleasure." She giggled. "Man, she looks really pissed."

"I'm sure she is," I said. Cripes, I was so paying for this.

My sister turned to the backyard door, then stopped. She pointed to the living room. "I'll just go out the front."

I made a shooing motion with my hand in that direction. "Good idea."

After she left, Linda animated, glared at me, then threw a rock at my head. I ducked, and it fractured the windowpane.

I looked at the chipped spot in the glass. "Damn it, Linda. I'm going to have to get that replaced now."

She blushed. "Tell your sister not to put her filthy mouth on me," she said sheepishly. "I'm sorry about the glass."

A *tap, tap, tap-tap* drew our attention. The pixies, a few dozen at a time, were flying into the window, widening the crack. I hugged Bob tighter, but not even his ju-ju could settle my stomach. The crackling sound as the crevice broadened made my chest squeeze. I glanced from Linda to Keir, and they both looked equally horrified.

My freaky-deeky shit was about to hit the fan.

CHAPTER 3

THE SINGLE-PANE GLASS BROKE INTO SHARDS, THE fractured pieces falling onto my counter and into the sink.

"Son of a bitch," I swore, jumping back as the troupe of pixies flew into my kitchen.

"Get out!" Linda screamed. "Out! Out!"

They didn't listen to her as they easily dodged all the rocks she threw at them.

"Linda, stop," I said. "You're going to break something else."

That shut her down temporarily.

"I will not be in the same space as that creature," Fair Konig declared, pointing a finger at Bob. "Get that horrible beast out of here."

His words deeply offended me. Bob, who was in my arms happily swatting at any pixie that got too close, appeared unbothered.

"You get out," I said. "This is Bob's home. This is my home, and if you don't cool your jets, I'll make you and your people go find another place to get jiggy with it."

The angry pixie blanched. "You are the reason my troupe and I are here," he bellowed. "We can't observe our rites without protection."

"Dude, if you think I'm going to watch a bunch of pixies bump uglies, you've got another think coming," I told him. I snapped my fingers and lit the tip of my finger on fire. I waved the flame at him. "So back off before I torch the lot of you."

Linda scoffed but didn't say anything.

The pixie tugged at his beard. I noticed that he was the only one with facial hair. Were there other males, or was he the only one? I stopped musing about it when Linda snapped a piece of wood off my center island cabinets and was swinging it two-handed at a batch of flyers swarming around her head.

Bob scrambled from my arms and let out a yowl as he skittered across the kitchen tile as he narrowly avoided getting brain-panned by the determined gnome.

"Stop!" I yelled, but like the tornado from earlier, no one listened.

My frustration level was at eleven as I watched the cacophony and mayhem play out in my kitchen. Linda swinging wood like a bat. The pixies diving at her with their tiny swords. Keir tried to reason where reasoning was impossible. I heaved a sigh, wishing there was a way to blow them all out of my house.

"Where's a good tornado when you need one?" I muttered.

A brisk wind blew into the kitchen through the broken window. With unnatural force, it swirled around the center island, picking up glass, a gnome, and a couple dozen pixies in the process.

Linda gave a shout of surprise. Gnomes were fluent in earth magic, and I could feel the shift in the elements as spikes of rocks and minerals shot up from below my house and through the kitchen tiles. They acted as a windbreak, dropping Linda to the floor where she hastily burrowed underground to escape the air stew.

The shrieking of the pixies had me scrambling to undo what I'd started until I saw that their shrieks weren't fear-based. They were riding the currents like miniature body surfers getting carried by waves. And they were laughing. Even Fair Konig's scowl had been replaced by a toothy grin as he dove into the turbulence with his troupe.

Their unbridled joy softened my feelings for the tiny creatures. Even so, Keir was pressed against the wall, trapped, my kitchen was destroyed, and the tornado had started ripping pans from the hanging rack. I had to cut their fun short before it started doing structural damage. With a burst of heat at the top of the tornado cone, I took it down.

When it evaporated to nothing, I gave a silent thanks to Linda for her tutelage. The grouchy gnome had become a surrogate mother of sorts for me, and she'd saved my bacon more than once when it came to my unpredictable magic.

"Quite enjoyable," Fair Konig said with a laugh as he alighted onto my counter. "I feel a hundred years younger."

"How old are you?" I asked.

"You stop counting after a couple of thousand," he replied.

He hadn't really answered my question, but I let it pass. I looked around my kitchen. The floor was full of holes, thanks to Linda, and there was broken glass and tiles littered over the smooth surfaces. "What a mess."

Fair Konig waved at his people, and they all went to work cleaning up the area. I watched with shock and awe as they managed to mend the floor, the tiles, and the window in just a few minutes.

"My God." My eyes had to be as big as saucers as I took it all in. "How is that even possible?"

Keir leaned close and asked, "Have you ever heard the fable about the elves and the shoemaker?"

It was a popular children's story when I was younger. The shoemaker went to sleep, and a bunch of elves finished his shoes for him. He became a success. After, he thanked the elves by making a bunch of tiny shoes for them.

"It was based on a true story," Keir said. "But it was a seamstress. She made warm clothes for a troupe of pixies during a harsh winter, and as a thank you, the pixies created fabrics from the finest materials available and made several show-stopping dresses for her to sell. She became one of the most requested dressmakers for the nobility."

The story made me reassess Fair Konig and his kin. However, there was still the problem with Linda and her animosity for the wee folk. "What did you do to Linda?"

"Who is Linda?" the pixie leader asked.

I narrowed my gaze at him. "The gnome."

"*Wroxishighomas Lupesabeinfeltchner?*" Fair Konig asked.

"*Gesundheit,*" I said to him. Although, the words sounded familiar.

"Thank you," he said. "I wish you good health as well. But *Wroxishighomas Lupesabeinfeltchner* is the gnome's given name."

"Oh, right." Keir had called her that once, but she'd told him she preferred Linda, and I could see why. Her given name was a real mouthful. "Now, tell me why she hates you."

"You will have to get your answers from the gnome. The grudge is hers, not mine."

Which meant Linda had been the injured party.

"Where are you from? And how did my magic jump-start this fruitbaiting thingy?" I made a circle with my thumb and index finger then poked the circle with my other finger.

For the first time, Fair Konig looked amused. "Our mound is on protected land on the other side of this mountain. We have lived there undisturbed for the past two hundred years until we felt the breath of your power penetrate our walls." He tugged his beard, then frowned. "As to the how? Your magic sang to our blood and awakened our reproductive cycle."

I sat on a kitchen stool. "That explains everything and nothing."

"My kind only reproduces once a millennium."

"*Yish.* That's a long time to wait for some action. No wonder you're grumpy." I'd been grumpy for over a year before Keir came into my life.

"Stupid, *Hexe*. We get plenty of action, as you call it, but we can only bring new pixies into the world every thousand years."

"Oh, so babies." I tucked my chin. "You guys must live a long time."

"We survive four to five seasons."

"A season is?"

"Procreation." The pixie tilted his head sideways, similar to the way Bob looks at me when he's confused. "Were you born with brain damage?"

I gave the pixie a one-finger salute. "I'm about to

kick you out of my yard, and you can do whatever you're going to do somewhere else."

Keir, however, was suddenly very interested. His narrow face and aquiline nose in profile made him look very much like a professor getting ready to quiz a student. "When did your quickening start?"

Fair Konig stirred up a breeze as he threw his arms in the air, waving them like he really, really cared. "Did you not see this as a possibility, seer?"

"That's not the way the future unfolds for me," Keir told Fair Konig. "There is a divide between what is seen, what is known, and what actually occurs."

"She has no control over her magic." The pixie's anger had returned. "I can feel the wild inside her now, turbulent and waiting to break free. It has awakened the life in our *Feenstaub* eight hundred years early. And it's not even Spring! Where will we find pollen at this time of year? This is unimaginable. She has a lot to atone for. Protecting our *Kinder* is the least she can do to make up for her mistake."

"Excuse me?" I glared at him.

Keir stepped in. "Iris is remarkable, considering she wasn't raised with any knowledge of her tru-craft nature."

"Exactly," I agreed. "I'm doing the best I can."

Keir took my hand. "And she owns her mistakes."

"Right on." I nodded my head and then looked at Keir. "Wait, what?"

Fair Konig flew up into the air to get eye level

with Keir. "Her power has restored us too early, and now she has to protect what she has wrought." He shed a leaf-woven jacket, and I was amazed at the muscle definition on the little guy's arms, back, and chest. In other words, he was jacked.

"Damn," I muttered appreciatively.

Fair Konig cast a look back at me and gave me a knowing smile as his wings beat faster. Keir gave me a flat look, and I would've laughed at the absurdity if the situation had been less serious.

A pixie female, the one Bob had been toying with outside, flew up in front of my face. "Eyes off my man," she hissed as she held a tiny sword aloft.

Dang. Pixies in heat were territorial. Her rapid darting movements reminded me of the time a hummingbird attacked me near a feeder at my dad's house. I thought the bird was going to stab me in the eyeball and suck out my eye juice with its beak. I had the same feeling now, except for the eye juice sucking.

"Annibish," Fair Konig said with patience and tenderness. "Take our people outside, my love, while I finish here."

Damn it to hell. I didn't want to like him. Not if he hurt Linda. But I had to admit, the little dude had his charms. Loving his family was a big one. It reminded me of how my father loved my mom and how he loved my siblings and me. I felt a stab of guilt. He'd fallen, and I hadn't been there for him. I was thankful Rowan had found Dad as soon as he had and that his injury hadn't been worse, like a broken hip. I'd had a lot going on since coming into my tru-craft ability, but I had to be better about being there for my family.

The pixies had gathered at the door, and I realized because the window was fixed, they needed some help getting out. I opened the backdoor without delay. Annibish glared at me, but the other pixies smiled and waved politely as they flew out into the garden. I knew a certain gnome wouldn't be thrilled, but they had to go somewhere.

Sorry, Linda.

When it was just Keir and me with Fair Konig, the pixie continued his explanation.

"A fortnight ago, *die Magie*," he waved his finger, "Magic, yours," he reiterated, "saturated our mounds and forced its way into my skin."

I winced. "That sounds unpleasant."

Keir's brows furrowed, creating a deep crease between his eyes. "And how did it start your mating cycle?"

"I am the king," Fair Konig said. He held out his arms. "I am blessed every thousand years with excess *Feenstaub* to help grow our little ones." Hundreds of deep blue symbols formed on the pixie's skin, covering his arms, chest, and back. Taking off his shirt made a lot more sense now. "These markings are my birthright, and without them, my troupe would eventually cease to exist. Our dust is a gift from the goddess Freya. She grants fertility in our females for two cycles. Their eggs are fertilized with my dust, and a new life begins." He held out his hand and made a gesture like a blooming flower.

"Is this *Feenstaub* semen? Because if it is, that's a bit TMI for my taste."

"It's pixie dust," Keir said.

"Oh, the magical stem cells." I stepped forward for a closer look. The symbols looked familiar, but not. "What is that?"

"Elder Futhark," Keir answered. "It's a runic alphabet that came about in the first century."

I let out a low whistle. "That's pretty old."

"Old goddess," Keir said.

I squinted at the stiff, straight-lined runes. "Does it have any meaning beyond go forth and procreate?"

"My rune reading is rusty," Keir admitted. "I can pick out a few of them, but I think it probably says more than that."

"It's a blessing from the goddess Freya, bestowing life to me and my kin. And now you have to prepare for what's coming," Fair Konig insisted.

"And what's coming?" I asked. "Pixie dust hunters?"

The pixie stared at me, then pivoted his gaze to Keir. "So you have seen what is to come?"

"I only know a little history about your people,"

he said. "I haven't seen your future, though. Can you tell us more?"

"Yeah." I jerked my thumb toward Keir. "What he asked."

"Any creature who covets magic and wants it for their own."

"Oh. Oh, no." I'd played the magic coveting game before. Bogmall, a particularly nasty druid, had tried to kill me and take my terra-craft. I gave Keir a sharp look. "You don't think...."

"Sorcerers," he finished. "They could be a problem."

Talk about an understatement.

Fair Konig's wings beat even faster. He spat to each side of his body as if warding off a curse.

"Have the druids heard anything about Bogmall's whereabouts?" The blonde druid disappeared after her narrow escape. I was pretty sure Keir's sister Luanne had been sent to find her, though Keir couldn't get confirmation on her mission. "Do you think she would come back to the mountain?"

Keir arched his brow. "I wouldn't put it past her. She was willing to risk everything to take your magic. She's not the kind of person to give up so easily."

The Hexenmeister-wannabe had drugged me, dumped me on an altar, and was going to sacrifice my ass to fuel her cabal of other druids who she'd turned to the dark side. I'd saved myself by tapping into Earth magic, then I'd kicked some major Hexenbitch ass by wrapping them up with bindweed. Granted, Lu had helped with clean-up, and Keir, in pooka form, had come running in at the last minute. In the chaos, Bogmall had escaped. It was easy to disappear when you didn't care what happened to the people who looked to you for support and protection. Blondie had left her cabal behind. I'd killed some, captured others, and she hadn't cared.

I couldn't be a Bogmall. I couldn't ignore the people who needed my support and protection. I turned to Fair Konig. "Can you relocate your family to Keir's property? It's isolated. You and your family won't be disturbed."

"I need pollen," he said. "Late summer isn't optimal, but the garden can meet our needs."

Keir interceded. "If Iris can procure pollen for you, will you relocate?"

His wings hummed as he rubbed his beard. "Will you both swear to protect us until the birth of our children?"

Keir looked to me for an answer. I nodded. "If you relocate, I will find you pollen, and I will find a way to protect you." I prayed I was capable of the last part. I'd taken on some baddies and won, but only by sheer seat-of-my-pants luck. "Do we have a deal?" asked Keir.

"Wait," I said. "How soon will the hunters come?"

"When *die Fruchtbarkseitriten* starts." He tugged

his beard and grimaced. "But our window of fertility is short. The rites must begin soon."

I understood the urgency, but I needed one more day before I could deal with the supernatural fallout. Michael had his first football game of the season. I wasn't going to miss it. "Can the deal start tomorrow? I have a family thing tonight."

The pixie king nodded. "Family is everything. I can give you one day, Iris Everlee."

"Then I agree to help protect you and your troupe." I held out my finger to shake.

Fair Konig quickly flew several feet away.

I gave him a bland look. "I'm not going to torch you. I was just going to shake on it."

"No need to shake me, Iris Everlee. I accept your deal."

Well, at least come tomorrow, they would be out of Linda's garden, and if they weren't here, hopefully, my house wouldn't become a supernatural battleground.

CHAPTER 4

FAIR KONIG HAD JOINED HIS FAMILY IN THE garden while I tried not to hyperventilate. My anxiety and panic levels were rising.

Keir rubbed my back as I dropped my head between my knees. "It could be worse," he said.

I sucked a breath in through my teeth. "I'm a supernatural bouncer for a hundred or so randy pixies. I would hope it couldn't get much worse." I gave him a flat stare. "Unless you're seeing all my possible futures again and know something I don't know."

"My seven gazillion cable channels of Iris are still on the fritz," he said, using the metaphor I'd once used. "I really wish I knew why your magic started their cycle, though. That has me worried."

"If you're worried, then I'm worried." I sighed.

The wild aero-craft magic inside me hadn't acted like the terra-craft. It didn't feel as if I were being cooked from the inside out. Other than not being able to control it, it hadn't really seemed to affect me physically at all. But I knew that all magic had a price. Maybe protecting the pixies was the cost this time. Better than my life, right? Although, losing my life wasn't completely off the table.

I turned to meet Keir's gaze. "It's moments like these that I hate my birth mother. She could've filled in a lot of the blanks, and maybe I wouldn't be such a shit tru-crafter."

"I wish I had the answers for you." He raised his brow at me. "If only there was some kind of book that might provide insight."

I groaned. "You know I love books." After all, I'd majored in English, taught for several years at the university, and for the last seventeen years, I'd worked as a non-fiction editor. But he wasn't just talking about any kind of reference book. He was speaking of my grimoire. "Just not that one. Besides, I'm not sure this problem can be solved with cryptic riddles."

"Knowledge is the only true way to solve problems," Keir disagreed. "While ignorance is usually the source."

"I'm proof of that."

"Iris," he said softly. "I didn't mean you."

"I know, but still, you seem to have hit the prover-

bial nail, or in this case, problem-child, on the head."
I had a sinking feeling in the pit of my gut. "Do you
think it's because I'm both Fade and Bright?"

"I told you that neither is good or bad. They're
just different." He lifted my hand to his lips and
pressed a kiss to my fingertips. "You're a once-in-a-
lifetime miracle."

"You're only saying that because you love me."

"I do love you," he said. He kissed my palm, and I
could feel a tingle of magic flow into my skin. "But
that's not the reason it's true. Whatever happens
next, we will get through it. Together."

"Thanks." I chewed my lower lip. "I hope you're
right." I'd been so wrapped up in my misery I hadn't
heard the front door open. My seventeen-year-old
bounded into the kitchen.

He was over six feet tall, and in the past couple of
months, he'd really started putting on extra muscle.
"S'up?" he asked as he grabbed an apple from the
counter on his way through.

*Just finished negotiating with a pack of hot-to-trot
pixies who were itching to get it on,* I thought. *Not that
much different than teenagers, really.* Aloud, I said, "Oh,
you know, same old-same old."

He paused and stared at me. "Are you crying?"

"No," I told him, then realized that I had been. I
forced a smile as I wiped the tears away from my
eyes. "What are you doing at home?"

"I live here," he said.

"Don't be a smart ass," I told him.

"Better than a dumbass," he replied. His dimples deepened as he grinned, adding to his adorable factor, and while I knew he was having a little fun at my expense, I was just happy he was having fun. For a few weeks after my ex had left the village, I worried Michael would never smile again.

"You're hilarious. If you're thinking about a career in comedy, don't give up your day job." I chucked him under the chin. "I thought you were going over to Doug's after school." Doug was one of Michael's best friends since kindergarten. They both played on the football team. "Weren't you going to ride to the game with him?"

The corner of his lips turned up in a smile. "I just came home to get a change of clothes."

"For what?"

"I need it for after the game. If that's okay."

"Is there something going on after the game?" I asked.

"Duh, Mom. The bonfire at Silver End Lake tonight."

Of course. I'd forgotten the football boosters threw a big party at the lake with live music, food, and a big bonfire for the team and fans to celebrate the first game and kick off the season every year.

"Coach Jordan wants the team there," Michael added. "His band is going to perform."

I wrinkled my nose. I hadn't heard much about

RENEE GEORGE

Coach Jordan, aka Jordan Sonnavilsa, other than Michael and his friends really liked him. I was looking forward to finally meeting him tonight. "The coach has a band?"

"He plays a lot of that old rock-n-roll." He ran his hands through his curly blonde hair.

"Like Chuck Barry?"

"Nah. More like Radiohead and Nirvana."

I smacked the kid's shoulder with a backhand. "That's not old rock-n-roll. I grew up with that music."

Michael shrugged, mischief in his eyes. "Like I said, pretty old."

"Cheeky," I countered. "I remember when you thought I hung the moon."

"When dinosaurs still roamed the earth."

"You're feeling your oats, aren't you?"

Keir, who'd witnessed the banter play out, chuckled. He held his hand up, and Michael gave him a high five.

I shook my head. I wasn't irritated or annoyed in the slightest. Seeing my son back to his happy, smart-assy self felt like a point in the win column. I'd take it.

"Go," I told Michael. "Get your clothes and get out of here." I went up on my toes and kissed his cheek. "I'll see you tonight. Kick some serious ass on the field."

My son grinned. "That's the plan." He gave me another quick assessment. "Are you sure you're okay?"

"Absolutely," I lied. "Your Pop-Pop took a tumble this morning, and I just found out before you got home." Less of a lie. His expression turned dark and worried, so I added, "He's fine, though, according to your Aunt Marigold. Just a little bruised."

The tension around Michael's soft brown eyes eased. "You sure?"

"Yes. He'll be at the game tonight." I ushered him toward his room. "Get going. You don't want to be late."

When we were alone, Keir put his arms around me. "You know I love you, right?"

"And I love you." Loving each other was not the problem. I pressed my palm against his chest. "What am I going to do?" I poked a finger into his peck. "And if you say research, I'm going to turn your tongue to stone."

"Then I wouldn't be able to do this." He nuzzled my neck, then ran the tip of his tongue along the edge of my earlobe. "Or this." He kissed me, his mouth moving over mine before sliding his tongue between my parted lips.

I moaned as my body reacted to his every touch and caress.

"God," Michael complained as he reentered the kitchen. "You guys could've waited until after I left."

He held his duffel bag up to his shoulder to block his view. "I'm going to need therapy again."

I snorted a laugh. "You better hurry up and go unless you want to see a lot more than some kissing and heavy petting."

"Gross." He race-walked to the living room and out of the front door.

Keir and I were laughing and kissing again before Michael's car started. Then Keir picked me up and started toward the hall to my room.

"Wait," I said as we passed the kitchen window. I looked out. Pixies were behaving. "Okay, we're good."

He grinned at me. "I'm about to demonstrate how good." Then he carried me back to the bedroom and proceeded to show me all the other ways his tongue was useful.

"Go, BIG GREEN!" I shouted from the stands. "Look, there's Michael." I pointed to the end zone as the Southill Howlers took the field. Our mascot was a giant bear-cat called the Ozark Howler. A mytholog- ical creature I was pretty sure didn't exist. At least, I hoped not. But it was the only real legend we had in our neck of the woods.

"Go, Mikey!" Marigold shouted. She'd arrived shortly after Keir and me, and she was the only one Michael let get away with calling him that.

I went ahead to save bleacher seats for the family while Keir went to the concession stand for sodas and popcorn.

Michael, number eighty, was the middle linebacker, an important position on the team. He was sort of like the quarterback for the defense, calling all the plays on the field. At least that's the way I'd understood it when he'd first described the position. While I wasn't really into football, I loved watching my kid play. "Go, Michael!" I screamed. "Go, Howlers!"

Several other moms around us were shouting their support as well. A hand on my shoulder made me turn around.

"Reba," I said, not surprised to see the brunette in the stands. Her son was a wide receiver. The kid was smaller than most of the players on the team, but he was really fast on his feet. Reba and I had been friendly for years. "Hi, there."

"I'm so glad you made it, Iris," she replied as she looked around. "Is Evan coming?"

I tensed. "No, he can't make it." I didn't elaborate about his move and such because every football parent damn well knew Evan and Adam had relocated to St. Louis. Enough time had passed that I'd hoped the focus would've shifted away from me and my personal life. My husband leaving me for the old football coach had been one of the biggest scandals to hit our town, but after a year, my heartbreak should've been old news.

Reba frowned. "Oh, that's too bad. I'm glad we were able to replace Coach Hauser on such short notice." There was a tinge of condemnation in her tone that I didn't like.

Friendly wasn't the same as intimate. I had no intention of having a conversation about my ex-husband or his current partner with her.

"Yep." I changed the subject. "Have you met Coach Jordan yet? Michael seems to like him."

"All the boys like him," she said. "And a few of the single moms. Maybe even a few married ones." She waggled her brows at me and grinned. "Now that you're on the market, you should get yourself in the running."

"I don't run," I joked, offended at her off-handed remark. "Besides, I'm not looking for a man."

"Too soon?" Reba's expression was full of pity. I wanted to punch her in the nose.

Lauren Reynolds, mom to Michael's best friend Doug, scooched in next to Reba. "Are we talking about the new coach?" She touched her arm and made a *ssss* sizzle sound. "He's smoking hot."

Marigold nudged me. "Maybe you could introduce me to the new coach."

If I thought introducing my sister to anyone would get her to stop pining for a fire djinn named Zev, I would do it. I thought for a minute that Zev and Marigold might come to something, but he had left Southill Village without so much as a "see ya, wouldn't want to be ya."

My sister had always been carefree. A real lover of life, and she deserved someone who could love her with the same zest. "We could go down there right now," I half-teased.

Carla Porter, the quarterback's mom, squeezed in between Reba and Lauren. Ugh. She was one of the moms I couldn't fake friendly with. She was always trying to stir up the drama. Her son Roger was a friend of Michael's, which was the only reason I tolerated the intolerable woman. She put in her two cents about the new coach. "If I was ten years younger...."

"And divorced," Lauren added with a laugh.

Okay, I hadn't met the new coach, but I was getting the idea that he was handsome and young. Maybe the PTO gossip had moved past Evan and me.

"Oh, my," Carla said. "Who's that tall drink of handsome?"

"He looks like that actor. Tom Hiddleston," another mom added.

I glanced over and saw Keir with three bags of popcorn and a drink carrier with three sodas. He smiled when our eyes met.

I waved, even though he'd seen me, and patted the bleacher next to me. If I was being completely honest, a petty part of me wanted the "moms," specifically Carla and Reba, to know I'd landed on my feet.

The players were doing their warm-up routines, Michael leading the defensive team.

Keir handed the soda carrier to me, and Marigold took two of the popcorns off his hands as he sat down.

I placed my hand on his thigh. "Thanks for getting the snacks for us."

"No problem." He leaned my way and gave me a kiss. "I like doing things for you."

I loved that my guy knew how to read a room. I rewarded him with another quick kiss.

"Who's your friend, Iris?" Reba asked.

I pivoted and looked back at the moms. "Keir Quinn, meet Reba, Lauren, Dana, Terry, Carla, and...." I didn't know the woman on the other side of Carla.

"This is Yolanda Carver," Carla supplied. "She and her daughter Maddie just moved to town about a month ago."

Yolanda smiled. Her blue eyes were bright with humor. She pointed to the sidelines where the cheerleaders were warming up. "That's Maddie over there. The one on the far left."

Maddie was cute. Dark-haired like her mother. Slender and petite. She was several inches shorter than most of the other cheerleaders. "She's beautiful."

The compliment seemed to make Yolanda happy. "She's a special girl."

Carla thrust her hand out to Keir and giggled coyly when he politely gave it a shake. "I'm Carla," she told him as she leaned forward, touching her throat to draw attention to her plunging v-neck, and added, "My son's the quarterback."

As loath as I was to admit it, Carla was attractive, superficially, with her perfectly coiffed blonde hair, expertly applied makeup, hourglass figure, and designer clothes. However, Keir barely acknowledged the woman and certainly didn't make any lingering eye contact. God, I loved the man. If we hadn't been on a crowded bleacher, I would've shown him just how much.

I gave Carla a tight smile and a silent neener-neener. "Keir teaches at the university with Marigold."

"I hooked them up," Marigold said, happy to take some of the credit for our inevitable meeting.

"Any more friends you want to hook-up?" one of the moms asked her.

I let Marigold field the question as I handed off the drinks to Keir and stood up. Rose, her two sons Drake and Dustin, and her husband Don wheeled Dad in a wheelchair toward us. "Be right back."

The moms started in on Keir with a million questions as I went down to meet them.

"Hey, Dad." I gave my father, a big man with an

even bigger heart, a hug. "I'm so glad you could make it."

"Your sister insisted I ride in this contraption." He patted the wheelchair. "I tried to tell her I could walk, but you know how she gets."

My sister Rose was a force of nature. She was the president of the PTO, she was active with several charities in town, and she'd even taken to training me in Crossfit four days a week. She would have done it seven days a week, but I'm also a force of nature, and I refused the offer. I smiled at my younger sister. "It's hard to say no to Rose."

I gave Rose, Don, and the boys hugs. "I've saved us the first and second row over there where Keir and Marigold are sitting."

"Are Rowan and Dahlia here yet?" Rose asked.

"Not yet." I felt more guilt. Before the grimoire had activated my tru-craft powers, our family saw each other on a weekly basis. We usually had dinners and sometimes played poker. While my siblings and I had all been adopted, as a tribe, we were closer than blood. Since magic had come into my life, the last time I'd been with all of them in the same place was in the hospital when my terra-craft had almost killed me.

I hadn't realized until this moment that I'd been distancing myself from them, even if it hadn't been consciously.

Back on the bleachers, I slid my hand into Keir's.

He must've felt my unease because he gave me a questioning look.

I shook my head.

"Oh, there's the coach," I heard Carla say. "Dang, that man is dreamy."

I searched the sidelines until my gaze landed on a man who stood a head taller than most of the teenagers on the team. He had blond hair and a neatly groomed beard and mustache. His shoulders were as wide as his hips were narrow.

"Cripes. The guy looks like Thor," Marigold gasped." She shook her hands. "Hubba hubba."

Keir's grip tightened on mine. I knew it couldn't be jealousy, but something was wrong. "What is it?"

"The coach," he said. "I know him."

"How?"

Keir leaned close so no one but me could hear. "You remember Bogmall?"

I swallowed the hot knot that had formed in my throat. "Yes." It was hard to forget the blonde bitch who'd tried to suck me dry of magic so she could become a sorcerer.

"He's what she wanted to be. He hit our radar a few years back when he absorbed a tru-craft witch's power when she died. That was in Wisconsin. Her coven turned his name over to us, but we never had any proof that he caused her death and took her magic. Only her coven's word. He's been on the Iron

Grove's watch list since, though we haven't had any more reports on him."

Tru-craft witches were rare, and not just anyone could absorb their powers. Jordan had to have been something else first. Something magical. "Was he a druid like Bogmall?"

Keir shook his head. "We're not sure what he is or was. We'd never heard of Jordan Oldsen before the incident."

"His last name is Sonnavilsa, not Oldsen."

His brow furrowed as he leaned forward, elbows on his knees as he stared at the football coach. "He's changed it then because that guy is hard to mistake."

The coach was pretty unique in his stature and looks. I believed Keir. "Is he here for the pixies?"

"They haven't started the rites yet." His eyes never left the coach. "So, he couldn't know about them."

"He's here for me, then, isn't he?" Cripes. Of course, he was. My tru-craft was having a three-way with the elements, and it was crack for pixies and *Hexenmeister*, as Linda called them. And now, one of them was coaching my son's high school football team. "How do we get rid of him?" And we needed to figure it out before the four-inch magic magnets started their mating frenzy.

Keir took his phone from his pocket.

"Who are you calling?" I asked him.

"Reinforcements." He put the phone to his ear.

"Lu, Iris needs you." He paused for a moment, then added, "I need you."

I blinked as I watched the deadly Adonis direct our teenage boys to take the field. The audacity of him infiltrating my town in such an insidious manner made me rage-y. I didn't know what game he thought he was playing, but he wasn't going to win.

CHAPTER 5

MY STOMACH KNOTTED AS THE FINAL SECONDS OF the game counted down. Our Southill Village Howlers were up by a field goal, and the ball was in the Ballycore Bulldogs' control.

The game was the least of my worries. I'd spent the majority of my time watching Coach Jordan. He seemed so...normal. Other than the fact that he was extremely action-movie-star gorgeous. I had a million questions for Keir, but none that were appropriate for the non-magical company. Why hadn't the Iron Grove already done something about this guy?

Keir's phone call with Lu hadn't gone as well as he'd hoped. She was currently in Nevada, just north of Reno, and it would take her at least two days of driving to get here.

"Come on, Kid!" my dad yelled. "Take his head off!"

Rose was up on her feet, too. "Defense!" She clapped her hands twice. "Defense!" Half the crowd joined in with her chant.

I looked at the field in time to see Michael speeding past the offensive line and right at the quarterback. My pulse kicked into high gear as my adrenaline spiked. "Hit him!" I screamed. "Sack 'em!"

As easy as slicing butter, Michael slipped past the last defender, came around behind the quarterback and took him down. The ball popped out of the quarterback's hand.

"Yasssssss!" The Howlers' fans went wild. I flew up onto my feet, jumping and screaming along with everyone else when Michael crab-crawled to the fumbled ball for a defensive turnover.

"Oh my gosh, oh my gosh." Rose was holding on to Don's shoulders, shaking her six-foot-four husband like a ragdoll. "Did you see that?"

Don was laughing. Dad was grinning from ear to ear. Rowan, who had shown up in the first quarter, turned around and high-fived me. He wore a Howlers' hat over his dark red hair and a Howlers' hoodie in a show of team spirit. Even stoic Dahlia, our eldest sister, was hooting and clapping.

Lauren grabbed my hands, and we raised them over our heads. She spoke loudly to get over the crowd noise, "We're going to have some happy boys this week."

"We sure are." I was smiling so hard my cheeks

hurt. There was nothing better than returning home a conquering hero to boost morale. Michael was going to be walking on cloud nine all week long.

"Finally," Carla said. "Coach Jordan is the leadership our boys deserve."

Leave it to Carla to sour a perfectly awesome moment. Music blared over the speakers as both teams left the field to gather their gear and head to the locker rooms. Game over. Final score was 10-7.

"Whew, that was a nail-biter," Marigold said as the crowd began to disperse. "Both defenses were tough. Really pinned the offenses down."

"They sure did," I agreed.

"What happens now?" Keir asked.

"Now we go down to the sidelines and wait for the boys to come out of the locker room. Then the moms get to embarrass their sons with congratulatory hugs and kisses." I raised my brows. "Plus, it'll give me a chance to assess the new coach."

Keir's brow furrowed. "I'm not sure you should go near him until we find out why he's in Southill Village."

I gave him a bland look. "We know why, don't we? Besides, he's wormed his way into my kid's life, which means I'm going to look him in the eye."

Keir took my hand. "Can I come down there with you, or is it just the moms?"

"You can come," I said, grateful for the backup. "But I doubt Coach Jordan plans to attack me in front of a crowd of people." Still, it made me feel better to have Keir nearby.

I said goodbye to my family and promised Rose I'd be at the family meeting tomorrow. After, Keir and I made our way to the field. I couldn't help but wonder why the Iron Grove hadn't handled this guy. It didn't seem as if he was trying to hide.

"Why haven't they taken Coach Jordan out? Or imprisoned him or something?" I asked. "The druids, I mean. Isn't that part of their job, to make sure magic isn't being used or taken illegally?"

"We haven't been able to touch him because we can't prove how he obtained his magic or if he even has magic."

I frowned. "He stole tru-craft to become a sorcerer. Isn't that enough proof?"

Keir sighed. "He hasn't technically stolen his power."

"How is that possible?"

Keir's hard gaze met mine. "There's no proof other than the coven's word. Besides, catching an unstable witch as the spark of tru-craft kills them, then taking the magic, isn't a crime. At least not a crime that we can prosecute and punish him for."

"But Bogmall...."

"She kidnapped you and was going to sacrifice you. Besides, she had also taken an oath to the Iron Grove. This sorcerer is not one of us. The original source of his power is unknown."

It took about twenty minutes for the boys to retake the field. Michael, wearing jeans and a green sweatshirt, saw me and grinned. He made a beeline for me and gave me a hug. It was awesome. My teenage son was not only happy to see me, but he was also cheerfully hugging me in a public setting. My elation made me feel feather-light.

"Uh, Mom," Michael said, still hugging me tightly. "You're floating."

"Yeah, I am," I replied. "You were fantastic tonight. I'm so proud of you."

"No," Michael said. "You're floating, and I'm having a hard time keeping my feet on the ground."

I blinked as I flutter-kicked my feet. We slid a foot to the right.

"Not helping," Michael said. "I thought you were working on getting your air stuff under control."

Since telling Michael about tru-craft, I'd kept him mostly up to date with my progress. However, I might have exaggerated how well I was doing. "Down," I hissed to my powers. "On the ground."

I dropped like a stone, and Michael's hug was the only thing that kept me from falling on my ass.

"Cripes, Mom." His wet hair dripped on my face.

"Sorry," I told him. "My emotions are messing with my control."

He chuckled, then let me go. He parroted a phrase I used with him sometimes. "Do better."

I patted his sweet, scruffy cheek. "I'm trying."

Uncharacteristically, he gave me a quick peck on the forehead. "I know you are. See you tomorrow."

"Yep. Great game out there tonight."

"Thanks."

Keir put his hand on Michael's shoulder. "Congratulations. Well-played."

Michael nodded, then gave us peace signs with both hands as he trotted backward, grabbed his buddy Doug, and headed down the field toward the parking lot.

Coach Jordan was talking with a handful of the moms. I looked at Keir. "I'm going over," I said. "Safety in numbers."

"Careful," he cautioned.

"That's my middle name."

"I thought your middle name was *Kleinkind*."

"According to Linda, that's my first, middle, and last name." I steeled my courage and cut through the new coach's adoring fans. Keir hung back a few feet but stayed right behind me.

I thrust my hand out. "Congratulations, Coach," I said. "Great game."

His intensely blue eyes met my gaze. Then he smiled. "You must be Mike's mom."

"Michael," I corrected automatically. He'd always been Michael, never Mike. "And yep, that's me. His mom." I was so smooth. Not. "And you have to be Coach Jordan."

"You can call me Jordan." His eyes softened as he held my gaze. "And what can I call you?"

As if he didn't already know my name. Hah. Though I had to admit, he was as charming as he was good-looking. "You can call me Ms. Everlee," I said out of spite.

Jordan arched a curious brow. "Mike, Michael," he amended, "is a Callahan."

"You are correct." I didn't elaborate. "Well, I just wanted to meet you and congratulate you on your first win."

I hadn't realized I was still holding out my hand until he took it. A surge of energy, almost like grabbing an electric fence, shot up my forearm and into my elbow. Uncomfortable and painful, but not lethal.

The man leaned in closer and said, "It's nice to meet you, Ms. Everlee."

The tingling sensation intensified but turned alarmingly pleasant. As I stared into Jordan's eyes, I wanted the sensation to continue. Warm, silky comfort filled me. I was safe, I thought. Safe, happy, and relaxed.

A touch on my shoulder snapped me out of my reverie of contentment. Jordan's touch was once again buzzing, electric, and prickly. I narrowed my gaze at the tall man as I drew upon metals and minerals in my blood and focused on my right palm.

I wanted nothing more than to wipe the smug expression from the coach's face, but I settled for his hand. I stifled a squawk of pain as I shot short spikes of iron and bone out from my skin and into his firm grip.

His face pinched as I felt my magic strike. He jerked his hand away and gave me a wary, surprised look. "What the hell was that?"

I shuddered as my hand dropped to my side. Now that we were no longer connected, I felt suddenly, nonsensically, at a loss. "I could ask you the same question," I accused him. Though, I wasn't the one who'd gotten stabbed through the palm.

The touch on my shoulder chased the feeling away and replaced the emptiness with so much love.

Keir. My anchor.

I stared down at my hand for a moment. It was smeared with Jordan's blood. Eeep. I wiped my hand on my jeans and then settled my gaze on him. "Don't get comfortable in Southill Village."

"I guess we'll have to wait and see," he said. He rubbed his hands together for a second, and when he was done, the puncture wounds were healed. "It's been interesting meeting you, Ms. Everlee." His frown shifted up again into a smile. "Until the next time."

I needed "next time" to be as I watched him leave town. I needed this guy out of Southill Village and away from my son and me as soon as possible. Only, next time I wouldn't be dumb enough to let him touch me.

There was a line of parents and boosters behind me, waiting to talk to their new hero. I gave Jordan a thin-lipped smile back. "Until then."

I reached up and touched Keir's fingers on my shoulder, the extra contact clearing any fog left behind by the sorcerer, as we walked down the sidelines toward the parking lot.

"You okay?" Keir asked when we were out of earshot.

"No," I replied honestly. "I'm not. He...." I wasn't sure how to put into words how Jordan had made me feel, but I tried. "He made me feel taken care of. Like, he was my protector." I shivered. "It also felt...violating."

"Magic?"

"It had to be."

Keir put his arm around me. "He wasn't expecting you to bite back." I could hear the pride in his voice. "The look on his face when you hit him with Earth magic. Priceless."

"I made him blink first." But I'd also revealed some of my cards. "He knows I'm on to him. Do you think he'll move faster on me now?"

"If he's here for you, then it's a possibility," Keir said.

"Who else would he be here for?"

Keir shrugged. "Sorcerers gain power from unstable users of tru-craft. While you haven't quite mastered your powers, you're no longer unstable, Iris."

"What does that mean?"

"Maybe there's someone else on the mountain who has had their magic triggered."

A laugh behind us kept me from asking who as my sister Marigold threw her arms over our shoulders and wedged herself between us. "Guess who's got a date?"

"Who?" I asked, still thinking about the idea that another tru-craft witch might be in Southill Village.

"The spectacularly hot coach asked me if I was going to the bonfire tonight at Silver End Lake." She made a teeth-sucking noise. "I guess that's not a date-date, but at least he asked."

I stopped and looked at her. "You can't date Coach Jordan."

"Like I said," she started. Her tone sounded hurt and confused. "It's not technically a date. I mean, he probably asked a lot of people if they were going to be at the booster bonfire."

Crap. Michael was heading to the bonfire now that the game was over. I didn't want him within a thousand miles of the sorcerer. Then another awful thought popped into my head.

I dug my phone out of my jacket and called my son's cellphone. The call went straight to voicemail. Damn it, Michael. "Hey, call me as soon as you get this."

"What's wrong?" Marigold asked.

We were in the parking lot, moving quickly as I searched for Michael's car. It was gone. Shit. He'd left already.

Marigold grabbed my arm. "You're scaring me, Iris. What's happening?"

I shook my head as my stomach turned icy cold with fear. "Michael," I said to Keir. Michael hadn't shown any spark of tru-craft, but maybe Jordan could sense something I couldn't. "What if he's after my son?"

CHAPTER 6

SILVER END LAKE WAS INSIDE THE STATE PARK A few miles from town. The scent of wood-burning smoke and grilling meats, combined with the blast of loud music over the speakers and the jovial conversations of the football lovers from all over Southill Village, greeted us as we got out of the car.

I'd kept calling Michael, but I knew from experience that the cell phone reception at the park was nonexistent. The lake had a large, paved parking lot, four giant pavilions, and an enormous ten-foot fire ring that made it a perfect spot for family gatherings, parties, and, of course, the Booster's Kick-off Bonfire. A stack of logs blazed in an open field where people, young and older, congregated to ward off the late summer chill. Just past a thin line of trees, the surface of the lake glittered with the moon's reflection.

I took several deep breaths to calm myself as Keir,

Marigold, and I searched for Michael. Even with the fire and the moonlight, it was dark, and half the town had shown up. Finding my kid was like trying to find a needle in a stack of moving needles.

The stage near the second pavilion had a high school band playing country-pop music. I recognized the bass player from Michael's class. We'd driven as fast as Keir's hybrid car would take us, which wasn't fast enough by my estimation. Still, I hoped we had been able to beat Jordan to the place. I didn't want that asshole anywhere near my kid.

"Let's split up," I told Keir and Marigold.

"Is that smart?" Marigold asked.

"We need to cover a lot of ground. And splitting up is the quickest way to find Michael. I can't let that man get near him." This was one instance where I really hoped I was making a mountain out of an anthill. As much as I hated being in the supernatural line of fire, I would take the hit a thousand times if it kept my son safe.

I grabbed Marigold's arm before we parted. "Steer clear of Jordan."

She nodded. "Don't worry. I'm happy to steer clear of supernatural men." She glanced at Keir. "No offense."

"No worries." Keir pointed toward the parking lot. A huge white truck had pulled in, and Jordan stepped out. "We need to find Michael now."

His sense of urgency to protect my son made me

love him even more. No matter what, I needed Michael to be a priority.

Keir headed toward the lake, Marigold left to circle the bonfire, and I took on the pavilions. I accidentally made eye contact with Quarterback Mom Carla, and I cringed as she hustled over to me.

"I'm so glad you came to the game tonight, Iris," she said with too much sympathy. "I know it's got to be hard for you, what with Evan being gay and running off with another man."

First of all, Evan was bisexual, but I wasn't going to explain the nuances to Carla. Secondly, how I felt about it was none of her business.

"Watching my son dominate the field on defense is never hard." I bared my teeth in a feral smile. "If our offense pulls together, we'll be unstoppable this season." Was I being petty? Yep. Did I care? Not really.

Carla, however, wasn't going to be out-bitched. "Let's just hope your new boyfriend isn't into coaches."

Her comment was meant to raise my ire, so I called up my ignis-craft and raised her body temperature.

I watched Carla's face as it flushed. A bead of sweat broke out over her lip and forehead. She frowned and sucked in a breath. "Did it suddenly get hot out here?"

I shrugged. "I feel fine," I told her. "Maybe you're starting menopause."

Her eyes widened, and her mouth dropped open as I eased off the heat, and her temperature returned to normal.

I didn't have time for this pissing contest, so I excused myself. "Have to run. Looking for Michael."

Carla, uncharacteristically helpful, said, "I saw him head down to the lake with Maddie Carver."

"The new cheerleader?"

"Yeah. You met her mom Yolanda earlier at the game. She's over there." Carla pointed a finger at the woman who'd been sitting behind us at the game.

Did Michael have a girlfriend? Why hadn't he told me? He was getting older, and she wouldn't be the first girl he'd dated. Still, it would've been nice to know. For the time being, I'd put the questions away. I had bigger fish to fry.

"Uhm, thanks." I rushed past Carla, uneasy about our encounter. I had enough problems in my life, what with pixies to protect and sorcerers to suss out, without adding a war with another mom to the agenda.

I saw Marigold come around the far side of the bonfire. I waved, but she didn't see me. I gave up after a few more waves in her direction and headed to the lake. Keir would already be down there. Hopefully, he'd found Michael already. I wasn't sure what I thought would happen. After all, Jordan had taken over as head coach several weeks ago. If he'd wanted to hurt Michael, he could've done it at any time without my knowledge. Maybe that had been the point. Jordan had been waiting to meet me. Maybe he'd wanted me to see him coming. A tightness gripped my throat. How powerful was the man? Would he be too formidable for me to stop?

I hustled past the Treese memorial bench on the path to the lake. The Treese family had planted gardenias on either side, and the late August blooms scented the night air with a sweet floral fragrance. There were people, adults and teens, walking up and down the path. It was a clear night. The three-quarter moon's reflection on the water was like something out of a painting. Beautiful. Even so, it was too dark to make out faces until I was a few feet from anyone.

Once when Michael was little, maybe four or five years old, he disappeared from the front yard. My imagination had taken me through every horrific possibility, and the panic I'd felt had been crippling. Evan and I had found him playing on a swing set one block over. I'd gotten angry and sent him to bed as soon as we got him home. I'd never been so terrified in my entire life, not even when Volres had taken me to his molten lair. I was starting to feel that same intense fear.

"Michael," I shouted, knowing it would embarrass

him, but I didn't care. Not if it meant keeping him safe. "Michael!"

"Mrs. Callahan." Doug Reynolds waved at me from the dock. He was with several other boys from the football team and a few girls.

I jogged over to him. I didn't correct him about my last name. I had been Mrs. Callahan to the boy for twelve years, and aside from that, I had bigger worries than whether someone got my name right. "Hey, Doug. Have you seen Michael?"

"Uh…Uhm, yeah," he said. "He's around here somewhere."

Since the teen was stepping about the answer, I took a more direct approach. "Mrs. Porter says she saw him come this way with Maddie Carver."

"Oh, yep." Doug nodded emphatically. "Yeah, I think he was with Maddie."

"Where?" I asked.

"I'm not—"

I balled my fist and set it on my hip so that I wouldn't call up the earth to swallow the teenager. "It's important, Doug. Point me in the right direction."

He pointed toward the Silver End walking trail, a two-mile hike around the lake. "That way."

"Thank you." I made my way to the marked start. The path followed the curves of the lake but was nestled in the trees. There were several benches where people could sit and take in the sights and a couple of paths that veered off to longer trails that went through the woods and came out at the special use camp area. I didn't like the idea of Michael using the trail in the dark, but I was a teenager once. The trail being dark and isolated was a selling point for someone young, dumb, and full of teenage hormones.

Just in case he was making out with Maddie, I called ahead as a warning. "Michael. Michael Callahan!"

Cripes. My heart rate quickened to the point that I had to pant for oxygen. Panic and anxiety were setting their claws into me, and I couldn't untangle myself from what was and what might be. Chances were good my son had a girlfriend, and they were making out in the woods. But my brain was cycling through all the other awful possibilities, such as he'd been drugged and kidnapped by a sorcerer who wanted to kill him for his spark.

"Michael!"

The trees rustled in the wind making the soft sound of a hand percussion shaker. *Shhhh-shh, shhhhh-shhhh*. I could still hear music playing at the pavilions, but crowd sounds had all but faded. Where was my son?

"Damn it, Michael," I hissed. "I swear I'm going to ground you until you're old enough to run for president." A rustling of leaves to the right of me made me jump. I went stock-still and listened. The crunch-crunch was there again, then stopped. I looked around, ready to fight if anything or anybody tried to attack me from the woods.

But nothing happened. I started walking. The rustling noise started back up again. When I stopped walking, it stopped again.

"Son of a bitch. Whoever you are, come out now if you want to survive."

I peered into the woods toward the sound. It seemed as if it were close, but there was nothing there. Were the woods around the lake haunted? Eeep. Or maybe the Ozark Howler was on the prowl. Legend had it that the animal with the head of a cat and the body of a bear patrolled wooded areas and forests, searching out wicked children. It was an old wives' tale meant to frighten.

When I took a step, and the rustling started and stopped with my movement, I had to admit that the story meant to scare kids was having a similar effect on me.

"Halt. Who goes there?" I said, yanking a line from my dad's favorite Monty Python film, *The Holy Grail*. Only, the sounds weren't coming from knocking together coconuts. I swallowed the knot in my throat. "Whoever you are, show yourself. Coward." I reached inside and pulled on my ignis-craft and, at the same time, searched with my terra-craft for rocks or minerals I could manipulate into weapons. This Howler or ghost or Hexenmeister was messing with the wrong witch. The wind began to stir above me, raising my hair until my ponytail was standing straight up.

I started walking again, determined to find my son but ready to wage war if I had to. The crunch and rustle of dead leaves continued.

"Michael Evan Callahan! Where are you?"

A loud boom sounded in the distance and sent me to the ground as I waited for a barrage of bad to rain down on me. Nothing happened. And once again, the noisemaker following me had ceased its movements. It had rained earlier in the week, and the ground was still damp. I'd accidentally willed the wet earth to act as a shield, and I had sunk down a good foot in what my terra-craft had turned to muck. The mud had created a vacuum around my hands and forearms, and I had to use magic to get myself out. Wow, if a bad guy had tried to jump me then, I would've been a sitting duck.

"Make your intention known, *Kleinkind*," Linda would say. "Or the magic will guess at what you want." My intention was to get my son and get the hell out of here. And maybe take a hot shower.

I wiped my palms on the back of my thighs since it was the only part of my jeans that were clean. This was getting utterly ridiculous. My cell phone had fallen out of my pocket. Useless with its no-bars, but I turned on the flashlight app and held it in the direction of the noise.

I screamed, scrambling backward, as a scaled

monster rushed out from under the leaves, then I tripped over a fallen branch, the phone flying from my hands as I fell into the lake. I sucked in a breath as I splashed to the surface. The stupid armored creature paid me little mind as it crawled inside a hollow log.

"A fucking armadillo," I sputtered. "Arrrrrgh!" I smacked my hands onto the surface as I tried to walk out of the water. The mud made it difficult to move, and I resigned myself to the loss of my tennis shoes as I finally managed to crawl up the small ravine and back onto the path. "Stay hidden, armadillo," I growled. "Or I am going to add you to the barbeque menu."

I collapsed onto the path and rolled onto my back when I made it out of the water. My phone was lit up like a beacon a few feet away. Even so, I stayed supine for a moment as I reexamined my life choices when a man said, "Nice night for a swim."

I blinked at the silhouette towering over me. I grabbed my phone off the path and scrambled to my feet. "Coach Jordan," I said coolly as I prepared to put some real intention into my magic and go crazy on his ass. "What are you doing here?"

"Just taking a walk," he said. He studied my wet clothes. "Most people wear bathing suits."

He was trying to be cute with his banter, but I wasn't having any of it or him. "No," I told him.

"What are you doing here in Southill Village, sorcerer?"

His expression went from surprised to amused. "You think I'm a...," he held out his hands, palms up. "I'm not a sorcerer."

"I know you are." I took a step back. He was tall and had a long reach. There were only two ways to take on someone with longer arms than you, get inside or get away. "Now tell me why you're in Southill Village, masquerading as a football coach."

"I'm not masquerading as anything," Jordan said. "I'm a coach. I'm also a math teacher." He put his hands to his side. "What I'm not is a sorcerer."

"Bullshit." I took another step back and saw the outline of a vine hanging from a tree several feet over his head. Since the bindweed incident, I'd been practicing incantations with climbing plants, and I'd found the magic was stronger if it was added, so I sent out my thoughts to the hanging line, *vine and twine protect mine and thine, twist and wrangle, this man you will tangle*.

The vine came to life, stretching and moving like a snake. I smiled as I met Jordan's gaze. "I hope you like hanging from a tree."

"It wouldn't be the first time," he said. Then, as the vine lashed around him and lifted him off the ground and fifteen feet into the air, he smiled back. Then his eyes flashed silver and began to glow.

My breath caught in my throat. "Not good," I whispered.

The vines holding Jordan fell away from him. He landed on one knee in a superhero pose as the light faded.

So not good.

CHAPTER 7

"Stay back," I warned the six-and-a-half-foot glowing dude—because, make no mistake, he now had a silver glow emanating from his skin. "I'm not going to warn you again." I gestured up to the tree. "You've seen what I can do."

He pointed to the lifeless vines on the ground. "And you've seen what I can do."

"Fair point," I admitted. He wasn't making any moves to attack me, and the glow on his skin faded. "The druids think you're a sorcerer."

"Not a sorcerer," he said again.

"Then what are you?"

"It's complicated."

"Try me."

"I'm half human."

"And the other half?"

"God."

I shook my head. "That wasn't all that complicated."

"You believe me?" he asked.

"I wouldn't go that far." I knew that gods, of a fashion, existed. I'd dealt with Volres, a fire god who had been worshiped for thousands of years. His followers tried to give me to him as a sacrifice. However, I'd learned something really important in the exchange: if gods can be killed, are they really gods? Nope. They were just really powerful beings that convinced a bunch of yahoos they were worth deifying. "Gods don't really exist."

"My father would disagree."

I snorted. "I'm sure he would. Gods don't like to be called on their bullshit."

Jordan grinned. "You're not wrong about that."

I narrowed my gaze at him. Tall, blonde, strong, and looked a lot like.... "Uhm, you're not Thor are you?"

He literally guffawed.

"What?" I asked. "It's a good guess. You have all the mythological traits."

"Only my half-brother is a foot taller than me," Jordan said.

"Half-brother, what?" I did a gazillion mental calculations. Math wasn't my strong suit, but one plus one usually equaled two. "You're Thor's half-brother?"

"One of hundreds of half-brothers and sisters," he admitted. "Maybe thousands. Our father likes to dabble in the mortal realm."

If he and Thor shared a father, then it could only be one god. "Bullshit," I scoffed. "You're telling me that your father is Odin? The Norse god, the Allfather, head of Asgard, etcetera, etcetera, blah, blah."

"Yes, mostly accurate. He has a lot of names."

"So, you're what, a couple thousand years old?"

"Hardly," Jordan said. "I'm fifty-eight."

Jordan barely looked forty, but I let that go.

"This is not computing. Aren't Odin's kids all old as shit?"

"He's got more children than I have time," Jordan told me. "As I said, he does like to spread his seed amongst his people. My mother, Ilsa Oldsen, was a middle school teacher in Wisconsin when Odin seduced her under the name Forni."

The teenage boy inside me giggled. "Like fornication?"

"No, like the ancient one." But he smiled. "But there was some fornication, and then nine months later, I came along."

"Interesting." I knew I should be on guard, but once again, Jordan made me feel peaceful and safe. I shook my head. "Cut out the mojo, man. I'm listening to you, and I'm not trying to lasso you or fry your ass. The least you can do is not cast your voodoo on me."

He sucked in a breath through clenched teeth.

"About that.... I can't help it. I'm not actually doing anything. It's just part of my, uhm, gift. An ability I inherited from my father. People tend to take from me what they need. What are you feeling?"

I shook my head. "Nah." Truthfully, I wasn't surprised about wanting to feel safe or at peace. Even before sparking to tru-craft, I'd felt scared all the time. Not of personal bodily harm, but I had been afraid of being left again. Evan's betrayal had done a number on me. And now, I was getting attacked every few weeks. So...yeah, did I want to feel safe. Absolutely. Still, if Jordan didn't know, then I wasn't going to tell him.

"You still haven't told me why you're in Southill Village, and don't lie to me. I'll know."

He arched a brow at me. "Really?"

I didn't answer because, no, not really. I didn't have a built-in lie detector in my magic, but Jordan didn't know that. "What's the real reason?"

"I've told you the real reason. To coach football and teach math. Even a demi-god who is mostly human has to work," he joked.

I shook my head. "I know that you were involved in the death of a tru-craft witch," I said. "Did you absorb her magic? That's what her coven reported to the Iron Grove."

His eyes reflected the moon as he stared out over the water. "I did, in a way, but not in the way it sounds."

"Is that so?" Keir strolled from the woods, his eyes like puddles of tar and his claws four-inch black diamonds, hard enough and sharp enough to cut through a gargoyle's chest and pierce its heart. He wasn't full pooka which would've put him at ten feet tall, but enough to let Jordan know that he was a seriously dangerous man. "Why don't you tell me how it was when Anna Crestfield drew her last breath, and you took what was rightfully hers?"

Keir had brought the facts.

Jordan crossed his arms over his chest. "She needed to give up her burden, and she needed me to have it. It wasn't what I wanted, but I think she sensed a need in me as well." His voice held grief and loss.

"You loved her," I said.

He gave me a sharp stare. "Yes. It wasn't enough. Look, I have nothing to hide. I just want to live my life."

I narrowed my eyes at him. "Why change your name if you don't have anything to hide?"

"Anna's coven accused me of being responsible for her death." He toed a tree root crossing the path. "I tried to make it work in our town for several years, but after my mother died, I didn't see the point. I changed my name for a fresh start. I'm the son of Ilsa, and no one else, so I changed my name to Sonnavilsa in her honor."

He didn't sound like he was lying, but some

people were better at it than others. "I don't want you—"

"Christ, Mom. What in the world happened to you?" Michael said, cutting off my warning to the coach as he came up the path toward us. "Did you fall in the lake?"

"Uhm." I looked from Jordan to Keir. Luckily, Jordan wasn't glowing anymore, and Keir was back to regular human eyes and fingernails. I made an oops face. "I did fall in, actually."

A short girl with dark hair peeked out from behind Michael. "Wow, you're soaked," she said. "You have to be freezing." She took off her oversized coat, which I noticed was Michael's letterman jacket and handed it to me. "You need this more than me."

I gratefully accepted. "It's a little chilly now that you mention it." I peered at the girl. She really was adorable. I could see why Michael was attracted to her. "You must be Maddie."

Michael shrugged. "I heard you hollering for me. What's up?" He glanced past me to Jordan. "Oh, hey, Coach. Am I missing something?"

I still wasn't sure that Jordan was as harmless, or at least meant no harm, as he was leading us to believe. But I also knew that if he'd wanted to hurt Michael, he could've done it before now. Still, I would be keeping a close eye on him.

"It's fine," I said. "I, er, was just wanting to let you know that I was going to be at Pop-pop's tomorrow, and your phone kept sending me to voicemail." I would tell Michael the truth when we didn't have a non-magical person around. "Then I fell into the water right before your coach showed up."

My son pivoted his gaze between the three of us. Finally, he gave a quick head nod and said, "Whatever."

"What was that explosion?" Maddie asked.

"I don't know." I'd been so focused on finding Michael, not getting killed by an armadillo, and trying to interrogate a demi-god that I'd forgotten about the explosion. "It sounded like it came from the booster bonfire," I said. "Maybe Michael and Maddie should stay out here while we check it out."

Michael furrowed his brow. "I'm going with you."

"Fine," I said. "But if things look sketchy, you find a place to hunker down."

There was a shift in his expression that went from annoyed to alert. "Okay," he agreed. Unlike his father, my teenager was no dummy.

It didn't take long to get off the trail and up to the pavilions. People were sectioned off in groups as the Southill Village Fire Department hosed down the bonfire. Marigold and Rose hurried over to greet us. Rose looked excited. Marigold looked relieved.

"Some kids threw a propane canister into the bonfire," Rose said quickly. "It shot fifty feet into the air."

"At least," Marigold agreed.

Rose nodded to Jordan. "Oh, hey, Coach. Sorry about all this. I'd hoped your first game of the season would end with a bang, but not like this."

I rolled my eyes. Of course, my youngest sister knew the coach. She was eyeball deep in school and town stuff.

Marigold eyed Jordan warily, then asked me, "Are you guys, you know, safe?"

"For now," I told her. "I guess no one was hurt?"

"No." Marigold shook her head. "But it's ended the bonfire. The police have shut down the festivities."

"That's a good way for the chief to lose an election," Rose said. "The boosters are pissed." She pointed to a man who was getting heated with the police and not because of the fire. "That jackass Alan Matheson is going to get us banned from the park." She gave me a quick hug. "See you tomorrow, Iris. Noon sharp. Don't be late. It's for Dad."

I felt the punch of guilt. "I'll be there."

The boosters and parents might be mad at the cops, but I was glad someone had called it quits on the evening. I'd planned to order Michael home to keep him away from his coach until I could learn more about the dubious demi, but thanks to fate and some delinquents, I wouldn't have to drop the hammer.

"We're going to get out of here," Michael said. He

gestured toward the parking lot. "See you tomorrow, Mom."

"Are you staying the night with Doug still?"

"Yep," he said. "That's the plan."

I put my hand on his forearm. "Call me when you get there and settled in for the night," I told him. "I don't care what time it is."

He nodded. "Can I go?"

"Yep." I gave him a quick kiss on the cheek. "Be careful out there."

"I will."

"It was nice to meet you, Ms. Everlee," Maddie said.

At least the young cheerleader had gotten my name right. "You too," I told her.

After they left, I turned on Jordan. "We're not done talking."

"I hadn't thought we were," he said. "But I promise you, I didn't come to Southill Village with the intention to harm anyone."

Keir snarled at Jordan. "We'll see about that."

The man raised his hands in surrender.

"He's one of those Hexen-creeps, right?" Marigold shook her fist at Jordan. "You better not be trying anything with my sister."

Jordan arched a brow at her. "Sister? I would've never guessed."

"Right." Marigold scoffed. "Like you didn't know

I was Iris's sister when you oh-so-casually asked me out."

"It was more of a see-you-there situation," Jordan clarified. There was a smirk of amusement playing on his lips. "But we could make it a date."

I stepped between them, shielding Marigold from his handsome features and his give-you-what-you-need mojo. "No, you could not."

"Oh, look," a woman said. "I've shown up just in time to save Iris from a guy who wants to date her sister."

I was shocked to see Luanne. She smiled, baring her teeth at Jordan. "Imagine my surprise to find you all socializing with a sorcerer like you were at a Sunday picnic." She cracked her knuckles. "I really thought I was going to get to kill something." She quirked her head to the side. "Of course, the night is still young."

"I thought it was going to take you two days to get here," I told her. "That was a fast drive."

She shrugged, easing herself from Marigold's embrace. "Keir seemed freaked, so I hitched a ride with a friend."

The tough act was foiled when Marigold launched herself at Luanne and threw her arms around the druid warrior's neck. "Welcome home. I've missed you."

"And me?" Zev stepped out of the shadows. He

lowered his sunglasses, and his eyes blazed with fire as he stared at my sister. "Did you miss me?"

CHAPTER 8

"THE NERVE OF THAT MAN!" MARIGOLD SAID FOR the umpteenth time. "He did not just show up willy-nilly, all flirty and fiery, and expect that I'm just going to melt in his presence. No way. No how."

"He is a fire elemental. Melting isn't out of the question." I poured us both a cup of coffee and moved it to the center island. "Donut?"

"Yes, please," she said, snatching a cinnamon twist. "Since I brought them."

After the bonfire, Keir had taken me home when the festivities closed, then he, Lu, and Zev had set about relocating the pixies to their new nesting digs on the mountain. I told them I would join them after I met with my family to talk to dad.

Michael was still at Doug's. I would tell him about his coach this weekend before he went back to school on Monday. I had some breathing room before Michael had to confront the fact that his coach was a magic-sucking sorcerer or demi-god. Ugh. The fact that I had to talk to my teenager about this stuff was mind-boggling.

I hadn't been surprised when Marigold had come over this morning with donuts. I was pretty sure she'd been sent by Rowan and Rose to make sure I showed up at Dad's for the big family meeting. I had missed a few...okay, all the family dinners because, hello, unstable magic. Yep. Did that make me someone irresponsible who needed an escort? Maybe. Still, I was glad for the company and the sugary, fried pastry.

My sister dragged her finger around the rim of her mug. "Jordan is really sexy."

"Nope." I put my hand on hers to stop her musing. "He's dangerous."

She clucked her tongue. "Then he's just my type."

"Hah. But no." I still wasn't sure why Jordan was in Southill Village, but I didn't buy his explanation. What kind of demi-god needed a job? Even if he didn't have an ulterior agenda, I didn't want his "you might not get what you want, but you get what you need" juju near Marigold. I didn't know what she needed in her life, but an immortal dude whose last love died in his arms wasn't the answer. "Stay away from him, Mar. I mean it."

I walked to the window and peered out at the garden. Linda wasn't in her normal place facing the bench. It dawned on me that I hadn't seen her since the night before when my tornado tried to take out the kitchen. Not that you could tell. They might be a nuisance, but the pixies were handy little suckers.

"Are your flying guests still here?" Marigold asked.

"Nope. How's work?" I asked, changing the subject. I didn't want my sister entrenched in the troubles that surrounded the magical side of my world.

"Good." Marigold taught Women's Studies at Darling University. "I've tasked my students to identify and write a five-page essay on a woman in history who they believe has furthered the cause of feminism."

"You know you're going to be grading a dozen papers on Ruth Bader Ginsburg."

"They could pick worse than the Notorious RGB —may she rest in peace—but I'd love to see some of them get creative with their choices."

I snorted a laugh. "Be careful what you wish for."

She gave me the stink eye. "Are you going to tell the family?"

"I think they already know about Ginsburg."

"Don't get cute," Marigold said.

"Look at me." I winked at her. "It's too late for that."

"Are you going to tell our family that you're a witch?"

"With Dad falling and all, it's not really the right time, is it?" I sat down next to Marigold and nudged her with my shoulder. I inhaled the nutty aroma of the coffee as I took a sip. The taste, along with the caffeine, gave me life. "I'm not sure they're ready to know. I feel like I haven't had time to lay down the groundwork."

"Come on," Marigold said. "You're not ready. This doesn't have anything to do with them and everything to do with you. What are you so afraid of?" She cupped her mug with both hands as if to keep them warm. "You're pushing the family away. Distancing yourself. It's like you've discovered your real identity, and you're turning your back on your old one. The one that has a brother and sisters and a dad."

Her words were like a cold slap. "I'm not," I denied. "I'm not doing that at all. I would never turn my back on you guys."

"When was the last time you called Rose?"

"I see Rose four times a week."

"Because she comes over here to train you, but have you called her just to talk? Or Rowan? Or Dahlia?"

She was right about our oldest two siblings. I'd talked to Rowan a few times because of the medical scares my new magic had caused, but otherwise, I'd avoided him and his questions that I wasn't ready to answer. As for Dahlia, I couldn't remember the last conversation I'd had with her that wasn't more than a hi and goodbye. "I'm not doing it on purpose," I told Marigold. "My life has been crazy for a while. Like dangerous crazy."

"I get that." She dusted cinnamon and sugar off the twist and back into the donut box. I could tell the conversation was painful for her. She was the happy-go-lucky sister. The one who nothing bothered. Only, I knew that wasn't true. At the core of Marigold, she was a worrier, maybe even more so than Rose, but she knew how to make someone feel better without prying. This conversation was turning her into my personal crowbar. "All they see is that you've divorced, found someone new, and that you're throwing every bit of your time into making a new relationship work."

I was appalled at the observation. "That's not what's happening."

Marigold lifted her fingers from the center island surface in a "whoa there" gesture. "I know that's not what's happening," she said. "Because I *know* what's happening. You told me the truth, so I don't have to guess at it."

My stomach churned as I considered her words. From an outside perspective, I could see how the rest of my family might think that I was throwing myself at Keir and making him my whole world. They couldn't know that every day I was fighting for control, fighting for my life, and trying hard not to get anyone I loved killed in the process.

"You're right," I mumbled.

"What was that?" she asked. "I'm not sure I heard you."

"You're right." I rolled my eyes at her. "I've been terrible. Mom would be ashamed."

"Come on, Iris. A few months of ghosting your family doesn't make you a monster or erase forty-odd years of being the best sister and daughter around."

"Don't let Rose hear you say that."

Marigold giggled. "If you repeat it, I'll deny it."

I nodded, forcing a smile to my lips. With a lot of uncertainty, I fought the urge to run away and said, "I'll tell them."

"Today?" Her shoulders tensed. "I mean, we will all be together in a private setting where no one outside the family can overhear."

"What about Don and the boys?"

"Nope. They won't be there. Just us chickens. Or, in this case, Everlees."

"Does it have to be today?"

"I won't tell your secrets, Iris." Marigold's tone and expression grew serious. "But it's taking a toll on me too. Every time they ask or worry about you to me, I have to make up excuses. I don't like lying to them."

"Oh, man. I am the worst." I hadn't even thought about what keeping the secret would mean for

Marigold. "I should never have brought you into my mess."

"I'm going to throat punch you," she said. "You absolutely should've brought me into your mess. I'm not just your sister. I'm your best friend. These are the kinds of things you share with both. And as you recall, you didn't exactly volunteer the information. I had to watch you catch yourself on fire. If I hadn't, you'd still be keeping it from me." Her last sentence ended with a cute pout.

"I looooove you," I sang sweetly. With a coy smile, I bit into a powdered donut, then gave her a sugary, messy kiss on the cheek. "You're the best."

Marigold leaned away from me. "All right. Don't get carried away." She brushed the sugar from her face. "I'm just saying, before your magic goes all whack-a-doodle in front of the rest of the family, it would be nice for them to hear it from you first."

A tapping at the garden window drew our attention. Fair Konig, the pixie king, was hovering in front of the pane, frantically beating at the glass to get my attention.

Marigold's eyes widened. "You definitely need to tell them before they see something like this because, unlike your elusive gnome friend, pixies in heat don't seem to give a crap who sees them."

I got up and opened the window. "I thought you guys were moving up the mountain."

"Where is the monstrosity?" he demanded.

I winced at his tone. Even so, I had zero idea what he was going on about. "You're going to have to be more specific."

"The giant white and orange creature you call Bob!" His face was an unflattering shade of red.

"Bob?"

"*Ja*! Zee Bob!" His voice hitched up to a higher octave, making him sound squeaky. "He is a murderous, filthy imp."

"Bob wouldn't hurt a fly...." My mouth formed a small "o." He was actually well-known for hunting down flies. *Eeee*. "Who did he murder?"

"Annibish!" Fair Konig exclaimed. "She was coming up with the second group of my troupe, but when they arrived, she wasn't with them. I know my Annibish. She wouldn't have left our people for any reason. Not unless she wasn't able to fulfill her duty to our kin. It can only mean one thing."

I covered my mouth. "No, not my sweet, innocent Bob. He would never." But a part of me knew that he might, and that part was feeling sick with grief. "Are you sure?"

"She's missing," he hissed. "It can only be the Bob."

"It's just Bob," I corrected him. "You don't need the *the*." I waved my hand. "You know what, never mind. Why do you think Bob, uhm, ate Annibish?"

"Who's Annibish?" Marigold asked as she took a

bite of her cinnamon twist and then proceeded to lick her fingers.

Fair Konig stared at her with the horrified expression of a man whose mate had been eaten by a cat.

Marigold blanched. "Sorry," she said with a mouthful as bits of donuts tumbled onto the counter. She took a drink of coffee to wash it down. "My bad."

"Annibish is Fair Konig's wife," I looked at the pixie to make sure I got it right. He didn't say otherwise, so I continued with the explanation. "Last night, Bob got a little playful with her outside."

"He attacked her," the pixie revised. "He's a vicious animal."

Marigold shook her head. "Nah," she said. "That doesn't sound anything like Bob."

"Did you see him, er...eat Annibish?" The question made me queasy.

"No," Fair Konig admitted. "But she wouldn't disappear without telling me. It has to be Bob."

Bob was still in bed, the lazy chonky. I hoped he stayed there until I got this sorted. I nodded to the pixie king. "Okay. Let's search the garden."

His stare widened at me. "For what?"

I wasn't sure how to say this next part nicely, so I just spit it out. "Bob doesn't have a butthole, which means he doesn't poop. This also means he technically doesn't eat. Whenever he swallows bugs, he usually regurgitates them in a few minutes. Usually, somewhere around the garden." I made an *ick* face. "It's a bone of contention for Linda."

"Are you telling me that my Annibish is in a pile of sickness somewhere out there?" He made a gesture toward the garden.

I nodded. "If Bob got her, then yes, that's what I'm saying."

Fair Konig zipped out the open kitchen window, off to find what was left of his missing love.

Marigold stood up, dusting crumbs from her tunic top. "Iris, you can't do this right now. We have to go to Dad's."

I looked at my kitchen clock. "We have nearly an hour. I can't not help him look. I mean, Annibish is a person too." An extremely small person, granted, but a person all the same. "If Bob is responsible, I have to search for her. It's the right thing to do."

"You have thirty-two minutes to wrap this up. If you don't find her by then, we're going."

"But—"

She cut me off. "No buts. There is always going to be some kind of magical disaster going on some-where, but you have to make time for the people who matter."

I ran my hands through my hair and groaned. "You're right. It won't take long to search the garden, and if we don't find her, you know, chewed up, then this isn't Bob's doing."

"I'm helping you look," Marigold said. "It'll be

quicker that way." She opened the back door, then her mouth dropped open as she slammed it shut. She turned to me. Her expression aghast. "Uhm, Iris. There's a guy in your backyard with hairy legs and hooves, and I think he's trying to catch the pixie king."

CHAPTER 9

I LOOKED OUT THE WINDOW. SURE ENOUGH, AT THE back of the garden near Linda's bench, a man with furry legs and cloven hooves was hopping up and down trying to catch Fair Konig. "What the hell is that thing?"

"I don't know." Marigold came around me and peered out the window. "The little dude needs help. He is completely outsized. Why isn't he just flying away?"

It was a reasonable question. "I'll go find out." I reached for the doorknob. "Call Keir."

Marigold grabbed her purse and dug around for her cell phone. "Maybe you should wait for him."

"Maybe, but I'm not going to." I shooed her toward the living room. "Let Keir know what's going on. Tell him to bring Lu. We might need the backup."

"What about Zev? You know...if he's still in town."

I gave her a bland look. "Just call Keir. Whoever shows up, shows up. I'll go out and see what the, uhm, the goat guy wants."

"Sure, go talk to the goat guy," she said incredulously. "That'll turn out well."

"I promised to protect Fair Konig and his troupe." Apparently, I'd already failed miserably with his wife. I couldn't fail him again now. "No matter what happens," I told her. "Stay inside."

"You don't have to ask me twice." As parting words, she added, "Don't set yourself on fire."

"Good tip. But I'm not planning to use any magic if I can help it." I'd done enough damage to Southill Village in the past, including causing the community pool to crack open and drain while it was full of local kids, all because I was trying to use earth magic to split a pebble. Even though I'd managed to become one with earth and fire magic, my aero-craft magic had been unpredictable and difficult to control. I didn't want to accidentally send a cyclone tearing through my neighbors' homes by inadvertently calling on the one element I hadn't mastered.

"See you on the flip side." I tipped my head to her and ran out the back door, slamming it behind me.

The goat-legged creature howled as one of Fair Konig's sharp wings cut into its forearm. He had enormous horns, like a curled-horned mountain goat, that were coiled close to his head, acting as bookends for his skull.

The man-goat sprang seven or eight feet into the air, trying to grab its prey, but the pixie king kept flying out of reach. Why was the winged idiot hanging around and not trying to get away?

"Hey!" I shouted, flapping my arms to get the creature's attention. "Pick on someone your own size."

He turned his gaze on me, and I got a good look at his face. He had brown hair, light golden eyes, and extremely attractive symmetrical features that made him appear ethereal. Holy crap. He looked like an angel. An angel with horns and the legs and hooves of a goat.

Shit. Was he Lucifer? After all, the fallen angel had been depicted as having horns and hooves in a lot of books and artworks. "Uhm, get behind me, Satan."

Goat-boy smiled. "Well, hello."

He was so ridiculous. Still, I giggled. "You should go."

Fair Konig did a flyby near my head. "He's got Annibish!"

I couldn't help but feel a small sense of vindication on my familiar's behalf. "I told you it wasn't Bob."

"Not the point," the pixie admonished. "That hooved beast took my Annibish, and he won't give her back unless I give him my *Feenstaub*!"

"Give me the pixie, sweeting, and I'll give you a kiss," Goat-boy said.

I laughed. "You can kiss my ass."

"An attractive offer to be sure," he said. "I accept."

My ears grew hot. "Ew, no. That wasn't an offer."

"Too bad, sweeting." He tilted his head to the left as he examined me. "You have a comely arse." He stared at my boobs. "And methinks the apples are ripe in your garden. I would kiss them as well, plucking each stem until you beg me to taste your fruit."

This fucking guy, man. Who the hell talked like this? I'd been mildly amused initially, but he was pissing me off now. "You're barking up the wrong witch, asshole."

"Aye, it's true. I have an arsehole like everyone else. I'm fixing to show it to you if you don't hand over the wee one."

"Tell me where my Annibish is," Fair Konig demanded. "I'll not ask again."

"Truer than true," the goat-guy said. "Because I don't plan to answer. Not until you give me what I want."

"What do you want with the pixie dust?" I asked, stalling for time. If Marigold managed to contact Keir on the phone, he was probably twenty minutes from getting here. I wasn't sure how to stop the devil, so a little help from the paranormal expert would be much appreciated.

His gaze met mine. "I can feel your energy, love. It's strong. Powerful." He shook his head. "But there is a fight for control between you and the magic. You're very close to losing."

I was doing just fine, damn it. I didn't need some angel-demon telling me I was failing. "Thank you for the assessment, Dr. Horny. I didn't ask for a house call."

He made wet kissing noises, then narrowed his golden eyes, lowered his head, and sprinted right at me. Yikes, I was feet from a head butt.

"Get out of the way!" I warned Fair Konig, pushing him one way while launching myself in the opposite direction.

I grunted as my shoulder clipped a paving stone as I rolled away. The devil hit the aluminum clapboard siding on my house and put a dent in it.

"Hey!" I shouted. "Not cool." Goat guy shook his head as if the blow had rattled him, then he grinned.

Fair Konig flew up behind the hooved asshat, his sword out. I wasn't sure what his tiny sword could do against the creature. It turned out not much, as the hairy-legged dude whipped around and snatched the pixie king from the air. "Aye, gotcha, I did."

His human-looking fingers were bloody as the pixie's wings sliced and diced, but the goat guy didn't let go. On the contrary, he laughed and laughed as if the pixie were tickling him.

I'd learned a few fighting moves from Luanne, but

my next move was all Linda. I grabbed a handful of dirt and pea gravel from a nearby flower bed as I got to my feet, and then I chucked it right into the laughing creature's smug face.

He wiped his mouth with the back of his free hand and turned a menacing glare in my direction. "T'was not very nice, sweeting." He squeezed Fair Konig's body in his fist, and the pixie began to turn blue. "The wee beasty can give me his dust, or I'll kill him and his mate for kicks and giggles, then no one will get the dust."

"Wait." I was confused about how pixie dust was harvested, apparently. He had the pixie king literally in hand. Why couldn't he just take Fair Konig's magic sprinkles? "Just ease up there," I said. I held my hands up like a magician with nothing up her sleeves. "Don't be hasty."

In my peripheral vision, I saw the backyard gate slowly open. Marigold poked her head inside. Damn it. I told her to stay in the house. Even so, I tried not to react. I didn't want the goat guy to turn his attention to her.

"Heeeeeeeey," I said loudly, trying to cover the slight squeak of the hinges as she slipped inside the gate. "Let's all take a breath here." I twirled my hand with a flourish toward the pixie. "Literally. Fair Konig is turning an unflattering shade of gray. If you kill him now, you get nothing," I guessed because I didn't actually know. If I got the pixie out of this alive, I would have a much longer talk with him about his supernatural spunk, or whatever it was.

I wanted to give a head shake to Marigold, who was tip-toeing along the fence, but any warning might give her away.

"You know what," I told the half-man. "Why don't we find some common ground here? I don't want the pixie dead, and you don't want him dead. Not really." Fair Konig was still struggling, but his wings and swings were only moving half-heartedly. I wasn't sure how much longer he could survive getting the stuffing squeezed out of him. "Let's talk this out. What's your name?"

"All right, lover. We'll play your game. My name is Sylva."

"Sylva," I said. Then in a poor Groucho Marx imitation, I added, "You look like a gold to me." At least it wasn't Lucifer. It shot my theory of him being the devil out of the water. You know, unless the devil had decided to change his name. I mean, I did. These things happened. It wasn't unusual for someone, even Lucifer, to want a fresh start.

Sylva's forehead wrinkled. "Are you trying to be funny?"

"Unfortunately, I am. You know, you got gold eyes, not silver, so not Sylva. It was a poor attempt at humor. Just trying to lighten the mood." Poor Fair Konig. His movements were turning sluggish, and his head hung to one side. "No pixie dust if you kill him," I reminded Sylva.

He sighed, then eased his grip. I could hear the pixie's gasp as his normal color started to return to his face.

"That's a great start, Sylva."

"Now tell me your name, my witchy paramour." He smiled, and I noticed his teeth were almost squares, like that of a horse. It made his ethereal looks a little less angelic.

Marigold had picked up a large shovel and was sneaking up behind Sylva. *Oh, Marigold.* What in the world was she doing? This wasn't going to end well.

"I'm Iris," I told him. "Maybe we can come to some kind of arrangement with the fairy dust."

"I am *not* a fairy!" Fair Konig complained. "Don't ever call me that, you ignorant *Hexe*!" His rant lasted for several more seconds, and it distracted Sylva enough that he didn't notice my sister bringing the shovel down on his head. The move managed to do little but startle the cloven-hooved pixie squeezer as the shovel clanged off his dense skull.

Marigold dropped the shovel and stumbled backward as he turned his gaze on her. "Another nymph comes to play with Sylva's pipe. Your pouty lips will wet my reed, and together, we'll make beautiful music."

"Uh, no, thank you," Marigold said as her backside hit the fence. "I'm not really into music."

"You'll change your tune, dearest one, when I bring your song to its ultimate climax. You'll never want to play another instrument again."

"Cut the double-entendres. That's my sister, and she won't be coming anywhere near your...instrument."

His lips curled up in a grin. "You know what they say, once you go satyr, you're never a hater."

Oh, boy. This guy was a satyr. It made sense. Horny half-man, half-goat. I was kicking myself for not thinking of it in the first place. Only, the mythology didn't quite measure up to the guy standing in front of me. "I thought satyrs were dumb, clumsy, ugly creatures who only thought about drinking wine and screwing nymphs." I shrugged. "I mean, you don't seem all that clumsy to me."

His grin turned into a scowl. "You're a feisty one."

"That's what I hear."

Sylva stuffed Fair Konig into an opening in his fur.

I wrinkled my nose in horror. Unless he had pockets, I could only hazard a guess that the pixie king was currently nestled against Sylva's anatomical pipes and maracas. Eeek.

He whipped around and made a grab for Marigold.

"No!" I shouted when she let out a scream.

I considered calling on fire or earth to help me stop Sylva, but Fair Konig was tucked inside the satyr's hairy underpants—for lack of a more accurate term—and anything I did to the awful creature could hurt the pixie king. Instead, I ran at the jackass's backside and lunged at him. I grabbed both his horns, then jumped up and kicked the back of his knees with both feet.

Not my best plan. The satyr landed backward on top of me. His tail swished against my stomach as he paddled his feet, trying to get up. I wrapped my legs around his waist and squeezed as hard as I could. Damn, Rose's training had given me some rock-hard thighs. Sylva started throwing elbows back at me, and I had to tuck my arms under his back to maintain my grip on his horns.

"Let me go!" he bellowed.

I couldn't see what was going on above me, but he let out another howl of pain, and I heard Marigold say, "How do you like that tune, asshole? It's called shovel to the face." Then she added, "Next on the playlist is a shovel to the nuts."

"Don't!" I shouted. "Fair Konig is near his nuts."

"Got it," Marigold said. "Then I'll stick with an encore."

"Bitch!" Sylva wheezed. "You broke my nose." Unable to loosen my grip on his body or horns, he raised his head then head-butted me in the face.

Marigold shouted, "Iris!"

I saw stars as he pulled his head back up for another smashing blow.

I was dazed and most likely concussed, which

made it harder to fight Sylva off. He managed to turn his torso, and he punched me in the stomach and the ribs, knocking the wind from me. I couldn't breathe. On the verge of passing out, I prepared myself for the next hit. The wind began to pick up fallen leaves around me as I started losing consciousness. *He can't hurt the wind. It must be nice,* I thought, because I was in a lot of pain.

Sylva fell away from me. I heard some metal against rock and bone, then my sister Marigold stood over me, a bloody shovel in her hand.

I rasped out. "Run."

She knelt down next to me. "Don't worry about that goat bastard. He can't hurt you anymore," she said. Her dark hair was loose and wild, flying around her as if she'd rubbed her head against a balloon. Her eyes were wide with shock. "I chopped his head off. Are you...are you...Iris, are you okay?"

"I'll live." I hoped. "Hel...help me up," I told her. I went up on an elbow and collapsed to the ground as if there was nothing there to support me. I glanced over and blinked a few times to clear my vision. "Oh, God," I said. "My arm is missing." Where my arm had been, there was a swirl of dust and other garden debris as if my arm had been replaced by the wind.

"Iris, it's not just your arm," Marigold said. "Your whole midsection is gone."

I glanced down and groaned. "How is this my life?"

CHAPTER 10

"I DON'T KNOW WHAT TO DO," MARIGOLD SAID. "Should I try to move you? I'm afraid I'll pull you apart."

At least she hadn't insisted on calling 9-1-1. There wasn't a single thing modern medicine could do for me. My right arm was intact. I used it to push myself up. My mid-section was empty, but my upper body hovered above the space. Weirdly, I wasn't in any pain. As a matter of fact, I felt nothing in those swirling spaces at all.

Of course, my battered face still throbbed.

"How are you doing that?" Marigold asked. "It's like you got sawed in half."

My legs moved when I thought about getting up, and with the help of my one good arm, I got to my feet. "Where's Keir?"

Marigold got up with me and held my elbow. "I

couldn't get ahold of him," she said. "His phone kept going straight to voicemail." Of course, she couldn't. If he was at home, his place had no reception. "That's why I came out here. I wanted to help."

I glanced over at Sylva. Marigold had severed his head with the sharp end of the shovel like the snake he was. If she hadn't, I'm not sure I'd be alive.

"You did help," I said. "You saved my life."

Marigold blew out a long audible breath and shook her head. "I....I just reacted. After the way he almost killed that pixie, and then he was beating you. All I could think was I needed to stop him."

The pixie. Oh no. "Fair Konig," I said. "He's inside the satyr's pouch."

She looked at the dead goat guy's waist. "He's not wearing a pouch."

"Yeah," I shook my head. "Not that kind of pouch." My upper body gyrated above my hips as I awkwardly knelt next to the Satyr's legs, and I lightly probed where I'd seen him shove the pixie king.

"Don't touch him there," Marigold said.

"If I could avoid it, I would." My fingertips felt something sticky. "Yuck. I found it."

"Found what?" she asked.

"This." I slipped my fingers into the slit and touched a disgustingly slippery, uhm, pipe, though it felt more like a bratwurst. Gross. I pulled the opening to one side. "Help me."

"I don't think so," Marigold said, gagging. "There

are some lines that shouldn't be crossed." She made a face. "Like ever."

"Fair Konig is in there. I just need you to hold it open, so I can free him." She didn't look convinced, so I added, "He might die if we don't."

Marigold let out an exasperated sigh. "Fine. But if I touch his instrument, there will be hell to pay."

The situation was dire. Parts of my body were made of air, and I had no idea how to fix them. I was going to dig around a satyr's genitals to rescue an annoying pixie. And still, my sister could make me smile. "Noted," I told her. "Now get down here and stretch it wide."

"That pixie better be the only thing that comes out of there," she muttered.

"From your lips to God's ears," I agreed. I reached inside the split fur and tried hard not to think about what was rubbing against my skin. "Come on, pixie. Come out, come out, where ever you are?" I felt a sharp sting against my finger. "Ouch."

"What?"

"I think I found him." I hooked my finger around what I hoped was a pixie waist and gently tugged it toward the surface.

"That's not the pixie king," Marigold said.

"No," I agreed as I pulled the lifeless body of the female pixie free of the satyr. "It's Annibish. His wife."

"Is she breathing?" Marigold asked.

I shook my head. "She was trapped for too long."

I set her on my lap and then reached back inside the flap. Was I too late for the pixie king? I'd broken my promise to protect them from dust hunters, and Annibish had died as a result. If Fair Konig was gone, did that mean their mating rites were over as well? The king was the only one who could produce pixie dust. Had I doomed an entire troupe?

I probed until I found him, and like with Annibish, I gently removed the small king. If he was alive, how would I tell him about his mate? He loved her. He fought hard to win her back. And in the end, it wasn't enough. My upper body began gyrating harder as if I'd been set on the spin cycle as I drew him free of the satyr's prison.

"Fair Konig," I said. "Wake up."

"Is he...." Marigold let the question hang.

He wasn't lifeless, but he was unconscious. "He's breathing," I said, finally. "Poor pixie king." I set him down beside his love. The way my body was moving, it was a much harder task than it sounded. "How will he go on without her?"

I couldn't imagine what life would be like without Keir in it. I had a son, and for that reason alone, I would learn how to survive on my own. Would Fair Konig's children be enough to sustain him? I prayed it was so.

I tilted my head back as tears streamed down my

puffing cheeks. The swelling had made it hard to see, but my injuries weren't the reason I cried.

I realized something that should've occurred to me much sooner. I was a shit witch. I had no idea what I was doing, and my lack of knowledge was a danger to everyone around me. "You should go, Marigold. Go before something bad happens to you."

"Iris," she said.

"No." I cut her off. "I don't know what I'm doing. If I don't kill myself, I'm going to kill someone I love. If that happens, I'll never forgive myself. You have to go. Go to the meeting. Tell the family that I'm...." I shook my head. The swirling grew more intense as if any minute I would be lifted into the sky. Good. Let my power take me to the clouds. At least there, I couldn't hurt anyone. "Tell Dad I love him. Tell everyone else whatever you want to tell them. Tell them the truth. You don't have to lie for me anymore."

"Iris," Marigold said more insistently.

I lowered my chin and made eye contact with her. "I love you, Marigold. Never forget that. Thank you for always being there for me. I'm sorry I ruined everything."

Her frown deepened, cutting a crease between her brows. "Are you done having a pity party yet? Because if you are, look down."

"Harsh," I said but did as she ordered. Neither of the pixies was on my lap now.

"Your stomach," Marigold said. "They're flying."

I looked down and saw Fair Konig holding Annibish close to him as they flew around in circles where my lower torso used to be. He was smiling and crying as he kissed her all over her face. She was smiling and crying too.

My own tears flowed harder as I watched their reunion. "She's alive."

"You're aero-craft has brought her back to me," Fair Konig exclaimed. "Thank you, Iris Everlee. Thank you."

"See," Marigold said. "You don't ruin everything."

The back gate opened. A pooka, a druid, and an ifrit walked into my garden. A good start to the joke that was my life.

Keir ran over to me. "Goddess, all mighty," he said. "Iris, what's happening? You're…. I don't understand." He looked over at Zev. "Help her."

The fire djinn held his hands out. "I'm afraid this isn't something I can help with, my friend. It's her own magic, and that overrides a genie wish."

Luanne checked over Marigold as Zev kept his distance. The coward.

"Are there fairies flying inside Iris's stomach?" Lu asked.

"Pixies," I answered.

Keir's worried expression made me more worried. "I just got Marigold's messages when we were a few blocks from the house."

"You're a day late to the party," I said. "Well, about five minutes late." I almost touched my face with my existing hand, then remembered where it had been. "If you love me, you'll scratch my nose."

"It looks broken." He itched the bridge with his fingertip. "I can't believe you took on a satyr."

I glanced at Marigold. "I had a little help. She's the one who killed it."

"Seriously?" The druid warrior looked impressed as she nodded to my sister. "Respect."

Marigold looked like she was trying not to puke. "Uhm, thanks."

Zev's eyes blazed bright enough I could see the fire behind his sunglasses. "You shouldn't put yourself in danger. You're not equipped for the trappings of the supernatural world."

Marigold arched a brow at him. "Screw you."

I gave Keir a pained smile. "What do I do now? How do I get my body back?"

"I think we're going to have to consult the grimoire," he said. "I know you don't want to, but...."

I raised my good hand, mostly to keep it away from my body but also to stop him from telling me what I already knew. "Fine. I'll read the damn book."

He put his arm around my upper torso and helped me to my feet. My shirt was still pulled up, and he said, "I think Fair Konig has started the rites."

I glanced down and witnessed the king and his wife doing the naked, Humpty dance where my stomach used to be. "Nope." I yanked my T-shirt down to my hips. "They need to get a room." I pointed to my stomach area. "And this isn't it."

Luanne laughed. "Iris Everlee, bringing loved ones together."

"Har har." All I really wanted was to bring myself together. I gripped Keir's shoulder as he helped me inside the house. "You should throw your shirt in the washer," I told him. "And turn the hot water on in the sink."

"Why?" he asked.

"Like Star Trek, I went where no one should ever go."

"I don't think that's the tag line," he said. "It's where no one has gone."

"Well, I don't know about all that, but I had my hand in the satyr's pecker sack. I'm pretty sure there were some sweaty, slimy balls in there as well. It's where he'd packed the pixies away before we fought."

He let me go like I was a live wire and turned the hot water on.

I one-handed pumped some soap into my palm. "Can you help?"

"Uhm...."

"I can't scrub it myself," I pouted.

"Fine." He used his hands to scrub and lather mine.

"You really love me."

"I really do."

I heard a couple high pitched squeals and a few grunts over the running water. "I think the pixies are done." Thank heavens. Though, the fact that they had been in the same pouch as my hand and they had sex after without washing was super disgusting as much as it was disturbing.

"I have assembled my donsy," Linda announced, suddenly in my kitchen. "We have decided to leave zee mountain for good. Never to return." Then she saw the state I was in and gasped, "*Liebling,* what have you done to yourself now?"

CHAPTER 11

L U TOOK THE FRISKY PIXIES BACK TO KEIR'S
property on the mountain, Zev disposed of the satyr's
body, Linda agreed to not leave forever until after my
wind problem was resolved, and Marigold went to the
family meeting. Without me. I really was the worst
ever. Once again, Marigold was going to lie and make
excuses for me. I had no idea how I would make it up
to her, my siblings, and my dad. I'm not sure I ever
could.

The stepladder in my closet wobbled. Keir was on
the top of the steps, half-in and half-out of the attic
trap door in my closet. After I'd bound my grimoire,
I tossed it in the attic, hoping to never have to deal
with it again. Total pipe dream. Now, since I only had
one good hand and no abdomen, Keir was digging it
back out for me.

"Careful," I warned him. "I can't catch you if you fall."

My face and body that were still visible hurt from the beating. My left eye was almost swollen shut, and I worried that I had an orbital fracture. Linda had gathered some healing herbs then made me eat them. They'd helped somewhat, but not enough. I'd tried a couple times to return the portions of my body the air had replaced, but my efforts had caused more of my body to disappear, so I quit messing around. I definitely needed more information before trying again. Otherwise, I was going to turn into a morning breeze and blow away.

Keir coughed, then followed it up with a sneeze. "I think you have asbestos."

"Just don't inhale too deeply," I said.

I heard Keir's head smack a roof beam. "Ow. Please tell me you're joking."

"Is the big bad pooka afraid of a little asbestos?" When he didn't answer, I said, "No asbestos. I had the house checked years ago when Michael developed a cough." During his first few years, I worried all the time about every cough, sneeze, and hangnail when it came to my son. Honestly, I still worried, but thankfully for my kid, I was a lot less obsessive.

"Did you have to throw it so far back?"

"Yes," I told him. "I never planned to open it ever again. I thought I'd made that clear."

"Yeah, but did you really think it was going to be that easy?"

"A woman can dream." Bob hopped onto the bed, and before I could stop him, the adorable floof was curled up in my empty space. I didn't make him move. I mean, if two pixies could fornicate in the space, then Bob could hang out there.

Linda wobbled through the bedroom door, took one look at me petting Bob and shook her head. "Zis is disturbing. You are a mess, *Kleinkind*. I don't know how you'll survive without me."

"I don't have to find out if you stay."

She gave an angry wave with her arm. "You've given me no choice."

"I didn't do anything," I protested. "I mean, I didn't do anything to you. I can't help it if I'm not as homicidal as you are."

"Those pixies bring nothing but death with them." She pointed at me and then drew a bullseye in the air. "You'll see. This disappearing act you are doing is likely their fault."

"You can't really believe that," I told her.

"Silence!" She clapped her hands. When she got like this, she reminded me of Frau Blucher from the movie *Young Frankenstein*. Even so, Linda had become very important to me in a short amount of time. Granted, I'd had the gnome in my garden for years before I sparked to magic, so I hadn't known she was a real person until then.

I wished I understood why she was set on leaving the garden, so I could talk her out of it.

"All the pixies are up the mountain at Keir's place," I told her, hoping that would help. "They won't bother you anymore."

"Their existence bothers me," she replied.

Stubborn gnome. "What did Fair Konig and his people do to you?"

"I'm touching it," Keir said from the closet. "It's at my fingertips."

"Watch the stitching. The metal thread will cut you." That's how the book had sparked my terracraft.

Linda shook her head. "It doesn't matter what his people did to mine," she said. "You won't break your bargain with him no matter what I say."

"I might," I said. "For you." I wasn't sure I could leave his group to fend for themselves against the likes of Sylva the Satyr and whoever came next for them. But I could figure out a way to get someone else to protect them. Maybe Zev. Hah. He would as soon as light them on fire, I'm sure. "If they did something terrible to you, and I have to choose between you and my word to the pixies. I choose you."

"But you didn't, did you?"

Painfully accurate. I almost wished she'd thrown something at me instead of hearing the hurt I heard in her voice. "I'm sorry, Linda." I'd known she'd be mad when I agreed to protect the troupe until their week of mating and gestating came to its natural conclusion. But…. "I didn't think you'd leave."

"You don't think," she said. She pointed at my missing arm and stomach. "That's how you get in these predicaments."

"Got it!" Keir said excitedly. There was another wobble of the stepladder, then a "Whooa!" and my usually graceful guy came tumbling out of the closet and onto my hardwood floor. He was clutching the bound grimoire against his chest. He glanced over at me. "I found your book."

I raised my brows. "I see that."

He plopped it on the bed next to me. "Undo it."

I had changed twine to metal with an off-the-cuff spell. I wasn't sure I could remember it exactly enough to reverse the spell. "That might be a problem." With my corporeal hand, I traced the bindings. They turned back to twine and then charred to ash before they fell away without me casting any spell. "I take that back."

"Your grimoire is eager to help you, *Kleinkind*. That's what it lives for."

Well, poop. I'd forgotten the leather-bound tome was alive when I bound it and chucked it in the attic. I'd trapped a living creature because of fear, and I kept it locked away so I wouldn't have to deal with more new magic.

"I forgot," I told it. "I'm sorry." The elemental

symbols for Earth, Fire, and Air began to glow yellow, red, and light blue. It was keen for me to open it, but I couldn't shake my reluctance.

"Do you want to stay half-woman half-air for as long as you can live before you starve because you have no digestive tract right now?" Linda asked. Talk about getting down to the heart of it.

"Fine." I frowned. "No funny business," I told the grimoire. "Or next time, I'll throw you in the lake."

The symbols began to flicker in a pattern like disco lights.

"I think you're making it nervous," Keir said.

"Me?" The book had been nothing but a pain in the ass since I'd bought it at the auction. Or rather, it had manipulated me into bidding on it. "This thing has had an agenda since before we met. I'm the one who should be nervous." I sighed. "Will you open it for me?" I asked Keir. It was hard to brace yourself up and turn pages. The grimoire flopped open, and the pages fluttered for a second, then stopped. "Okay. This is new."

"I guess it didn't like being cooped up in a tiny attic crawl space," the gnome said.

"Zip it, Linda," I said automatically, then wished I could take it back. Being contrary wasn't going to get her to change her mind about going. "I mean, I totally get it." I ogled the book. "My bad, Grim. Won't happen again."

Keir chuckled, but the levity didn't erase the worry creasing his forehead. "What's it showing you?"

Blood of my blood, daughter of fade and bright.

Tears of my tears, prepare for a harrowing fight.

To fight what is not there, first, you must harness the air.

Ignorance is the greatest sin. Learn what you must or be dust in the wind.

Goddess, help you.

I sighed. "Once again, Ol' Grimmy has a lot to say about nothing. When have any of these fights not been harrowing? And if one more person or thing calls me stupid, I'm going to explode."

A chunk of dirt hit me between the eyes.

"Linda!" I locked gazes with the gnome.

"Intention," she reminded me. "Your magic is fueled by intention. Unless you really want to explode the next time someone calls you stu—"

I held up my hand as bile burned my throat. "I take it back. I will NOT explode if someone calls me stupid because that's exactly what I am. Sheesh."

"See, you're not so ignorant you can't learn." Her rosy gnomy face was a little too smug for my taste. "What's that line about dust?"

It dawned on me that Keir hadn't said anything about the cryptic grimoire poem. "Maybe the grimoire is a Kansas fan," I said, referencing the song *Dust in the Wind*. "I mean, it's possible."

Linda tsked. "I take back my previous observation."

"Oh!" I snapped my fingers and almost fell over before I slapped my palm back down on the bed. "What about pixie dust? Right. Fair Konig's dust is highly sought after, so maybe that's what it means. Maybe I'll turn to...." I paused and looked at Keir. "Dust. Shit. My magic is killing me again, isn't it?"

"We don't know that for certain, Iris." But I could see by his expression that he was really worried it meant just that. My terra-craft, before I got ahold of it, nearly turned me into magical dust that a dozen rogue druids had wanted to snort up to become sorcerers.

If I'd had guts, I'd have hurled. "It's happening again, isn't it?" I tilted my head back. "So much bullshit!" I let out a cry of frustration. Not even Bob's oxytocin-producing juju could ease my worry and frustration. Keir put his arm around me, and his hand slid into the empty space. I shook my head and leaned away from him, flopping sideways on the bed. "Don't touch me. It's too weird." A sob choked from me. "Let me blow away in peace." Or in pieces.

"Get up, *Liebling*. There is no giving up," Linda commanded in her brook-no-bullshit tone.

"Why do you care, Linda? You're leaving me anyway." Damn, like the force in *Star Wars*, the pity party was strong in me. "Just go. Both of you. If I don't make it, I leave all my aether dust to the two of you to use or dispose of as you so choose."

"Don't start writing your will and testament just

yet, love," Keir said. He crawled on the bed behind me and rested his hand on my hip. Bob began to purr louder as he rubbed his ears over Keir's fingers. My poor chonky-chonky was trying his best, but not even his feel-good vibes could lighten my mood. "I'm sorry, Bob. You've been a good familiar. I know you'll find a good home when I'm gone."

"You're being ridiculous," Linda said with an eye roll. "Get back into zee grimoire and, as your sister Marigold is so fond of saying, figure *die Scheisse* out."

I sniffled. I felt empty and defeated.

"You're not a quitter, Iris," Keir said. "Don't quit on me now."

He was right. I wasn't a quitter. So, why did I feel like giving up was the only option? "I think someone or something is making me feel this way? Maybe the magic. I don't know. I feel...despair. Like the bottomless pit kind." To some degree, I'd been feeling it since the pixies' arrival. Was it Fair Konig making me feel this way? "Do you think the pixies have done something to me? To my magic? Could it be affecting my mood?"

Linda could've used the opportunity to bash the winged creatures she hated so, but she didn't. "It's not the pixies," she said. "That is not the way of their magic. They make you want to protect them at all costs. Even if the price is your own family." She bowed her head. "I watched my mother and my papa die on this mountain two hundred years ago to protect Fair Konig and his troupe. I was barely ten years of age. My husband's parents took me in, and the elders left in our donsy cared for me." She shook her head. "Pixies don't fill anyone with despair. Their magic is hope. My parents were pixeled, as they call it. That's not what's happening to you."

"Oh, Linda." I started crying again. I lost my mom as an adult, and it was the hardest thing I'd ever experienced. I'd rather my husband had left me a dozen times for someone else than to go through that again. And Linda had lost both her parents at the same time. She'd been so young. Too young. Though, was there ever a time when any age was old enough to bear the loss. "I'm so sorry for you."

"It was a long time ago, *Liebling*."

"It's still awful," I said. Too awful. I wept even harder. Why couldn't I stop?

"Mom?" The sound of Michael's voice, quiet and scared, shook me out of my reverie.

"Don't come in here," I told him. "I'm okay."

"You're not okay," he said, entering the room. "What happened to you?"

He had honed in on my bruises and missing parts. "A little magic gone awry is all." Having him in the room made me feel stronger, less despondent. My son's presence was breaking whatever ill spell had a hold of me.

Keir must've felt it too because he said, "Michael, come sit next to your mom. Hold her hand."

My scared, brave teenager didn't hesitate. He sat down on the bed, his eyes as big as saucers, and took my hand. The melancholy retreated. Bob began to purr even louder. With Keir holding me, Bob curled up against my legs, and Michael holding my hand, I felt strong. It was the first time since the fight with the satyr that I felt my strength return.

My gaze flickered to the ceiling, where I saw a shadow resting in the corner of the room above my bedside table. It moved.

"Oh, shit." I tried to sit up, but I was on my empty side, and I couldn't use my non-existent abs. "There's something in the room with us."

Keir hauled me up, and Michael stood, looking around the room. "Where?"

I noticed then that Linda was an inanimate lawn ornament again because Michael was still non-magical. I pointed to the corner of the ceiling. "There," I said.

"I don't see anything," Michael said.

But Keir cocked his head sideways before reaching over to my tableside lamp and flicking it on. The scream that emanated from the shadow, filled me with fear, rage, despair, self-loathing, and hate. I screamed back.

It fled across the ceiling and out of the room. Keir chased after it.

"What in the hell was that?" Michael was clutching his chest.

"Are you all right?" I asked with frantic worry.

"Nope," he said frankly. "I am not all right. Not at all."

Keir hurried back into the bedroom. "It's gone," he said, his voice not quite human. "For now."

I looked at him. "What was that thing?"

His expression was stark. "A wraith."

"Oh, shit," Michael said.

My sentiments, exactly.

CHAPTER 12

I TOOK A SLOW BREATH AS I PROCESSED THIS NEW information. "A wraith," I said. "A wraith was in my house? In my bedroom? Why?"

"Wraiths are undead evil spirits that are bound to this plane of existence because of unfinished business," my son said. "They can only be killed with holy magic or a holy artifact, and if you attack one, you better damn sure kill it, because it will go serial killer on anything that makes it feel threatened."

I stared at the teen as if he'd just grown a nipple in the middle of his forehead. "How in the world do you know this?"

"Duh, Mom. Video games."

Oh, yeah. He spent a lot of late nights on the weekends playing Rogue Slayer Realm Guardians with his friends and every new incarnation of the series for the past decade. "I don't think video games are all that accurate to the real world." I looked to Keir for help. "It's more fiction than fact, right?"

He shrugged. "A lot of fiction is based on some truth. Michael's assessment of the wraith is accurate to a degree."

I could see the vindication in my son's body language. "Great. Then we just need something holy to take the sucker out," he said.

"I wish it was that easy," Keir told him. "Wraiths are not the undead. They aren't ghosts of humans with unfinished business. They're spawned into existence by foul magic as soulless creatures who survive by stirring up negative emotions in their victims and then feeding on the energy. Meaning, someone used magic to conjure the wraith. But the last part Michael said is completely accurate. Once attacked, it will go after anyone or anything that threatens its purpose. The only way to get rid of the wraith is to kill it, though I'm not sure how. Holy relics and prayers can't stop the entity. Honestly, I'm not sure what can. I've never heard of one being successfully killed."

"Then how do you get rid of one?"

Keir's eyes turned black as pitch as his anger triggered his beast. "That's the question. Usually, a wraith will feed until its target is dead, then vanish since its purpose has been served."

Awesome. All I had to do was let it kill me, and everyone else would be safe. Fun-fun. "How do I fight it when it comes back?" I didn't ask "if" because the when was inevitable.

Keir chewed the corner of his lip for a moment, his gray eyes darting back and forth as if calculating data, then he asked me, "How did you fight it this time?"

"Michael," I said honestly. I gave my son a tight smile. "This isn't the first time I've gone down a dark hole, but it's harder to stay there when I have someone more important than myself to rise up against the darkness for." I gestured to the voids on my body. "But if I can't get my aero-craft under control...." I left off the part about me turning into aether dust. I didn't want to scare my son. "I can feel the emptiness growing."

Keir sat down on the bed near me. He looked like a guy on the verge of a difficult decision. "Michael, can you give us a minute?"

My son shook his head. "I'm not leaving my mom. Whatever you guys have to say, I can take it. I'm not a kid anymore. You don't have to protect me."

"Oh, baby." I smiled sadly at him. This was his world now too, and for that, I would always be sorry. "I'll never stop trying to protect you, no matter how old you are."

Finally, Keir said, "I know someone who might be able to help."

"Then call them," Michael said to Keir. "What are you waiting for?"

"Thomas Darrencroft." Keir scrubbed his face. "He's an aero-craft witch. He might be able to teach you how to break this spell that's got a hold of you."

"Terrific. Like Michael said, give him a call."

His expression soured. "The help comes with a price."

"Is the price death?" I asked. Because that's what I was facing now. "Anything else would be preferable."

Keir's sister Luanne walked in from the hallway. "Calling Darrencroft is a bad idea." She wore black jeans, black Doc Martens, and finished the mono-chrome ensemble off with a black T-shirt. She bent over and looked at Linda. "Hey, girl."

"How long have you been listening in?" Keir asked.

"Not long," she said. "I just got back from drop-ping off Fair Konig and Annibish. They screwed all the way up the mountain." She sucked her teeth. "You can't even imagine the noises coming from the back seat."

"I don't have to imagine," I said. "You might've had a front-row seat to their frantic fornicating, but I was the freaking stage."

"About that," she said. "Fair Konig wanted me to thank you again for reviving Annibish."

"I still don't know what I did, but I'm glad she's alive."

"Your air magic took hold of her and brought her back. He said the wind picked her up from your lap and breathed new life into her. It also triggered her *oomatufeit*."

"Sounds painful," Michael said.

"It's not," Lu said. "It's a process of when a pixie female drops an egg. If it's not fertilized right away, then it will lose its viability."

"Ah. Hence all the screwing."

"Yep," she said. "Alllll the screwing."

"Wait." My son shook his head. "You're saying we had pixies at the house? And now a wraith? Freaking hell. I was gone one night."

"Don't forget the satyr," Lu added.

The teenager blanched.

I glared at her. "I'm sorry, Michael. You never asked for any of this."

"Neither did you, Mom. Sheesh." His tone was annoyed. Better than scared, I supposed. "Why is calling this Thomas guy a bad idea?" He asked Lu. "If he can help my mom, then we should try, right?"

Lu eyed her brother warily. "He's bonded to the Archdruid."

I knew the archdruid was Keir and Lu's grandmother. Finding out she was tied to a tru-craft witch piqued my interest. "Like Keir is bonded to me?"

"Not exactly like us," Keir said. "But yes, they have a druid-witch binding. He's very powerful."

"Because the Archdruid is powerful," Lu countered. There was an undercurrent of anger simmering below her words. "Darrencroft wouldn't have half his juice if it wasn't for her."

"Is he your grandfather?"

Luanne scoffed. "Hardly."

"Our grandfather was a druid," Keir said.

"And did he also have a bond with a witch?"

"He did not." Lu curled her lip in a snarl. "The Archdruid let our grandfather die to save Darrencroft's life. She chose him over her own husband."

"You know it's not that simple," Keir said.

When I had first learned what I was, Keir told me that ours was a bond of friendship, companionship, and devotion. A bond that makes a person willing to give up their entire life to save the other. If the Archdruid had that same bond with a tru-craft witch, then she would have the same compulsion. He also told me the compulsion only goes one way. Thomas Darrencroft wouldn't have the same need to protect the Archdruid, just as I didn't have the same driving need to protect Keir. I would because I loved him, but not because some metaphysical, supernatural power compelled me to do it.

He had also talked about Arthur Pendragon and Merlin being bonded like us. And that it only happened once in a millennium. "What happened to me being the Arthur of our time. I mean, if it happened to your grandma and this Darrencroft guy...."

"The Archdruid," Lu corrected me. "She is no

more our grandmother than your birth mother was your mom."

"Luanne," Keir chided. "Enough."

However, Lu's comment hadn't hurt my feelings. "No," I told him. "It's good. It gives me context. I understand exactly what she's saying. Family is more than blood." I looked at Lu. "Just like we're family, even though we're not related."

The hard lines around her eyes softened. "Too right."

"Anyhow, back to the whole, once in a lifetime. How did the Archdruid and this guy get bonded then?"

"It was a carefully crafted spell," Keir answered. "She couldn't know how it would turn out."

"I'm sure Grandfather was a sacrifice for the binding spell."

I scratched where my absentee arm was because it itched. It was a step up from the nothingness, but not by much. "You mean, you think the Archdruid killed your grandfather all so she could be attached to an aero-craft witch?"

"Not on purpose," Keir said. "There was a battle, and it came down to Thomas or our grandfather, and the Archdruid was compelled by the magical binding to save Thomas. She couldn't have known she would ever have to choose between them."

Lu barked a laugh. "You've always been more

forgiving of her." She shook her head. "And more gullible."

"Wow," Michael said. He had his arms across his ribs, and he was plucking at his chin hair. "And I thought I had family issues. You guys are making my Dad running off with the coach look like a walk in the park."

He wasn't wrong. "All the family drama aside, do you think this Thomas Darrencroft can fix me?" I wiggled my shoulder, which was attached to nothing at this point. "I don't want to find out what happens if this spell goes to my head."

Although, at this point, I wasn't certain it was a spell. I hadn't tried to use magic to fight the satyr. Which meant the theory I'd hypothesized earlier was most likely the right one. Like the terra-craft had tried to turn me into a pile of minerals, aero-craft was turning me into air.

I rolled my legs over the side of the bed and stood up. "Keir, I trust you. If you think you should call him, call him."

"You didn't tell her, did you?" Lu asked. Was she talking about the Archdruid, or was she talking about me?

Lu crossed her arms over her chest and tapped her foot. "You see, Iris. Keir has decided that the Iron Grove didn't need to know about your spark to aero-craft. He didn't want them sending anyone else to test you the way they'd sent Zev. And when he made the choice to withhold the information, he asked me to keep it a secret as well."

Keir winced. "I'll tell them you didn't know."

"The Archdruid will punish me anyhow." She narrowed her gaze on her brother. "And they're not going to be happy with you. Even so, I understood why you wanted to protect Iris. They wanted to study her after the second element manifested, and I knew it would be hard for you to keep them at bay if they found out about the third," she told her brother.

Wait? They'd wanted to study me? I knew Keir had been keeping some information about me from them. He'd said as much when I found out he had been reporting on my progress. But I hadn't realized they'd wanted to treat me like a lab rat.

Lu continued. "Believe me, I don't trust the Iron Grove where Iris is concerned either, so I'm not sure why you suddenly think they can be trusted."

"Because if I don't do something, Iris is going to die." His blunt words hung in the room.

"Call him," Michael said. He was clenching his fists as his jaw worked back and forth. "Save my mom."

"Michael," I said softly. "I'm going to be okay."

"Look at you," my son said. "You're disappearing in front of my eyes."

"Aww, damn." Luanne muttered a few more curse words. "I'm sorry, kid. I didn't mean to say that."

"But you meant it," Michael responded.

She closed her eyes and nodded.

My gaze traveled from Michael to Lu to Keir as I weighed my options. "Lu, you've been gone for weeks. I'll vouch for Keir that you weren't aware of my new status. If this guy can help me control my air magic, I have to try. I don't have the lifetime of tutelage from other tru-crafters to shape my magic." As a matter of fact, I'd never met anyone like me before. I tilted my head to Keir. "Make the call."

He nodded. "I'll be right back."

Lu unlaced her arms from across her chest and followed him out of the bedroom, leaving Michael, statuary Linda, and me alone. My poor kid looked sick with worry. I needed him out of here and out of harm's way. I never wanted to be without him, but a part of me wished he'd gone to stay with his father for his final school year.

"Come sit next to me." I patted the bed.

Michael didn't move. "I'm okay here."

I sighed and picked at the pilled fabric on my blanket. "I need you to get yourself away from here for a couple of days," I told him.

"I'm not leaving you, Mom." He swiped his hand across the air as if giving the final word."

Bob rubbed his face against my good arm. Absently, I stroked his head. I had to figure out a way to get my son out of harm's way.

Michael narrowed his stare at me. "Don't even try to Pikachu me, either."

I knew he was talking about the episode of Pokémon where Ash had told Pikachu he didn't want him around anymore and to go away because he didn't like the sad little electric Pokémon. Michael had been five years old at the time, and he'd come running into the kitchen crying as he told me that Ash didn't like Pikachu anymore. It was an old plot device. Ugh. Michael had been devastated. I'd had to watch the rest of the show with him until Pokémon and trainer were reunited once again.

A sentimental smile played on my lips. "I'm not trying to send you away for your own good," I lied. "I'm doing it for my own good." I pointed to the gnome. "I need Linda, but she can't come to life with you around. She'll protect me. Go to Doug's house. Go hang out with your new girlfriend."

My son quickly averted his gaze. "She's not my girlfriend."

"Whatever," I told him. "Just go."

His brow furrowed, and his blue eyes grew glassy. "Promise you'll text me and let me know that you're okay?"

"Cross my heart," I said.

Michael leaned over and kissed my cheek. "I love you, Mom."

I held back the sob threatening to choke from my throat. "I love you, too, son."

When he exited the room, Linda burst to life and yanked her cap down over her ears as she shouted,

"How could you lie to the young one? How am I supposed to protect you?" She tossed a rock at me, and it sailed through the empty, and that's when I saw the tears falling down the gnome's rosy cheeks.

Damn it to hell. I'd made Linda cry.

CHAPTER 13

I DON'T KNOW WHAT I THOUGHT WOULD HAPPEN next, but Keir coming back to the bedroom with a tablet so I could video chat with the Great Wizard of Air was not it.

"Uh, hello there," I said. I didn't bother to wave as I was keeping myself steady with my good hand. "I'm Iris." I nodded to my miniature companion. "This is Linda."

"Hello, Iris." Thomas had wiry gray hair that stuck out all over the place. I could only see his head and shoulders, so I couldn't tell how tall he was, but his face was thin and his shoulders narrow. "Linda," he acknowledged my gnome. "I'm Thomas." I could see in the corner of the tablet that Keir was holding that he was back far enough that I was visible to the hip. Thomas had shrewd but kind eyes as he looked me up and down. "You're in quite the predicament, young lady."

"Isn't that the truth," Linda replied.

I resisted the urge to stick my tongue out at her, then addressed Thomas. "I'm hoping you can help me undo whatever is happening to me."

"Your magic is in chaos." Thomas twisted and pulled at his hair. No wonder he was Einstein-chic. "Very dangerous."

"Yep."

"How did it happen?"

"I was fighting a satyr, and I thought about how lovely it would be to be made of air. Air doesn't feel pain. And then after...." I shrugged. "This was the result."

"Magic takes a sacrifice," he said. "Even air magic."

So far, he hadn't said a single thing I didn't already know. "Can you help?"

The old man wiggled his mouth back and forth, scratched the bridge of his nose, then began to pluck at his eyebrows. Finally, he put his hand down and said, "I can help you contain the element and slow down its destructive progression. But I can't stop it. You have to figure out a way to become a master of aero-craft and undo what you've done. Only you can save yourself, Iris."

"No, I can't." I heard the whine in my voice and

cringed. "I've tried, Thomas. This is worse than when the terra-craft ran amuck through me."

"It's because you have too many competing elements in you. Earth, Fire, Air." He clasped his hands together. "On top of that, your magic has to compensate for both Fade and Bright. It's like trying to light a fire in a vacuum."

"More like lighting a fire in a room full of gas," I said.

"Or that," he agreed. "You're either canceling your magic, or it's out of your control. You have to find the balance."

Had this guy been consulting my grimoire? Ugh. Was there even such a thing as balance? Not in my experience. "What can you do to help me slow it down until I can find the yin to aero-craft's yang?"

"I can't cast a spell from here. I'm good," he said, his eyes alight with gentle humor. "But I'm not that good." He held up a fine-boned finger. "However, I can teach you a containment incantation that should at least give you the semblance of a solid form while slowing down the progression of the magical flux."

I raised a brow at him.

"You'll stop disappearing."

I let out a sigh of relief. "Oh, thank heavens."

"Keir, I'll need you to help Iris. As her soulmate, you'll be able to anchor the magic."

Without any hesitation, Keir sat on the bed next

to me and held out the tablet in front of us. "What do I need to do?"

"Wait." I leaned against Keir, grateful for his warmth. "Can this do any damage to him?" I asked Thomas. "I won't do the incantation if it puts Keir in danger."

"It doesn't," the old man said. "I promise. It's a spell of minor consequence. It will cost you very little."

"Cost?"

"As I said earlier, magic takes its price. It has to come from somewhere, and when you take, you must also give. The Fade is destructive magic. You can use it to get rid of obstacles, but then something else has to return in its place. The Bright is creator magic. But when you create something new, the building blocks come from somewhere."

I'd known about the creation and destroying aspects of Fade and Bright, and I knew all too well that magic required sacrifices. It's why Linda instructed me on spell work and potions. The ingredients paid the price. And when I worked with fire, it cost me a little of my blood. Still, I didn't have any idea what price air would take, but my body seemed to be part of that bargain. "I hate that this is all new to me. That I don't really understand how my powers manifest. I feel like I've lucked into control of the past two elements." Fear, anger, and the threat of death, those had been the catalysts for control. "I don't want to have to almost die in order to learn a lesson I should've known from the beginning." Had I been raised by my birth mother, I mentally added.

"You would benefit from apprenticing with a tru-craft witch," he said. "But that is for a later conversation." He leaned forward, and I could see up his nostrils. "Have you done any big creation magic lately?"

"Uhm, no." I shook my head. "Not that I can think of."

"The tornados," Keir said.

"But that's not creation...." I frowned, then shook my head. "Yep, I made two tornados," I told Thomas. "I did that yesterday. I used my fire magic to stop it."

He steepled his hands and nodded. "Impressive. Of course, that's probably why your magic is in flux. You're using your other crafts to control the air instead of your aero-craft."

I shrugged. "It was that or keep getting tossed around like a rag doll."

"I'm not criticizing you, Iris. The opposite. You are the most unique tru-craft witch I've had the privilege to meet. Your ability to hold three elements is awe-inspiring. I am rooting for your survival."

"Good to know." I frowned. "Does this mean there are people not rooting for me to survive?"

Thomas bowed his head, gave it a slight shake and smiled. "We will need a few items, then we can start the incantation. Miss Linda, can you retrieve the items we need? A clear crystal, a white candle, and some yarrow root."

Linda practically preened. "Of course, Thomas." Maybe she was looking to trade up witches. "I'll be right back."

Thomas continued his instruction. "Keir, I'll need you to put both hands on Iris, so you need to put the tablet down."

"Then you won't be able to see us," I said.

"It's not necessary to see you for this part," he assured me. Keir followed Thomas's instructions and put the tablet on the bed, giving Thomas a view of the ceiling. After, Keir put his hands on the back of my neck and my solid shoulder.

Linda popped up through the floor. "I have what you require," she said. She leaped onto the bed and set the yarrow that I grew in my garden on my lap, along with a clear quartz crystal. She took her hat off, exposing her bald dome and a single white birthday candle. She smiled. "It was in the kitchen drawer where you keep the cake decorating supplies."

"You've done very well, Linda," Thomas said admiringly. "Thank you for your service to Iris."

"I am her earth guardian," she said formally. "It is my honor and duty."

Hah. An hour ago, she'd been threatening to leave me. I wondered how she'd feel if I told Thomas about that. I wouldn't, but the petty thought made me feel a little better all the same.

Thomas made a few flourishes with his hands as if writing on the air. "Centered," he said. "Iris, if you are ready to start, we can begin."

"Yes," I replied.

"Repeat after me. But, if you decide to adjust the language, try not to get too creative," he warned.

"I'll be word for word," I promised.

Thomas added, "Don't forget intention."

"I tell her that all the time," Linda said. "Your intention must be clear, *Kleinkind*."

"Gotcha." I gave her a two-finger salute. "Clear intention." In this case, my intention was to not turn to aether dust, to be whole again, and to protect my son, protect Keir, not lose Linda, keep the pixies safe, and stop being a lying disappointment to my family.

"Keep the intention simple," Thomas said. "It's easier to convert if you keep it simple."

"Kiss," I said with a wistful smile as I thought of easier times.

Keir tilted my head and kissed me in a way that made my toes curl.

"Whew." My breath released quickly. "That was great, but not what I meant. K. I. S. S. Kiss. It's what I used to tell my students when they would try to make a short essay too complicated. Keep it simple, stupid."

He smiled. "Oh."

"I'm certainly not complaining."

Linda cleared her throat. "If the two of you could

stop playing footsies for two seconds, we can get on with the plan to save Iris from herself."

I blinked at Keir. He kissed me again. I giggled when it ended, then said, "I'm ready. Intention clear." I wanted to be made whole. I didn't want to disappear. But I focused on what Thomas said I could have, containment. It would have to do for now.

Thomas said, "Visualize the candle purifying the air. Visualize the crystal as it bends the light in the empty spaces. Visualize the yarrow, as yellow is the color of air."

I closed my eyes and did all the visualizing. "Done."

"Now," Thomas continued. "Repeat after me. Eastern wind and spring divine, healing breath now entwine."

"Eastern wind and spring divine, healing breath now entwine," I said.

"As the storm will blow, time will slow, and the tempest I will bind."

"As the storm will blow, time will slow, and the tempest I will bind."

"Bend to my will."

"Bend to my will."

"Now blow across your skin to activate the magic. Then repeat the incantation again. Just hold the vision in your head of your hand, your arm, and your body where the air has replaced your flesh. The magic is neither creation nor destruction, so even if it fails, the cost will be minuscule."

Please don't fail, I thought. Aloud, I said, "*Eastern wind and spring divine, healing breath now entwine. As the storm blows, time slows, and the tempest I will bind. Bend to my will.*"

My skin began to tingle as yellow light glowed from the empty spaces. Solid, I thought. Solid and steady. Fingers, hands, wrist, forearm, elbow, upper arm, shoulder, ribs, stomach, top of hips, and anywhere else that might turn to air. "Bend to my will," I said again, this time louder and with more confidence, as I once again felt my fingers move on the hand that hadn't been there seconds earlier. "Bend to my will."

On that final call to my magic, a physical replacement of my missing parts solidified in place. I held up my hand, examining the slightly diaphanous appearance. It had a yellow tinge of yarrow, the waxy appearance of the candle, and it was as hard quartz when I tapped it on Linda's head. "It worked," I finally said. I flexed my fingers. "And I appear to have functionality."

"That's wonderful," Thomas said. "May I see?"

I reached behind me and picked up the tablet and held it at arm's length with my flesh hand while waving with my air one.

"Extremely impressive, Iris. Better than I hoped for. You're an excellent student."

I nudged the gnome. "Can you say that again? I don't think Linda heard you."

Thomas chuckled. "One more thing, you should avoid using magic beyond a simple incantation, like what we just did, for a few days. If you can avoid doing magic altogether, even better. The more power you pull from tru-craft, especially if you mix elements, the more unstable you can become. This instability might resolve itself if you allow the chaos to go dormant."

"And if I don't?"

He made a "who knows" gesture with his hand. "Probably better not to find out," he said. "I look forward to meeting you in person next week, Iris."

"What?"

Keir put his hand on my leg and gave it a squeeze I interpreted as, "Let it go." So I did, but he definitely had some explaining to do.

"Thank you, Thomas, for your help and expertise," Keir said. "Please give the Archdruid my best."

"I will, and please keep me informed of Iris's progress."

"Of course," Keir agreed. Then he slid his finger across the screen and disconnected us.

"Why am I going to the Iron Grove?" I asked. Lu had said that the Iron Grove would want to study me if they knew about the third element. Was that why? "I will not be probed by a bunch of robed scientists who want to treat me like a test subject."

"I swear," Keir said. "No probing will occur. The Archdruid wants to meet you, is all. It's what I promised for Thomas' help."

"I get the impression he would've helped even without a quid pro quo. Better to know what you must exchange than wait for a far worse favor to be asked."

I moved my hand around and touched my stomach. Solid and mobile. It was strange but also wonderful. It didn't feel like my body, but it didn't feel empty anymore. The nothingness was gone. "How come we did a video call?"

"He wanted to see you, and it's an eight-hour drive."

"No, I mean, couldn't he have hitched a ride? Like Lu hitched a ride with Zev, he could've done that, right? I mean, Zev works for the Iron Grove, after all."

"Zev doesn't work for the Grove, he freelances, and genie wishes are not cheap."

I gave him a sharp look. "What did Lu have to agree to in exchange for a ride here?"

Keir grimaced. "To be determined."

"Yikes."

"She loves me." He put his arm around me. "And she loves you."

"I'll ask Zev to exact the price from me."

"The hell you will," Lu said from the hall. "I'm a big girl, and I take care of my own debts."

"Come in, Lu," Keir said. "Thomas is no longer on the call."

"I know." She stood in the doorway. "I listened to the whole thing."

"What do we do now?" I asked. "I still have to get my aero-craft under control, but I also promised the pixie king I would protect his troupe while they mate and have babies. I can't go back on my word."

Linda made a noise of disgust.

"Zev has got them on lockdown right now. He'll keep them safe until we get back up the mountain to Keir's place," Luanne said.

"Good." It made me feel better knowing they had Zev to protect them, but I also wondered what this extra favor would cost Luanne.

"It wasn't a wish," she supplied as if reading my mind. "I made a friendly request, and he accepted."

"Even better." I turned to my grumpy gnome. "Linda, I need you."

She dropped her arms to her sides, and her shoulders slumped. "Fine. I will not desert you, *Kleinkind*, but know, if it comes down to you or the pixies, I will let them die."

"Noted." I heaved a sigh. It was easier to breathe now that I had the façade of a diaphragm. "But what I really want is some kind of early warning detection. We need to figure out what's coming at us above and below ground."

Luanne smiled as she placed her hand on her hip. "We're going to make a general out of you yet."

"If the satyr is any indication of the crazy, it's about to go full-on mental ward around here." I nodded to Lu. She was ex-special forces, mercenary, and all-around badass. She'd seen a lot of combat situations in her forty years. "But maybe you should handle the battle plans."

"I'll get on it," she said. "I know Keir's land about as well as he does. I can identify weak spots and try to fortify them. It's a big area, though."

"Just do your best." Keir helped me to my feet. "We should get going. Zev's not known for his patience, and the pixies could break Buddha's Zen."

The scent of sulfur and smoke seared the air as Zev flashed into the room. Damn, my bedroom was getting a ton of action lately, and none of it was the fun kind.

His wild stare made my pulse bound. "Leprechauns," he whispered with a shiver. "I can't stop them by myself. So many of them. They're everywhere."

CHAPTER 14

Lu and I rode with Keir up the mountain while Zev and Linda made their own way there. I wasn't sure what I expected. The cute little guy in green on the front of a Lucky Charms cereal box or the fun Irish gnome-looking dude sitting on a pot of gold at the end of a rainbow every St. Patrick's Day. I was quickly disabused of either notion.

Leprechauns are not cute or fun. They are assholes.

When we pulled into the driveway, the late afternoon sun highlighted the shit show taking place on Keir's lawn. Pixies zipped all over the place. Zev was hurling fireballs, and Linda was popping up all over the yard, taking down leprechauns in a reverse game of whack-a-gnome. By the time Keir got out of the car, he was in complete pooka form, including super pointy antlers, five points each jutting from the top of his skull, and arms the size of tree trunks. He snarled at the invading force on his property, saliva dripping from his frightening maw of razor-sharp teeth. He clicked his black diamond claws, then took off in a run to meet the ensuing battle head-on.

Luanne, heaven help her, was grinning from ear to ear as she slid a knife from a belt strap. She winked at me. "Let's have some fun."

Her idea of fun and mine were two totally different things. Even so, I retrieved Michael's baseball bat from where I'd thrown it into the back seat and tested it against my hand.

Lu's grin widened. "Right on," she said. "Batter up."

I tried to steel my nerves, but all I could think about was all the times I really messed up. I shook the doubts from my head. Leprechauns first. Doubts second. "Let's do this."

An hour into the fight, we were no closer to getting rid of the invaders than we were when we started. The truth was, we were getting our asses handed to us by skinny, old men with scraggly beards, wielding little more than wooden staffs. I'd been thunked hard more times than I cared to admit. Zev had been right. They were fucking everywhere.

"I think these guys are multiplying!" I shouted as one of Zev's fireballs exploded near me, sending two leprechauns flying. Every time we took out one guy, five more took his place. The pixie males were aiding in the fight, while the females who had taken part in the mating ritual already had been barricaded inside Keir's house.

Konig flew over to me and pointed at Keir's tiny home. "They're going for the women!" A dozen leprechauns had managed to get past our perimeter and were rocking the container home back and forth.

I was exhausted and in a lot of pain. Adrenaline was the only thing keeping me going at this point. Still, I ran—well, jogged—to the house to defend the soon-to-be pixie moms. I choked up on the bat and smacked the first leprechaun in the head. He careened backward and then fell to the ground. I hit him in the face a couple more times to make sure he wasn't getting back up. After, I made my way around the outside of the structure, swinging the slugger into every leprechaun I could find. They were so focused on getting inside the container house that they weren't even trying to defend against my blows. One by one, they went down like dominoes.

However, by the time I made it around the front, several more leprechauns had taken their places. "How many of these assholes are there?" My voice was high-pitched and strangled as I took in the scene.

Keir ripped the arms off one of the scrawny fuckers, then used his diamond-hardened nails to cut the head off another. Then twenty of them jumped on him at once. Fair Konig and Linda were dueting their fight. She would knock them down, and he would stab them in the eyes. Even so, more came. Lu was ducking, dodging, kicking, and cutting, but she wasn't gaining much ground either. Zev couldn't make fire-balls fast enough to keep a small horde of them from taking him down. He kept poofing out then re-poofing in outside the leprechaun piles before turning the thin, old men into barbeque pyres. The smell of roasting leprechauns was sickly sweet, like burnt sugar, as if their flesh had been made of cotton candy.

I let out an angry cry of frustration as the tiny home began to teeter. For every inch of ground we gained from the wily, multiplying leprechauns, we lost a foot.

Thomas had warned me not to use any magic until I could come to terms with aero-craft, but we were going to lose the house if I didn't act. I fell to my hands and knees, gripping the soil between my fingers. It felt weird on the hand that was made of magic, but I couldn't let that stop me.

"*Mother Earth and Goddess bound, move and shape this bounty of ground. Mineral, rock, and stone below. Shape, expand, stretch and grow.*" I felt the magic gather and disperse beneath me. "*Come to me and build a gate. Protect the pixies....*" I searched for a good word to rhyme with gate and landed on, "*...who are here to mate.*" I added my intention to keep the pixies safe and the house standing. As a final, I used Thomas's ending, "*Bend to my will.*"

Rapidly, tall spires of rock shot up from out of the ground all at once in a rectangle around the tiny house. The structures were close together, forming a sort of privacy fence that prevented the leprechauns from touching the house, let alone trying to tip it over.

It didn't stop them from climbing, though. "Sons of bitches." They were using their wooden staffs like ice picks on the roof, trying to break in through the top.

I called to the earth once more. "*Up, up, up,*" I told it. "*Bend to my will.*"

A platform of rock formed under my feet, lifting me as it rose from the ground. When I was high enough, I vaulted to the roof. Unfortunately, my bat was still on the ground.

Once again, I reached for my magic. Ignis this time. I called to the fire from one of Zev's stack of bodies because I needed the flame for the incantation. "*Blood and fire, ignite and fight. Bend to my will.*"

I yipped as fire burst from my body like a nuclear explosion. The powerful wave of flames and heat blasted the leprechauns from the roof. When the debris and the smoke cleared, I was the only one up there left standing. "Yes." I fist-bumped the sky.

From this vantage, I could see the whole battlefield. It was a much different picture than I'd seen on the ground. The yard should have been littered with hundreds of leprechaun bodies, but there weren't more than a dozen on the ground. Even Zev's fire piles were gone, with the exception of the one he was currently roasting.

Where were they going? I looked for the one that I'd smashed in the head. He was gone as well. Something wasn't right. Keir tore limbs off a half dozen more leprechauns, and I knew even more would replace them, so I scanned the area to see where the creatures were coming from. To my surprise, they appeared out of thin air behind Keir, already at a run.

Had that been happening the whole time? How had we not noticed? The same thing was happening to my friends. That's why we couldn't get rid of them. Like Zev, the leprechauns could poof. Only, where were the dead bodies going?

Three of them ran at Luanne from a blind spot. "Lu! Behind you!" I shouted. She spun around with the grace of a ballerina, and she avoided their staffs as she dispatched them with quick stabs of her knife.

"Yes!" Then four more popped up behind her. My friends might be better fighters, but the leprechauns were constantly replacing their fallen comrades. A few more hours, and we would be completely over-whelmed.

A red glint from the trees drew my attention. It came from a large oak above the waterfall. Then I saw the beard. It was a leprechaun wearing a red coat and a red beanie. Was the color and indication of status? Was he their commander, orchestrating the fight from a safe perch?

"Oh, hell no," I muttered. "Not on my watch." The grimoire had listed the oak as a tree of power, but all I really needed was the poison ivy and creeper vines growing up the sides and hanging from the branches. *Bind and twine, tether and knot. Cinch and clench, for what he's wrought.*"

I smiled when the watcher began to shout obscenities as the vines trussed him up like a giant butt roast ready for the oven.

The sudden quiet on the battlefield startled me from the celebration as the leprechauns that had been fighting vanished. All of them.

"What the hell is going on?" Luanne shouted up to me.

Keir peered up at me with a hand over his eyes as the sun shined in his face. "Did you do this?"

I grimaced. "Maybe. I don't know." I pointed at the leprechaun on the hill. "There," I said. "I think that's their leader."

"Hoe-lee shit," Luanne cheered. "Damn, Iris. You can come with me on my next mission."

Zev, whose perfect hair was a mess, and his leather jacket torn at the shoulder, blew out a ring of smoke. "I'll get him," he said.

In two shakes of a lamb's tail, Zev was gone and back, returned with the red-coated Leprechaun. The vines still held the dude, and his arms were strapped down to his sides, and his legs were bound all the way to his feet.

I climbed down the rock fence as our prisoner tried to hop away, then fell onto his backside. "You'll pay for this," he screeched. "All of you! I will shred your flesh and grind your bones. I will turn your bowels into sausage casings. Give me the pixie dust, or you will rue the day you crossed pikes with Blue Haggins."

I reached down and took his beanie off and stuffed it into his mouth. "There," I said. "Much better." I snapped my fingers. "Hey," I said. "Since I caught him, does that mean I get his pot of gold?"

"You might," Keir answered. "If he was a leprechaun."

Lu leaned over our captive. "He's not?"

Zev nodded. "He is not. Though he made good imitations of the freaks."

Up close, the asshole didn't look much like the guys we'd been fighting. He had huge red eyes, a hook nose and thin lips beneath his grizzled beard. His gnarled hands were bent like talons, and he had thin, emaciated arms and legs but a broad bird chest. "Then what is he?" I asked.

"He's a redcap. A type of goblin," the fire djinn explained. "Distantly related to the leprechauns but much more malevolent. They conjure physical illusions—usually for nefarious purposes."

"Legend has it that they soak their hats in their

victims' blood in order to increase their power," Keir said. "I've never actually seen one before in person, though. I've only studied them."

"What do we do with him?" I asked.

"Find out if he knows who else is coming, then dispose of him," Luanne said. The "of course" was implied. She looked at me and said, "Hey, are you okay?"

I was light-headed, but I'd been too hopped on adrenaline and magic spells to realize how bad I'd begun to feel. I started swaying as my head spun and spun...and then I fell into darkness.

CHAPTER 15

When I awoke, I sat straight up in bed and smacked my head on the ceiling.

"Ow." My first thought was, where am I? My second, is the bed this high or the ceiling that low? It turned out to be both. I crawled to the bottom of the loft bed and saw Keir conversing with Fair Konig in the living room of his tiny house. The space also doubled as the dining room, the kitchen, and the library. I couldn't understand how Keir could stand to be in such a tight space, but he'd said he didn't need much in the way of material things.

The cramped bookcase under the loft steps told me he liked some material things. I'd tried to talk him into an ebook reader. They were awesome and took up way less room. However, he reminded me that he had one solar panel that basically runs the hot water heater and the water pump, and he didn't want to have to sit in his car to charge the battery every time it got low just so he could read.

Touché.

His tiny house, like his vehicle, was eco-friendly. He even had a compost toilet behind a curtain just off the kitchen. I'd worked hard not to eat or drink anything before my visits to his place. It was twenty minutes to the nearest flushing toilets. Besides, this woman needed her privacy.

Annibish flew up to where I was perched. "I don't want to fight with you," I told her. My head still swam a little. "Whatever it is, you win."

She dove toward my face, came up short in a total Tinkerbell maneuver, then kissed me on my cheek. "Thank you, Iris."

Well, she sure as hell had changed her tune since the day before. Of course, I had saved her life. Twice. "Uhm, you're welcome."

Conspiratorially, she asked, "Do you want to see my baby?"

I shook my head then nodded; not sure this was a good idea. Were pixies' stomachs see-through? Did I want to see a translucent womb? Kind of. "Yeah, okay."

The gestation period was pretty quick, so I wasn't sure if I was going to see a peanut or a fully formed mini-pix. I was very surprised when Annibish pulled her skirt down to her hips and opened a pouch set right below her navel. Inside was the most beautiful glowing ball of light. It was surrounded by a colorful ring of dust. "Is that the *Feenstaub*?" I asked.

"Yes," she said. "It is bringing our daughter to maturity."

"A daughter?" I couldn't keep the wonder from my voice.

Her point was taken. When I was pregnant with Michael, his heartbeat was, on average, a hundred and fifty beats per minute. The doctor was certain he would be a girl based on the rate. He said that boys had slower heart rates, like around one-twenty. Imagine our surprise when Michael came out balls first. I smiled as I remembered the startled look on Evan's face. He was such a proud dad, and for all his flaws, he still was. He loved Michael.

"How do you know? That it's a girl, I mean."

"Do you see the pale green at her outer edge?"

I nodded. "I do."

"That indicates she will be female."

"Green is for girls?"

"No, the solid color indicates it's a female. It would be multicolored if she were a male."

"Awww. She's beautiful, Annibish."

She smiled and batted her eyelashes at me. "This is what you are protecting, Iris. Not us, but the precious cargo we carry. And now that all the dust has been used, the females in our troupe will be at risk."

"How can the bad guys take the dust now?"

Her mouth set in a grim line as her wings vibrated

with agitation. "They will kill our children and us, dry our bodies to separate the organic matter from the dust."

I sucked in a breath. "They wouldn't."

But I could tell by her expression that it was something that had happened before.

"Two more days until these babies are gestated," I said. "Can they harm them after they are born?"

Annibish alighted onto the mattress near my shoulder. "They can, but it will do them no good. The dust will be gone. But frustrated creatures are often the most violent."

"I will do my best to protect you and your children." I gave her what I hoped was a reassuring smile. "I can't wait to meet your daughter."

Annibish closed the pouch and adjusted her skirt. "I am certain Iverlee will be glad to meet you as well."

I gave Annibish a confused look. "Iverlee?"

"After you, Iris Everlee. After all, you are the reason she exists. We conceived her in your magical body. It brought me back to life and brought forward new life."

"I'm so flattered." And weirded out, if I was being completely honest. They'd made a baby inside me. Joy. "What's going on down there at the table?"

"Fair Konig and your man are discussing the best way to keep the troupe safe." She made a slight whistling sound when the pixie king stomped his feet on the table. "They're not agreeing on much."

"I can see that."

"You are still very translucent, Iris Everlee. I think this is a bad sign."

"You and me both, sister."

She smiled. "I accept your offer. We will be sisters now."

"I didn't—" I shook my head. "You know what, never mind. You're naming your daughter after me. I'm happy to be your sister."

Annibish preened as she squeezed her arms together and her rapidly flapping wings lifted her from the mattress. "I am happy too."

Keir pounded a fist on the table, and all the pixies scattered. His eyes had turned black. Not good. "I better go help."

She nodded, her eyes as big as buttons. "Good idea."

I got myself turned around on the bed, and considering I hurt in places that I didn't think would hurt again after taking Rose's fitness boot camp, it was a masterful feat that I was able to get down the steps without a serious tumble.

"Hey," I said. "Uhm, whazzz up?" I said it like the old Superbowl commercial as a poor attempt to lighten the mood. Nobody laughed. "So, any more redcaps or satyrs stop by while I was out?"

Keir sighed. "I was explaining to Fair Konig that you can't protect his troupe. Your magic is far too unstable, and we almost lost you as a result of this last battle."

"Nah," I said, waving a hand at him. "I just passed out. I've been through a lot worse than that. I mean, hello, I fought a rock troll that pummeled the crap out of me, and I ate a fire god. In my defense, he tried to eat me first," I added when the pixies chattered nervously. "I don't make a habit of eating things I fight with."

"You died."

"I what?"

"You died, Iris. You weren't breathing. Your heart had stopped. We had to do CPR. Nothing worked." He looked pissed at me, and I wasn't sure why.

"I'm okay now, though, right? I mean, other than being a little more translucent." My bladder felt suspiciously full. "How long have I been out?"

Keir's gaze met mine. "Nineteen hours."

That made it Sunday and about nine or ten in the morning. "Wow." Anxiety made my chest ache. "I missed an entire day." I walked over to the folding table and scooched in beside him. "How long was I dead?"

"Eight minutes."

Holy cow. Eight minutes was a long freaking time. Like kill your gray matter long. "Is my brain okay?"

He narrowed his gaze at me and frowned. "You tell me?"

"I have a headache, but otherwise...." I shrugged. "Tell me why you're so angry with me."

"You are the one thing in my life that I won't live without, Iris. I can't. When you died, I felt a vast nothingness that I never want to feel again."

"Oh, Keir." I placed my hand on his thigh. "I'm sorry. I.... What am I supposed to say to that? I never wanted this unequal tether between us. I love you, and it hurts knowing that I can cause this kind of pain for you."

"That's why you can't stick around to protect the pixie troupe."

I made a noise of protest. "I made a promise. A bargain I plan to uphold."

He took my hand in his and held it up. "Look at yourself, Iris. You heard Thomas. You need to take a few days off from magic to see if the break will realign your elements."

I looked out the two large windows. The rock barrier I had constructed was still there. "How did we get in here?"

"Linda took us through the stone." He made a gesture toward the yard. "Lu and Zev are seeing if it's possible to monitor the perimeter. That should give the pixies some warning when the next hunter arrives. They can hide in here with the stone fence to protect them."

"That's not going to keep ninety-nine percent of the supernatural world out of here, you know that, right?" I asked him. "The redcap's army almost got in through the roof already."

"The *Hexe* is correct," Fair Konig interjected. "And she promised her protection if we left her garden. Our mates are hungry. We need to leave this prison of a dwelling to feed. Our offspring need that as much as they need *Feenstaub*."

"What do you eat again?" I asked.

"Pollen mostly," Annibish said. "Some edible plants like dandelions."

"There's a health food store in town. I go there to get spell-making supplies." Of course, they just thought I had a healthy appetite for holistic crap. "My sister Marigold swears by the bee pollen capsules." Marigold. I knew she had to be out of her mind with worry. And Michael too. I'd promised him I'd text. "We could break open the capsules or see if the store carries the pollen by itself. Would that work?"

The pixie king tapped his chin, then stroked his beard. "It might be acceptable."

"Then you'll stay in here until we get back. No outings alone." I would call Marigold and Michael when I got to town and let them know I was alive. "Zev and Lu can stick around to make sure you're safe." I looked at Keir for confirmation.

He nodded. "What are you up to, Iris?"

"I think I can craft a protection spell." I'd created several spells after I mastered terra-craft that I believed I could adjust with a few key ingredients and a lot of intention. "It'll be strictly earth magic, so I know I can make it work. I just need to double-check my grimoire."

"No more magic, Iris," Keir pleaded. "Please."

"Thomas said I could perform simple incantations. The herbs and minerals will pay the cost. Not me."

Keir's hands balled into fists, his knuckles going white. I'd scared him, and he was still afraid of losing me.

"I'm sorry, Keir. I'm not trying to make your life more difficult. Honestly. But I'm going to be an auntie now." I cast a glance at Annibish. "So, I'm responsible for making sure that little one makes it into the world."

Nineteen hours had passed since I passed out. Well, technically died, but semantics. And I revived Annibish a few hours before the fight, so about twenty-four to twenty-six hours since mating occurred. "By my estimation. I have two more days to make sure the pixies survive another thousand years."

He wouldn't look at me.

I pressed my palm, the one made of flesh and blood, to his cheek. "Keir, I love you. I want you by my side in all things. I want you with me through every fight, victory or failure. I want you." I couldn't keep the sadness from my voice. "But I'll go it alone if that's my only option. I'll hate every minute of it, but I'll do what I have to do to keep this troupe safe, even if it's without you."

His gaze met mine, and the creases around his eyes softened. "With me," he said softly. "I am always with you, Iris. Even if I don't agree. You'll never have to fight alone."

"I hoped you'd say that." I kissed him until the droning buzz of fairy wings got too annoying.

"Food now," Fair Konig said. "Sex later."

"We weren't—" I frowned and shook my head. "Never mind." I glanced at the barricaded door. "How do we get out of here?"

"Trapdoor," Keir said.

"There's a what?" I looked around the small area. "Where?"

He gestured for me to scoot.

I scooted.

Keir got up and went to the curtain blocking off the toilet, kicked aside a bathmat and said, "Abracadabra."

Underneath, there was a wooden trap door with a hole to use as a handle to lift it open. "This is how I managed to sneak up on you the first time you visited me."

I felt giddy. "I can't believe you haven't shown me this before."

"You rarely come inside," he said.

I gestured to the compost toilet. "Get modern

plumbing, and I'll start spending more time at your place."

He chuckled. "Point taken."

"Where's the exit?"

His eyes sparkled with mischief. "Behind the waterfall."

"That's freaking awesome."

"I'm glad you approve."

Keir had told me that Linda had brought us through the rocks when I was passed out.

"How come you didn't use the tunnel to bring me into the house?" I asked.

"Because this is not a route you want to take if you have to carry someone. Are you ready to go?"

I had to pee, but there were at least a hundred pixies hovering around the toilet, and there wasn't a whole lot of room in this tiny house to move them somewhere else. I decided that while it would be a painful journey, I could hold it until I got home. "Yep. Let's do it."

Keir jumped down into the hole. It wasn't very deep. "I hope you don't mind crawling."

"Better than dying." I winced at the ill-timed comment. "I mean, you know what. Let's just go. I'm good with crawling." And on that note, I got down in the dirt behind Keir, thanked Kegel exercises for strong bladder control, and crawled my ass off.

BY THE TIME we got close to town, my cell phone was blowing up. I had twenty-plus texts from Michael from the night before, so he was the first person I texted back.

I'm ok. Heading home to grab some stuff. Stay with Doug. Text soon. Love u.

The other messages were from Rowan, Marigold, Dahlia, and Rose, wanting to know where I was and to call them immediately.

Oops, too late for that. I called Marigold, and she picked up on the first ring.

"Hey," she said. "Where are you at?"

"Coming back into town. Was at Keir's. You know he doesn't have any cell phone reception. How did it go yesterday? Is everyone pissed at me?"

Marigold sighed. "I need you to come to Dad's house."

"Why?"

"Because I need you to come here," Marigold said.

Fear knotted in my gut. Why was she at our father's house? "Is Dad okay? He didn't fall again, did he?"

Marigold sighed. "I'll tell you everything when you get here."

"It could be a problem," I told her. "You know, because of the wind—"

She cut me off. "Hey, you're on speakerphone," she told me. "Rowan is here too."

Great. That meant I couldn't discuss my current

condition. "I'm going to have to go home and shower first," I said. "I'll be there in an hour." I hung up the call.

"What's wrong with your dad?" Keir asked.

"I don't know, but Marigold sounded worried. It must be bad. Rowan's there too." Rowan was a doctor, so if he was keeping this close of an eye on our dad, then it had to be serious. "I need to go, but I can't let them see me like this."

"Long sleeves and gloves," Keir said. "That will cover up all the parts that need covering."

"And the bruises?"

He grimaced. "Makeup."

"It's worth a shot." My frustration and fear were on the same level. "Why is this happening now all at once?"

"I have a theory about that. I call it the all-or-nothing chaos theory. Either nothing is going on, or everything is going on."

"I think that theory has been around for a while." But I smiled, and I think that's all he was after.

When I got home, Linda was in the garden with Bob. She didn't throw anything at me, which worried me even more. "Linda, are we okay?"

"For now, *Kleinkind*," she'd said.

Bob walked next to me as I went inside, taking every opportunity to rub his face against my legs. Bob and I were always good. Keir made a few calls while I showered, dried my hair, lamented my slightly translucent parts and put makeup over my bruises.

I put on a turquoise turtleneck sweater I had in the closet as part of my fall wear, then checked myself out in the mirror. I gave the look a seven out of ten. It would do. I wasn't sure how I was going to get away with gloves, though.

The bruises were hardly noticeable under the makeup, so I tried some on the bad hand. The coverage wasn't bad. I dabbed concealer on for extra coverage, then applied foundation to both hands so they would look alike.

After, I went out to the living room, where Keir was finishing up a call. "You ready?" He gave me a once over. "Not bad at all."

"Not bad, huh?"

He chuckled. "You're beautiful, Iris. The makeup is not bad."

"I'm going to go by myself, if that's okay," I told him. "I don't know what's going on with Dad, and with Rowan there, he might get weird if I bring someone along. Even if that someone is the heart to my soul."

Keir smiled, his gray eyes soft as he stared at me. "I understand." He wrapped his arms around me.

"Careful of my hands," I said. "I don't want to get foundation all over you."

He kissed the top of my head. "I'll go to the health food store and grab the pollen."

"Leave it," I told him. "I'm bringing my grimoire, and I might need some ingredients for spellwork. I'll grab the pollen on my way back." I tilted my head back, and Keir kissed me properly.

"I'll wait for you in town. We can go up together." He rubbed his palms down my arms. "Text me when you're on your way home."

"I will," I promised.

FOUR MORE KISSES and twenty minutes later, I pulled into my dad's driveway. I counted four cars as I squeezed my vehicle in between Rose and Dahlia's vehicles. Why was the whole family here? My mouth dried as concern for my remaining parent overrode all my other emotions. Oh, God. What if Dad was dying? I could understand why Marigold wouldn't want to tell me that kind of bad news over the phone. Dread filled me with every step down the drive to the handicap ramp that led to Dad's front porch. I stifled a sob as I walked into the old ranch-style house and saw Dad sitting in his easy chair.

"Dad," I said as my breath whooshed from my body. I practically ran to him and gave him a hug. "Are you okay?"

"Fine, fine, Girly." He gave my hair a gentle pat. "Why don't you have a seat on the couch?"

That's when I noticed all my siblings had come

into the living room, and they occupied the other chairs and part of the couch.

"Uhm, hey, guys. What's going on?" I pivoted my gaze to Marigold. She widened her eyes, then flashed me a wincing frown and a slight head shake. Uh-oh.

My oldest sister Dahlia answered. "Iris," Dahlia said. "We love you." The rest of them, including Dad, nodded in agreement.

"I love you guys too." I sat down on the couch, focusing on controlling my breathing. Hyperventilation would not be a good look right now. "Why did you need me here?"

"We're worried about you," Dahlia said. She wore her slightly wavy, graying hair down, and she wore jeans and a floral top. She gestured to our youngest sister. "Rose, do you want to tell Iris why you're worried about her?"

Rose, who wore hot pink and black yoga pants, a hot pink top, and a black workout jacket, stood up and pulled out a piece of paper. "Iris, for the past several months, since your divorce, you have been secretive. You get ill for no reason. Some days, you have a lot of energy, too much, and other days, you are practically listless." She made an "I'm sorry" face at me. "I'm worried about you and your choices. And I'm worried about how those choices are affecting your family." She folded the paper and sat back down.

"Thank you, Rose," Dahlia said. "Marigold, would you like to go next?"

"Nope," replied Marigold. "I'm good."

Dahlia gave our sister a disapproving look.

"What is happening?" Then it dawned on me what Dahlia and my siblings were doing. "Oh my God. I can't believe you guys are staging an intervention." Of course, they were. Dahlia was a psychologist. This was right up her alley. I stood up and glared at them. "I'm out."

"Iris." My dad's voice contained a mix of anger and sadness, so much like Keir's had sounded earlier. His next words were a command, not a request. "Sit down. Now."

Because it was my father, I did the only thing I could do.

I sat down.

CHAPTER 16

I SAT THROUGH ROWAN NERVOUSLY PUSHING UP HIS glasses constantly as he talked about how I'd almost died and how he was worried I'd been doing designer drugs—I'm paraphrasing—and that he was worried about how quickly I'd moved on to another relationship. Blah, blah, blah.

I'll admit, their assumptions about what I'd been going through were making me squirm in my seat.

Then Dahlia took her turn. Unlike Rose and Rowan, she didn't need to write stuff down. She had a wealth of education and experience behind her words. "Iris, you know how much we love you. How much I love you. I know it's been difficult for you since Mom's passing. And then with Evan, I think we can all agree the circumstances would've thrown anyone for a loop. Since the divorce, you've been distant, depressed, missing family meals, you hardly return any calls, and I'm really worried that even if you're not doing drugs or drinking, you've been self-harming. We'll always be here for you, but you are going to have to take the next step."

I arched a brow at my oldest sister. "And what step is that?"

She got up from her seat and crouched in front of me. Dahlia, whose eyes were a blue-green hazel, met my gaze and took my hands in hers. "You have to want help."

I remembered that I had makeup on my skin, so I quickly tugged my hands away. To cover, I said, "I don't need help." Only I did. I was falling apart, literally, but there wasn't a single person in my family who had the expertise to put me back together again.

The corners of Dahlia's mouth dipped, and her frown lines deepened. "We can't force you to be honest with us, Iris." She gave me a slow blink of disappointment. Dahlia, who was ten years older than me, had perfected the look long before she became a family counselor. "But I hope that you'll think about what we've said here, and you'll be able to eventually be honest with yourself."

Dahlia had been Mom's little helper, babysitting Marigold and me whenever Mom and Dad had to work. Our oldest sister was kind, patient, intelligent, and a master at making me feel like a naughty six-year-old who got caught with her hand in the cookie jar.

I looked to Marigold for help. She shrugged. Nope. No help there. I narrowed my gaze at her, and she leveled me with a "you brought this on yourself" stare.

"Well," I said as I got up. "It's been interesting." I tried to keep my tone neutral. "I take all your concerns seriously. If there's nothing else, then I'm going to go. Lots to do today."

"Now, baby girl," Dad said. "We just want you to be safe and happy."

Safe hadn't been in my wheelhouse for quite some time, but I had the heart-stopping realization that even with all the danger and unpredictability, I was happier than I'd been in years. "I hear you, I do. And I'm okay, Dad. Promise."

Rowan got up and ran his hand over his balding head. "We can't stop you from leaving. But you can tell us the truth. We love you, Iris." That seemed to be the consensus. "We're on your side."

"Guys, really." I waved off their concerns, but inside I was dying. I wanted to be honest with them. Hiding what was going on with me, what I'd become, from my family, was harder than almost dying. But now, when my magic was so unstable, didn't seem like the best time to reveal my witchiness. "When I'm ready to talk, I'll let you know. Promise."

Dahlia walked over to me, her expression full of worry and consternation. She licked her thumb and wiped at my cheek. Shit. She'd revealed one of my bruises to the family.

I swatted her hand away.

"What happened to you?" she demanded.

"You should see the other guy," I half-joked.

Dahlia's face pinched with anger. "No," she said. "This isn't funny. Who hit you, Iris? Did Keir do this?"

"No, absolutely not." I couldn't tell her that my bruises were a combination of a satyr's horns and a bunch of faux-leprechauns with wooden staffs. "He would never hit me."

"Bullshit," she said. "He's a classic abuser. Why didn't I see it? He comes off as Mr. Perfect, seduces you, then little by little, he separates you from all the people who love you so that he can completely control you."

"Stop it, Dahlia." I moved out of her reach. "Keir didn't lay a finger on me. He is not trying to control me or keep me from you all."

"Then who?" Her mouth dropped open. "Oh. Please, no. Is it Michael? Is he lashing out because of trauma over Evan?"

"His dad is bisexual. He didn't beat him." Rowan was trying to give me a physical examination now. I side-stepped my two oldest siblings. Rose had started crying. My poor dad was getting red in the face. This was the last thing he needed.

Then Marigold stood up. "Enough!" she yelled.

She was usually the chill sister, so her outrage made everyone shut up. "Everybody, sit down," she ordered. "And quit badgering Iris. I know for a fact that neither Keir nor Michael have been abusing her, so let that shit go." She snapped at Rose. "For the love of Pete, Rose. Quit crying. You're not helping things here."

"I'm sorry. I can't help it," Rose said, then cried some more. "It's hormones."

I looked at our youngest sister. "Are you pregnant?"

She nodded as she choked on a snotty sob. "It's still early, so Don and I were keeping it under wraps until the second trimester."

Holy crap. Rose was forty. I couldn't imagine starting all over with a new baby. "It's good news, right?"

She nodded and hiccupped.

"Nope," Marigold said. "Congrats, Rose, but today is not about you."

Dahlia was like a pixie with a boner. She wasn't going to stop, no matter how inconvenient it was for me. "Someone is abusing you, Iris. I've been doing this long enough that I can't believe I missed the signs."

Rowan started in on me next. "We should go to the hospital and do a full work-up complete with nail scrapings for DNA and take pictures. You might not want to press charges now, but someday you could change your mind."

Dear Lord. This intervention was never going to end.

"Oh, for fuck's sake," Marigold said. Then she turned to our father and winced. "Sorry, Dad."

He shook his head. "I'm thinking far worse."

"I'm a witch," I said quietly as Rowan and Dahlia fought over what I should do next, Marigold simmered, Dad looked confused, and Rose would not stop crying. "I'm a witch." This time I said it louder.

Marigold did a slow clap. "Finally. The truth comes out."

"Stop trying to make jokes," Dahlia said. "It's a coping mechanism."

"Jokes can make bad situations better," Rowan disagreed. "At least she's saying something."

"Yeah," I told him. "I'm saying I'm a witch. I have a familiar and a grimoire and everything. I can even cast a spell or two. But I probably shouldn't right now because the last spell I cast killed me."

Marigold was sipping tea when I'd said the last bit and ended up spraying it all over the floor. "You what?" she asked sharply.

I shook my head at her. "I came back to life. Not a big deal." Only it had been a big deal. A really big deal that had nearly broken the love of my life. He said I'd been dead for eight whole minutes. I'm still not sure how he managed to bring me back to life. "Anywhoooo," I went on. "My magic sparked to life a day or two after the divorce. That's why I've been distancing myself from you all. Granted, I hadn't realized that's what I was doing. It's hard to see all the stuff from the outside when you're constantly being put in the thick of it, you know?"

My sisters, brother, and father looked dumbfounded.

"She's hysterical," Rowan said.

"That's not an actual diagnosis, Ro," Dahlia said. "Just because a woman has a breakdown doesn't mean it's hysteria. Men have breakdowns all the time, and no one accuses them of hysteria, do they?"

"I'm not hysterical, and I'm not having a breakdown. I'm a tru-craft witch. And the reason I'm bruised is because I am protecting a pack of mating pixies until they have their babies in like two or three days."

Marigold groaned. "Baby steps, Iris. That sounds crazy to me, and I know it's the truth."

"Well, I'm being as honest as I can be. I don't want to hide who I am anymore or what I'm going through from you guys. I love you. I'm really not trying to cut you out of my life."

"Prove it," Rowan said.

"Like I said, I can't do magic right now because I can't afford the cost. Magic comes at a price." I rolled my hand at my brother as if the gesture could turn back time. "Remember when I thought I'd been roofied, then I almost died?"

"That's not something I'm likely to forget," he said.

"That's when my magic had been triggered. I was learning about terra-craft, earth magic, and it was basically burning me up from the inside. It nearly killed me until I learned how to control it. Right now, I'm having a similar problem with air magic."

"This is delusional and fantasist," Dahlia said. "Often when someone's abused, they make up stories, especially if they love their attacker, in order to protect them."

"Thank you, Dr. Bill," I said, knowing how much Dahlia hated Dr. Bill and his armchair psychiatry. "But I'm not making this up." The makeup on my right hand was smudged, and I could see some shiny bits showing through. "Okay, I've got proof, but no one gets to freak out."

Marigold shook her head. "Too late for that."

I yanked my long sleeve up, exposing my slightly transparent arm.

Dahlia frowned and took a step back.

Rowan took a step forward. "Is that an optical illusion?"

"No," I told him. "That's air magic. It's consumed part of my body." I lifted the shirt at the waist.

Collectively, my siblings gasped.

"This isn't possible," Dahlia said. "Magic doesn't exist."

"You'd be surprised," Marigold told her. "All kinds of things exist."

Rose sniffled. "What about Keir and Luanne? Are they witches too?"

I shook my head. "Druids. Keir is my soul-bond. We were born two hours apart, and he has spent his entire life getting strong so that he could be my defender." I held out my hands. "We're a team. He would sooner take his own life than harm me." Without a doubt, I knew it to be true. "And Luanne is a warrior. She has been fighting for me and beside me since all this started. There are people who have hurt me or tried to hurt me because of my magic, and Keir and Luanne have helped to keep me safe. So, as you can see, there is no hospital, rehabilitation center, women's shelter, or law enforcement agency that can fix my problems. That's something that I have to do myself." I took a deep breath and held it as I tried to center my feelings. The emotional turmoil was causing the air magic I'd slowed down to stir beneath the surface. "I'm keeping my distance," I told them all, "because I couldn't live with myself if something terrible happened to any of you because of me."

For a few seconds, all I could hear was the whirring sound of Dad's old air conditioner as it kicked on. Dad put down the footrest of his easy chair, then got up and walked over to me. He put his arms around me and held me tight. His hug was perfect, a healing balm on my wounded heart.

"I wish I knew what to say or do for you, baby girl," Dad said.

"This is it," I told him. "This hug. It's everything."

"You are loved," he said. "Always."

Marigold wrapped her arms around both of us. Then Rose got up and joined in. Then Rowan and Dahlia.

After a few moments of holding my family, breathing in their scents, taking in their love, I was crying as hard as Rose.

"Keep this up, and someone's going to think we're all pregnant," I said.

Everyone laughed except Rose, who said, "Hey, now."

Then we laughed some more.

I'd finally come clean to my family. I wasn't sure if they all understood everything I'd said about the supernatural world, but at least I wouldn't have to lie anymore. On top of that, Marigold no longer had to lie for me.

Still, I had responsibilities that required tending. "I have to go," I said as we broke the group hug. "I have a bargain to keep. But I promise to tell you all more as soon as I'm finished."

Dahlia grasped my wrist before I could leave. "You know I'm here for you."

"I do," I told her. "I never doubt that."

She nodded, then let go of me. "If you need anything, call me. Day or night. I will always pick up the phone for you."

I felt a pinch of guilt over the handful of times I'd let her calls go to voicemail. "Thanks, Dahl. Sorry, I'm such a shit."

Her eyes softened when she smiled. "Little sisters are good at being shits. I forgive you."

"Because big sisters are good at that."

She smirked. "I'm still not sure I believe all this hocus pocus stuff."

"That's okay," I said. "You'll have time to get used to it." At least, I hoped she would. I'd unloaded a lot of information on my family in a short amount of time. Eventually, this was going to require a bigger conversation.

Marigold walked me out to the car. She draped an arm over my shoulder. "It took me a few weeks to embrace the new Iris. Those guys will come around."

"I need to hire you as my publicist." I leaned my head on her shoulder, thankful to fate for not only giving me an awesome family but a sister who was also the best friend I could've asked for. She was always there for me, no matter how bad I screwed up.

Marigold sucked her teeth and shook her head. "Nope. I have a job, and it doesn't include fixing your life."

I smiled at her. "Could've fooled me."

CHAPTER 17

IT WAS EIGHTY DEGREES OUTSIDE. THE turtleneck, while necessary, made me feel like a microwaved burrito—hot and sweaty and past my expiration date. I pulled up to the curb in front of Nature's Natural, the local health food store and parked.

There was a pair of mittens left over from winter in the glove box. I put them on before I got out of the car and went into the store. The personal protection spell called for ylang-ylang oil, six blue candles, and black tourmaline. I could stop at the mart for candles, but I hoped like hell the health food store had the essential oil and the stone because otherwise, I was shit out of luck and would have to find another way to watch over the pixie troupe.

I grabbed a handbasket on the way in and made a beeline to the bee products. There was an entire row of raw honey with honeycomb, lip balms, hand creams, and other stuff, but I didn't see the pollen.

I'd been so locked in on searching the shelves I hadn't noticed that Carla Porter had snuck up behind me. "Well, hey, there, Iris." Her blonde hair was flat-iron straight, and she was wearing rhinestone-studded jeans and a v-neck teal green t-shirt that flattered her chest. "Great game Friday night, huh? I can't believe the booster bonfire was cut short. Stupid teenagers. Throwing a propane tank in the fire could've gotten someone really hurt."

There was a woman next to her that I recognized as Maddie's mom.

Carla smiled. "You remember Yolanda Carver, right?"

"Hi," I told her. I just wanted them both to leave me alone. I was looking crazy in cold weather gear on a hot late summer day, and I didn't want to give the football moms more gossip. "It's nice to see you again."

Yolanda smiled, and she nodded. "My Maddie talks about your Michael all the time."

"That's, uhm, nice. She's a sweet girl," I told her because I wasn't prepared for awkward encounters with the mother of the girl my son was crushing on.

"And Michael's very cute." She held out her hand.

I went to take it, then remembered I was mittened. "Oh. Sorry. Skin rash." Quickly I added. "Nothing contagious." I'd tied Coach Jordan up with poison ivy, so I further explained, "Poison ivy. There so much of it at the Silver End." Yolanda was wearing a t-shirt like Carla because it was eighty degrees outside. "The turtle neck is for the same reason. Rash everywhere," I finished. God, I was an idiot.

"You poor thing," Yolanda said. "You must be so itchy."

I gave a quick shake of my head. "Sure. Itchy." I scratched my arm with my mittened hand, silently cussing when my arm really started itching. *Damn you, power of suggestion!*

Carla looked at my empty basket. "Watcha looking for? Calamine lotion?"

"Stuff," I told her.

"You should pick up some antihistamine gel from the drug store," Yolanda suggested. She brightened. "Oh. They do have colloidal oatmeal here. Add that to your bath, and it will help soothe the rash."

I already regretted saying I had a rash.

"I don't need any gel right now, but thanks all the same."

"Then what are you looking for?" Carla eyed me suspiciously. "Come on now," she poo-pooed. "I shop here all the time," she said. "Maybe I can help you find your...*stuff.*"

Since there was nothing catastrophic about what I was looking for, it didn't hurt to tell her. "I need bee pollen. Pure pollen," I added. "No preservatives or anything extra."

She arched her brow, and a smirk tugged at her lips. "Bee pollen is good for a lot of things. Inflammation, boosting your immune system, and," she paused dramatically, then nonchalantly said, "menopause."

I forced a smile. "Has it worked for you?"

Yolanda giggled. I gave her a quick wink, and she covered her smile with her hand.

Carla frowned and narrowed her gaze at me. "I'm a long way from menopause. My doctor says I've got the ovaries of a teenager."

I shrugged. "I didn't mean to imply that you're old or anything. Middle age is the new twenty, after all. You just seemed so knowledgeable; I made an assumption." She looked so outraged that I had to stifle a snicker. "It's for a project." Not a complete lie. "Do you know if they have some here?"

Carla pointed toward the back wall. Her fingers were dripping in jewelry, including a large diamond wedding ring. "If the store has it, it will be on the supplement aisle."

"Uhm, thanks. Do you know if they have ylang-ylang or crystals and stones?"

She gave me a wide-eyed stare. "What kind of project are you doing?"

"It's for Michael," I said, surprising myself with how easy the lie rolled off my tongue. "Trying to get an early start on his senior project." All of the parents had been dreading the much-hated senior project. When my ex-husband worked as a teacher at Southill

Village High School, he'd said the projects were almost as big a nightmare for the staff as it was for the students. Doing poorly on a senior project could be the difference between graduating or repeating the twelfth grade.

"Interesting," Carla mused. She took a rose-colored lipstick from her purse and refreshed her lips with color. "Luckily, I have another year before I have to worry about that."

"Me too," Yolanda said. "I've heard they are a time-suck for the parents."

"Truth." I nodded. "I better get to it."

Yolanda commented, "As for the ylang-ylang, maybe by the essential oils up by the register, but I've never seen rocks or crystals in here."

"Thanks," I said. "See you at the next game."

"Go, Howlers," Carla said.

"Yep." I waggled my finger in the air. "Go, Howlers."

BEE POLLEN. Check. Candles from the Mart. Check. Black Tourmaline and Ylang Ylang. Total bust.

I called Keir after I'd exhausted all the possibilities, including a tobacco shop just outside of town. "I can't find all the ingredients," I said when he answered.

"Meet me at your house," he said. He sounded

angry and frustrated. "We have a few things to discuss."

That was never a good sign. "What's up?"

"A drake attacked my house and burned a hole in the roof to get to the pixies." Quickly, he added, "Zev and Lu were able to take the creature out. None of the troupe was harmed."

I let out a noisy breath. "I'm glad everyone is okay but tell me again. A what did what?"

"A drake is a small dragon-like creature."

"I'm familiar. I just didn't know they were real."

"I'm surprised you're still surprised."

"Every day," I told him. "You're sure the pixies are okay?"

"Well, they're waiting in Lu's car for you to get home and decide what to do with them, but yeah, they're okay."

"These dust hunters aren't going to stop, are they?" I asked.

"Not until the pixie zygotes mature. The dust will be worthless at that point."

"Got it," I said. "I'm a couple minutes away. Be home in a bit."

"Love you," Keir said as a goodbye. He sounded less unhappy with me, which made me feel less crappy.

Since I had a minute to myself, I called Michael to check in. The phone went straight to an automated voicemail box. "Hey, kiddo. I'm doing okay.

Hope you are too. I may be staying in town tonight, but call before you come home. Lots happening. Love you, babe. Bye," I rattled off into the phone. I didn't want Michael walking into a shitstorm at the house by accident, so I hoped he bothered to listen to my message. I'd text him when I got home to be safe.

Luanne's white SUV was parked at my curb, and Keir's electric car was in my driveway. When I drove past the sports vehicle, I raised my brows at the pixies flying around inside. The windows were closed. That couldn't be healthy for the babies. Or maybe it was. I mean, most creatures' eggs were hatched under heat. I parked next to Keir's car. Luanne came outside the house.

I opened the door and grabbed my grimoire. "Why is the troupe locked inside your SUV?"

"Talk to Linda. She's having a major meltdown about them being back, but I didn't know where else to take them," Lu said.

Damn it, Linda. I knew she felt like she had her reasons, but this was ridiculous. "I'll talk to her. The pixies can't stay in the four-runner, though. It's too hot out here. Have the troupe go in the house and stay there until I get this sorted."

Lu cocked a brow at me. "I left it running with the air on. I'm not a dummy."

"It's so quiet," I told her.

"New vehicles are quiet. If you bought something in this decade, you'd know that."

"As soon as I can figure out the spell for money, I'll trade up."

She laughed. "If you figure out how to make money, we'll travel the world and take this show on the road."

"Don't be plotting to run off with my girl," Keir said as he came out on the porch. He crossed his arms and leaned against the door frame.

Lu gave me a peculiar look. "Your face is melting."

She had to be talking about the foundation. I hadn't powdered it, and I'd been perspiring profusely. "This is not sweater weather," I said in my defense. The makeup was all but gone from my hands, thanks to the mittens I'd worn in the store. I tucked the grimoire under my arm. "I'll go through the garden gate. You guys get the pixies settled while I confront the gnome."

The second I stepped through the backyard gate, I ducked. I'd been playing this game with Linda long enough to know what came next. A clump of dirt and rocks smacked the fence behind me.

Linda stood near her bench, looking ready to spit gravel.

I smirked. "Missed me, bitch."

The gnome was not amused. "I accept that you must protect the *Luftdämonen,* but I refuse to allow them to defile my garden with their foul ways and ill winds." She waved at me as if to say, See? "Look at what they have already done to you. This unstable magic wouldn't be happening if not for them."

"That's not fair, Linda. That's like saying you were responsible when my terra-craft was threatening to return me to the earth. It wasn't your fault, and it wasn't theirs."

"Bah!" She threw her stubby arms into the air and turned in a circle. "Zis is different! They are evil, vile creatures."

"No." I sighed, remembering the look of pure joy and love in Annibish's eyes as she showed me her baby—the daughter she was naming for me. "They are not evil."

If I hadn't been convinced before, that moment showed me that the pixies were a vulnerable species who had something that every bully thought they could just come along and take because they were physically strong enough to do it. That was caveman thinking, and I wasn't going to ignore it while the pixies were killed for their magic.

I shook my head at her. "Fair Konig and his people didn't do anything to provoke what's happening to them. If anything, their situation is my fault, not the other way around. My magic is in flux, and the chaos aspect started their mating season eight hundred years earlier than it should've started. And now all the awful creatures are trying to kill them, to kill their babies, to grind them down to pixie dust to use for any number of reasons, but none of them good. Is that what you want? You want me to abandon them to that fate?"

The dirt clump hit me that time. "Son of a bitch," I ground out. "Damn it, Linda."

"Do what you must, *Kleinkind*, but do it somewhere else."

"Please don't make me choose between you and the lives of a hundred pixies and their incubating babies. I love you, like seriously love you. You're like a second mom to me. I don't know what my life would be like without you. I know it would be much worse than it is now, but all that said, I'm willing to find out if you can't make room in your heart to put your differences aside for a couple of days. Because that's all they need. A couple of days. Once their kids hatch, or whatever, the pixies will be out of danger, and they will move on."

"No!" Linda said sharply. "You will die like my parents did. All because of them, and I will not stay around to watch it happen. Not again. I will never put my differences aside. I will not forget my mother and father as they were slaughtered by banshees, all because of those flying demons."

"I remember your mother and your father," Fair Konig said as he flew over to Linda and alighted onto the bench. I sat down next to him and put the grim down.

"I don't want to hear your words," Linda told him. "Nothing you can say will make a bit of difference."

"I understand. I was a pisky at the time. I hadn't yet been raised to King, but my father was friends with your parents. They agreed to help out of friendship and community."

"They were fools," Linda hissed. "And they died for it."

"They were heroes," Fair Konig disagreed. "I remember the fight well. The banshees captured several of our troupe, and my father tried to get them back, but he was captured as well." His stare was far off as he recalled the ordeal. "Annibish carried two children, a boy and a girl. The banshees took her too." His voice was hard with anger. "I tried to fight them, to get her and our people back." He pivoted his gaze to Linda. "If it hadn't been for your parents....my mate, along with son and daughter, Broxishowna and Ghomandawn would not have survived.

Linda looked dumbstruck. Speechless. "Broxishowna and Ghomandawn."

He nodded. "It is our custom to name our children for those who lend us their strength so that we may survive. It is our way of honoring the debt and the sacrifice. Your parents were our saviors that day, and in our troupe, they have never been and never will be forgotten."

Linda turned her back on the pixie king as she yanked her hat off and crumpled it in her hands. She gave a curt nod with her bald head. "They can stay," she said quickly, then in a blur, she tunneled underground and disappeared.

"She'll be back," I said, hoping like hell I wasn't wrong. I looked at Fair Konig. "Thank you for telling your story." Picking up the grimoire, I placed it on my lap. I prayed I could figure out a protection spell that would keep them safe. Keep us all safe. "You go inside with your people. I'll figure something out to protect the troupe."

I sent a silent plea to the damned book.

Please don't let me fail.

CHAPTER 18

My dearest Michael, I wrote, if you are reading these words, I am no longer alive. I'm sorry that you have to find out about me, about your heritage, like this, but I've only known for a short time myself, and I thought I'd have more time.

I traced a finger over the letter I'd written to my son over a month ago before I had told him about tru-craft. I'd found out that I was in grave danger, and if I would've died, I hadn't wanted him to be left alone without any explanation. Thank heavens, I'd survived, and the letter hadn't become necessary. Still, the penned last letter to my son was a stark reminder that my life was a complete shitshow, and I was the star.

I read through the names of my ancestors, sending up a request that they give me some guidance. *Aideen Magee, 1678. Clionna Doon, 1705. Siobhan*

Adrian, 1782. Mary Ann Langford, 1834. Brigit O'Malley, 1880. Mira Roberts, 1912. At the end of the list, I had added my own name and the year.

I flipped through page by page, reading spells that I'd created along with notes in the margin like, *don't use too much agar unless you want the giggles all day.* One day, this book would pass to my child and, perhaps, to his children. From what Keir had told me, grimoires were family-specific living entities. They were drawn to the bloodline of the witch who crafted the book, and they were able to manipulate their existence until they found living heirs. This grimoire had found a way back to me, though it hadn't found my birth mother or her mother. Or maybe it had, and they'd known how to repel it. *Mira Roberts, 1912* had been the last name before mine. I assumed she had to be a great or great great grandmother. She'd landed in New York as a refugee during the first world war in 1914. She'd had a child with her, but the name had been illegible, and her husband had been listed as deceased on her immigration card. Keir hadn't been able to find any other information about her.

I didn't resent my birth mother for giving me up. If she hadn't, I wouldn't have known the love of my family, and that would be a tragedy. I'd had a happy childhood, and I wouldn't have traded it for anything. It didn't stop me from wondering about the woman who'd let me go. Had she been a tru-craft witch? Had wild magic killed her? It had almost killed me.

My stomach clenched as I looked at my hand and arm.

Wild magic hadn't killed me yet, but it wasn't from a lack of trying.

The terra-craft spells in the book were fairly useless for the purpose I needed. The closest one was a perimeter incantation that warded against pestilence that Linda had helped me with when we got leaf miners, mostly moths and sawflies. They were destroying several plants, and the spell repelled them from my yard. If I needed to fend off Japanese beetles or Gall mites, then I was all set. Unfortunately, I needed something to keep every pixie-hunting paranormal asshole from entering my garden. Better yet, something to keep them entirely out of Southill Village.

I kept flipping pages, wishing the book would magically show me the way.

It did not.

The fire spells were a total bust. Its pages of charms and defensive magic offered nothing that could cover the yard and the house. I had mixed feelings about continuing. When I'd first mastered earth magic, I'd eagerly cataloged every spell and incantation I'd learned. I'd been less enthusiastic with fire, and it showed in how few spells I'd written in that element's section.

The next page after the ignis section was empty.

There were no aero-craft spells, incantations, or journal entries. Nada. Nothing. Zip. Totally my bad.

Help me out, I silently pleaded with the leather-bound tome. *Show me the way*.

It didn't respond.

Keir walked out into the garden. "Can I sit?"

"Yep." I scratched my head. "I'm stuck."

"Anything I can help with?" He put his arm around me.

I laid my head on his shoulder and inhaled the scent of bergamot and sandalwood. I'd bought him some homemade organic, non-sudsing goat milk soap from a shop out of Garden Cove, Missouri. Marigold, a self-proclaimed expert in natural products, promised I'd love it. I did. I loved it even better on Keir.

Damn, the man smelled terrific.

"I was so quick to put the book away when the air symbol showed up. Is it too late for me? Did I blow my shot to master aero-craft by not embracing it right away?" I closed the book and placed my palm on the cover. The grimoire was a living thing. Living things could get angry. Maybe the book was punishing me for tying it up and tossing it in a dark attic. "You think the grimoire is pissed at me? I've ignored it for a month. It's possible, right?"

Keir gave me a crooked smile. "I don't think your grimoire would keep anything from you. Especially if your life was on the line. It wants you to survive."

"Hah. I haven't seen any evidence of that, or it wouldn't keep throwing element bombs at me." My fingers trembled as I traced the alchemy symbols for earth, fire, and air. Cripes. I was afraid of the book. Of course, I was. It had turned my world topsy-turvy, and the hits kept on coming. "I'm scared of it," I told Keir. "I'm scared every time I touch it. Maybe it senses my fear."

Keir was quiet for a long moment. "I don't know the answer, Iris. I wish I did."

Luanne came out. "Hey," she said. "The pixies are getting hungry."

Crap. "I left the pollen in the car."

"You got something figured out yet?" she asked.

"Rub it in," I said.

Lu's brow arched. "What you really need is a lead box."

I gave her an incredulous stare. "For what? Storing plutonium?"

Keir snickered.

Lu put her hand on her hip and struck a badass pose. "Lead hides stuff in an x-ray. I just thought that something like that might keep the pixies off the supernatural radar."

"Oh, like the cloak of invisibility."

Luanne squinted at me. "Do you have one of those?"

I chuckled. "Didn't you ever watch the Harry Potter movies?"

"Uhm, no," she said. "I'm not an adolescent who wishes magic was real. I'm an adult who knows it exists."

I could see how that might turn someone off to the series.

"Well, Michael loved the books and the movies." So had I. It was a love I could share with my kid. "Harry has a cloak of invisibility that allows him to go around unseen."

"Too bad it doesn't exist," Keir said.

"Something like that would make my job easier," Lu agreed.

I opened the grimoire back up again, hoping to find some kind of hint in the cryptic message it had given me the day before.

Blood of my blood, daughter of fade and bright.

Tears of my tears, prepare for a harrowing fight.

To fight what is not there, first, you must harness the air.

Ignorance is the greatest sin. Learn what you must or be dust in the wind.

Goddess, help you.

I glanced at Keir. "What do you think it means by fighting what isn't there?"

"Maybe it was talking about the wraith," Lu guessed.

Keir gave a slight head shake. "That was unseen, mostly, but it was definitely there."

A shiver ran through me. "Speaking of which, if

the wraith isn't done with me, does that mean it will show up again?"

"Likely," Keir said.

"It's like the universe is trying to kill me," I said.

"There are easier ways to off someone." Lu huffed a breath. "When you weave your invisibility cloak, you need to get under it with the pixies."

"Hardy har." I rolled my eyes. I reread the message. "If ignorance is the greatest sin, then I am definitely going to hell."

Lu kicked a pebble off a paving stone. "Hell is a construct. It doesn't really exist."

"It doesn't really exist," I repeated in a mutter. "Hey, how does the pixie dust attract all the hunters?"

"The dust sends an energy signal that acts as a beacon to all supernatural creatures."

"Then why can't I feel it?" I was a witch, after all.

"Because you're a person," Keir said. "Not a creature."

"But you're a creature," I told him. "Sometimes. Do you feel it?"

He nodded. "It's like a compulsion. A calling. It feels like the dust wants me to find it and use it to transform myself into something more than what I am."

"What?" I asked.

Keir frowned. "I'm not sure, but I can understand the draw."

"Could you feel it even when they were at your

place and you were here in town with me?"

He nodded. "Yes. It's like a signal, but I don't want to change, so it's gotten weaker since the first time I resisted."

"What about Zev?"

Lu looked back over her shoulder. "Zev!"

He came outside. "Yes?"

"Are you getting drawn in by the pixie mating dust?" I asked.

He held out his hand and tilted it back and forth. "Sort of. But it's not strong."

"Maybe because he's human-ish," Lu said. "What are you thinking, Iris?"

"I have a pest spell in the book that wards the perimeter, and there's a transformation spell that turns a mum into a carnation." That was one of my prouder moments.

Lu made a face. "Why?"

"Because carnations smell nice and mums don't," I said.

"Or you really liked carnations," Lu countered. "How does a flower spell and a pest spell help us?"

"I'm not sure I can make it work, but they're both earth spells, and I think I can maybe twist the two of them together to make a transformation spell." I shook my head. "More of a masking."

"Of what?"

"The signal," I said. "If I can change the signal going out—"

"Then the pixies basically become invisible," Lu said excitedly as she caught where I was going.

I grinned. "Exactly!"

Zev nodded. "If you can mask the signal, there is no need to hide the pixies. It's a good plan if you can make it happen."

Keir had been reservedly quiet. He removed his arm from around me.

"You don't think it will work?" I asked.

"I think it could work," he said, but he looked miserable.

"Then what?" I reached for his hand, and he tucked it between his knees. "What are you thinking?"

The corners of his eyes were wrinkled and pinched with worry. "I think it sounds like the type of spell that might kill you."

"Keir," I said softly. "I don't know what else to do. The monsters aren't going to stop coming. I'm going to be forced to use my magic one way or another. And if I can block or change the signal the pixies are putting off, isn't it better than panic magic during a fight?"

He shook his head, but he wore a hint of a smile. "Probably. Can we at least consult with Thomas beforehand?"

"Absolutely." I kissed him. "Because I'm not as ignorant as the grimoire would have you believe. My momma didn't raise no fool."

CHAPTER 19

THE WIZENED OLD MAN ON THE OTHER END OF THE video call only looked mildly surprised to hear from me so soon. "What can I do for you, Iris?"

"I need your advice," I told him. I'd taken the call to the bathroom for some privacy. I didn't want Keir worrying and Luanne scowling over my shoulder. I wanted Thomas's counsel, but I also knew that, ultimately, whatever I decided to do, the decision would be mine to make.

He inclined his head. "I am at your disposal."

"I have this idea for a spell, and if it works, it will not only save the pixies, but I think it could protect them down the road."

"What does this spell entail?"

"I want to change the signal."

"The what?"

"You know, the signal the dust puts out there that attracts all the baddies."

He steepled his thin fingers. "I see. Sort of like switching channels on a two-way radio. If everyone is on channel nine, they hear the broadcast, but if the broadcast switches to channel one, then the broadcast is no longer heard by everyone still on the old channel."

"Uhm...okay, sure." His analogy was spot on, actually.

He smiled. "Sorry, I used to be a police officer when I was a young man. When we wanted privacy, we'd switch channels. Your idea made me think of that."

"Then we're on the same page." I cracked my neck and adjusted the laptop on the counter so that the camera was centered on me.

Thomas's eyes crinkled with mild amusement. "Are you sitting on the toilet?"

"Yes." I chuckled. "There's not a lot of privacy in the house right now." Even in the bathroom, I knew Keir could hear me with his ultra-sonic pooka ears. Zev could probably as well, and if I knew Lu, she had some techy listening gadget pointed at the bathroom.

"Do you have any powder available?" he asked.

"I have some talc."

"That'll work. Get it."

I retrieved the talcum powder from the medicine cabinet and then sat back down. "Now what?"

"Pour some in your hand."

"How much?"

"A quarter size amount should do."

I did as he asked and shook a small pile of the white powder into my left palm. "Done."

"Excellent." He smiled. "Picture your bathroom as a soundproof booth in your mind."

I smiled back, seeing where he was going. "Soundproof. Got it."

"Say these words, beyond these walls, no sound to hear. Inside these walls, our path is clear. "

"Then what?"

"Then clap your hands together, spreading the talc around the room. It will soundproof your bathroom."

I smirked. "That could come in handy for other reasons."

Thomas laughed. "And it has," he agreed. "It certainly makes living with someone easier."

Did Thomas live with the archdruid? Keir hadn't said, but maybe that was part of the reason for Lu's continued animosity. Had Thomas replaced their grandfather in all aspects? After all, Keir and I had gotten romantic. A soul-bond made intimacy of some kind unavoidable. "Okay." I repeated the words and clapped the powder around the room. At the end, I added, "Bend to my will," a phrase Thomas had me use in the first spell I performed with him.

"Finished," I said as I sat down. I'd barely felt any

magic flow during the spell. "But I don't notice any difference. Did it work?"

The corner of his mouth tugged up, and he tugged on his scraggly beard. "You'll know in—"

A knock at the door sounded. "Iris? Are you okay?"

Thomas grinned. "It's working."

"I'm good," I said loudly.

The knock came again. "Iris? Everything all right?"

"Well, poop. How am I supposed to answer him?"

"You could slip a note under the door."

"And what do I write with? This is a bathroom, not an office."

Thomas covered his mouth and shook his head. "You're a resourceful young woman. I'm sure you'll think of something." I suspected the old man was extremely amused by my predicament.

The knocking became more insistent. I hurriedly dug through my makeup drawer until I found my eyebrow pencil, then I took a few sheets of toilet paper from the roll. *I'm good*, I scribbled, *privacy spell*. The pencil tip broke off on the last L, but the words were clear enough to get my message across. I used my nail file to shove the toilet paper under the door. Then I passed a flat barrette under to get his attention when he continued to knock.

"Oh," I heard him say. He stopped knocking. I

went back to my throne. "It's sorted. How do I dispel the sound barrier when we're done?"

"It's temporary. It will last about five minutes, though you can shorten the time by opening the door." He nodded to me. "Now, tell me your plan."

I wiped my palms with some facial tissue. "I have a question, first."

"Go ahead."

"I barely felt that spell. Even the one we did earlier didn't take hardly any energy. Were those aero-craft spells or something else?"

"You ask the right questions, Iris. I'm glad we are finally speaking. Those were aero-craft since that is the only element I can harness."

The grimoire had said I needed to harness the air. Coincidence? Maybe. Or maybe it was just commonly used language. "So, if both those spells were me tapping into my air magic, why is it still running wild in me?"

"Yours is a unique situation. I've never encountered a multi-elemental witch, so it's only a guess. From what you told me earlier, I think whenever you cast aero-craft, like the tornado you spun up, you try to use the other elements to control it. Earth to block, fire to smother, instead of utilizing air, the element used to create the magic."

"Can it be that simple?"

"And that hard," he agreed. "The damage aero-craft is doing to your body is a culmination of your efforts and failures, not just one incident."

I didn't love thinking about myself as a failure. "How do I fix this? How do I stop failing?"

"Failing at times is inevitable." His eyes were kind and his voice gentle. "Living through failures is how we know when we succeed."

"I'm going to fail myself right out of existence before that happens." I clenched my hands, trying to tamp down my frustration. "So why didn't I fail when I cast the spells you gave me? Is it because they came from you?"

"No," he said. "It's because you had faith in me that I wouldn't give you something that you couldn't handle. That faith made you less apprehensive, more confident."

"Confidence is key, huh?" I took a deep breath as anxiety squeezed my chest. "You make it sound easy."

He laughed again. "Then I'm doing my job wrong. There's nothing easy about mastering any tru-craft. The fact that you survived two of the elements is a miracle."

"Why did earth and fire play nice with each other, but air can't seem to get along with either?"

"Because earth and fire are natural antagonists. Fire burns the earth, and earth can smother fire. However, air stirs up earth and acts as fuel for fire. When those three mix...." He made the gesture for *boom* with his hands.

A chill ran through me at the implication. "That's terrifying."

His expression turned grim. "It is." He sat back in his chair. "Tell me what you have in mind."

"I want to take the perimeter part of the pest spell, you know, but instead of bloodstone to keep out bugs, I want to use amethyst for a type of purification. Then use the transformation spell to change the way the pixie dust signal feels, sounds, and such." I was excited talking about the possibility of crafting. I hadn't felt this way in two months. "What do you think?"

"You should use lapis lazuli," he said. "It will amplify a communication spell."

"So you think it can work?"

"Maybe." He was leaning forward. His thumb on his jaw and his forefinger on his temple. "There's the possibility that if you change the dust's...frequency, so to speak, you might also change the way it does its job. It might prevent the pixies from completing their rites."

"Damn. No babies."

He nodded. "No babies."

I hadn't thought about the possibility that it might alter the DNA of the pixie dust. If anything happened to their developing pixies because of me, I wouldn't be able to forgive myself. "Scrapping that plan."

"I'm sorry." His brows hooded his eyes. "I wish I could give you the assurances you want."

I couldn't believe there wasn't a better solution than Luanne's idea of putting the pixies in a lead box. Not an option because a) it wouldn't work, and b) suffocation was only marginally better than dying at the hands of a monster. Still, the box scenario sparked an idea. "What about this soundproofing spell? Could I use the transformation spell to make it a magical signal blocker but on a bigger scale?" I remembered the limited duration. "And can I make it last longer than five minutes? I only need a couple of days."

Thomas twisted the ends of his wild hair as he considered my idea. "What you're asking, I'm not sure it can be done."

"Why not?"

"The impenetrable spell's magic is simply using air magic and dust to erect a barrier. Once the dust settles, the magic dissipates. What you're asking would take more than just a handful of powder. On top of that, to modify the spell to block a supernatural frequency...." He sighed. "It could prove dangerous for you." He tugged at his hair some more, and I could almost see the wheels spinning in his head.

"What are you thinking?" I asked.

"Doing this alone will fail at best. At worst, it will kill you."

Been there, done that, I thought. I didn't want to put Keir through it again. Not if I didn't have to. "Or?"

"Or, you could form a coven."

"Hah." I laughed at the ridiculousness of the suggestion. "Where in the world am I going to find a coven in the middle of the Ozark Mountains?"

"All you need is six people plus you for an even seven." He said it as if it were that easy.

"Sure, I'll put finding six tru-craft witches in the next hour or so on my list of impossible things to do. Easy peasy." I shook my head. "I only know two. Me and you."

Thomas spread his hands. "Your coven doesn't have to be witches."

"It doesn't?"

"Maybe coven was the wrong word. You need a circle. A group of people who you share a bond of love, that you trust enough to share power with and take energy from. They must swear allegiance to you and each other."

"That sounds like an impossible task."

His expression softened. "Oh, my dear Iris. I think you underestimate the attachments you form with the people you love. Who love you back. You only need six."

"I have Keir, Luanne, and Linda," I told him.

"It's a start."

I'd forgotten that part. "How am I supposed to

manage more? Activate the PTO phone tree?" I mumbled the last part.

Thomas leaned forward more and turned his ear to the computer. "Excuse me? I didn't catch that."

"It was nothing." I wasn't going to explain the brilliance of *Practical Magic* to him. "Except, there isn't anyone else I can call." I mean, there were the pixies, but if the circle required me to love the other members and for them to love me back, then Fair Konig and his people were out. I mean, sure, there was some mutual respect, but that's not the same thing.

"Your son?" Thomas asked.

"I don't want him involved," I said. Between satyrs, hobgoblins, and drakes, I didn't want Michael anywhere near the house. Not until the pixies hatched or came out of their pouches. "Besides, Michael's non-magical, which means if he's in, then Linda is out."

"Ah." He gave a nod of understanding. "Gnome. She can't animate in front of humans."

"Yeah." Even if I could find three magical people who loved me, would Linda even be around for the circle? She'd allowed the pixies to stay, but she hadn't actually forgiven them, had she? "I'm not sure I can count on her, though."

"Six is best, but you could try with five," he said. "One for each point of the pentagram and representing an element." He lowered his gaze. "It's hardly enough for a proper circle, but it might be enough to make the spell work."

"And if it doesn't? Will it kill me?"

"Not if you kiss." When I raised my brows, he added, "Like you said yesterday, keep it simple."

"Stupid," I finished with a smile. "Can I call you if I have any questions?"

He inclined his head. "It would be my pleasure to assist you."

I knew Luanne had a bug up her butt about the old man. Family stuff was complicated. I knew that as well as anyone. Keir trusted him, though, and I was inclined to trust him as well. "Hey, Thomas?"

"Yes, Iris?"

"I'm looking forward to meeting you in person, too." I shrugged. "If I survive."

His lips spread in a pleased grin. "Then survive, Iris."

"Working on it," I said, then ended the video chat.

Now all I had to do was form a coven, save the pixies, and not die.

No problem. Hah.

CHAPTER 20

Luanne sat in the kitchen sipping hot tea. There was a pile of shortbread cookies in the middle of the center island. There was no sign of Keir.

"Someone's on a shit list," Lu said.

"From who?" I went to the fridge and grabbed a diet soda.

She gave me the "you know who" stare.

"Keir?"

"Oh, don't look so grumpy, goose. You won't stay on the list for long," she assured me. "I frequently make the top five shits, and he still loves me."

"You're family," I said. "He has to love you."

She took a cookie and dipped it in her tea. "That's not been my experience." She frowned, looking a bit crestfallen. "Damn, half the biscuit fell into the cup." She shrugged and gobbled the end still in her hands, then grabbed another. "Keir will get over it."

I didn't like being on Keir's shit list. He and I were soul-bonded, and I had gotten used to him supporting all my hair-brained schemes no matter how dangerous they proved to be. On top of that, I didn't want him mad at me. "I can't believe he left just because I kept him out of my conversation with Thomas."

Lu snorted, then gagged on her tea and cookie. "Damn it, Iris. Don't make me laugh when I'm eating. I almost choked to death."

"Drama queen."

She chuckled. "Keir didn't leave because of a tantrum. That's not in his wheelhouse either. He went up to his house to see if he could salvage a few of his things, books and such, before the rain hits."

"Is it supposed to rain?"

"There was a thunderstorm warning."

"And Zev?"

"He's babysitting the pixies at Keir's request."

"I'm surprised he's sticking around," I told her. "But I'm thankful. I could use all the help I can get right now."

"I'm not sure helping is his only reason for sticking around."

I arched my brow. "Oh yeah?"

"I think Zev is drawn to a certain free spirit by the name of Marigold. He's asked me a dozen questions about her."

"So he does like her." I shook my head. "Men.

Why doesn't he just say so? She's completely into him."

"He's an ifrit," Luanne said. "He can't date a human. He can't date most supernaturals either."

"How come?"

"Let's just say, when he brings the heat, he brings the heat. Ifrits are fire creatures, and they burn when they have sex."

"Yikes." This was a conversation with Marigold I wasn't looking forward to having. But later, much later. I had too many other things to worry about than her love life right now.

My phone made a loud warning sound. I took it off the counter where it was charging. There was a storm alert starting at seven tonight until eleven in the morning. Automatically, I checked to see if there were any messages from Michael.

There were none.

I opened my favorites and called him. The call went straight to voicemail. "Hey, call me when you get this," I said after the beep.

"Everything okay?" Lu asked.

"I've tried to reach Michael several times today, and he's not picking up his phone or returning my texts."

"I heard he has a new girlfriend," Luanne said. When I gave her a sharp look, she added, "Rose and I talk."

Rose and Luanne had developed a tight friendship over the past couple of months.

"He was going to hang out with his friend Doug yesterday and stay the night, I hope. Still, he should've gotten back to me." I didn't want to be an alarmist, but with everything going on with the pixies and the wraith, I was worried. I texted Doug. He didn't text me back either. I scrolled through my contacts until I found Lauren Reynolds' information and tapped her name.

Lauren picked up on the second ring. "Hey, Iris," she answered.

"Hey." I tried not to sound as panicked as I felt. "I've been trying to get a hold of Michael, and he's not answering his phone."

"Boys." I could almost hear her headshake. "They're at Coach Jordan's house with the football team. Coach wanted to go over Friday night's film with them. You know, go over the good, the bad, and the ugly." She chuckled. "Coach is going to feed them too. Fine by me. One less thing I have to do tonight."

It wasn't unusual for the football team to congregate at the coach's place for team bonding. When Adam had been the coach, he'd hosted team nights a handful of times during the season. The difference was that Adam was human, while Jordan was a demigod. And the fact that Michael wasn't answering his phone while hanging out with the guy made me feel as if my skin would crawl from my body. Of course,

I only had his say-so he was a demi-god. He might not be a sorcerer, but that didn't mean he wasn't a liar.

"Uh, okay," I said to Lauren. "Do you have the coach's address?"

"I don't have his address, but he lives out on Crookshank Road. Once you pass the old mill, take the first drive on the right. He's got a lovely place nestled back in the woods."

Well, that didn't sound creepy at all. "Thanks. Sorry to bother you."

"No worries. I'm sure Michael is just having a good time and hasn't been paying attention to his phone. You know how teenagers are."

"You're probably right. Talk later." I dropped the call before she could say bye.

"Iris, you're white as a sheet," Lu said. She pushed the plate of cookies away from her. "Is something wrong?"

I grabbed my purse. "Michael might be in trouble."

"Iris, wait." She grabbed my arm.

I yanked away. "I have to go find Michael."

She flicked her gaze to my arm and hand. "You better cover up first."

I stared at my hands. The swirling beneath the waxy surface moved faster than earlier. "Damn it." My eyes were hot with tears. "He's at Jordan Sonnav-ilsa's place."

Lu stood up and wiped her hands on her pants. "I'm going with you."

"The pixies...."

"Zev can handle it. I'll get the gear packed."

"No guns," I told her. I didn't want to chance a showdown with the entire football team caught in the crossfire.

"Noted," she said. "I won't need one. Go get camouflaged. I'll meet you in the car."

In less than fifteen minutes, we were on the road.

"Where does this jackhole live?" Lu's grip on the steering wheel shifted from one hand to two, her knuckles going to white.

"Take a left on Main Street, and we'll follow it all the way out of town."

Lu nodded, then punched the gas. "I swear to the goddess, if he's even looked cross-eyed at Michael, I'm going to stab him through the ear and scramble his brains."

"There won't be any brains to scramble after I explode his head," I told her.

"Brutal," Lu said. "Much respect."

"Tell me what you all know about Jordan," I said, needing more information so my own head wouldn't explode. "I know he's on your watch list because he was with a tru-craft witch when she died but is there any other reason?"

Luanne shook her head. "Honestly, no. After I found out he'd changed his name, I did a thorough check for Oldsen and Sonnavilsa. I couldn't find anything. Either he's keeping his nose clean or—"

"Or he's really good at hiding all his nefarious activities."

She frowned. "Too right." It didn't take long for us to leave town. The mountain had gorgeous views when there weren't a lot of houses to obstruct it. When I was a kid, I used to wish I had one of the big houses overlooking the world below. I pointed when I saw Crookshank Road. "There it is," I said. "Take a left."

Luanne turned onto the gravel, kicking up dust behind us as she gained speed. Up ahead, there was a covered bridge over a stream. Nearby, there was a tall, narrow brick building with a high-pitched roof. On the side was a giant water wheel revolving as the water flowed. I pointed at it.

"There's the old mill. Jordan's place should be the first road on the right after the bridge."

Lu, with laser focus, drove toward the bridge with butt-puckering speed. I knew the mill was at least a hundred years old. I prayed the bridge had been given some updates since then.

We survived. I only knew this because when I opened my eyes, we were turning right onto a short-leaf pine-lined road. When we got to the end of the drive, there was a large white house with a wrap-around deck at the end. A dozen cars and trucks littered the side of the road and the driveway. I began to rub my hands together nervously as we pulled in and parked.

"Stop that," Lu said. "You're rubbing the makeup off."

"Shoot." I put my hands at my sides.

Teenage boys were running around the side of the house, playing some kind of game of tag. There was an above-ground pool with an attached deck. I recognized all the boys. Monty Croner, David Smith, Craig Donaldson, Allen, George, Dave, Jake, Josh, and more. Mostly juniors and seniors. They were having a good time. I took a few deep breaths to calm myself. Nothing scary or violent here. However, I didn't see Michael. I wouldn't feel better until I saw my son.

Luanne was strapping up several knives.

"Let's take it easy, okay? There are too many kids here," I said, "for a lethal confrontation. Let's just assess the situation first."

"Okay, mamma bear," she told me, putting the weapons back in her console. She kept one knife out and slid it into her boot. "But just in case...."

"I can live with that." A single knife wouldn't cause any collateral damage if she had to use it.

We exited the car. Craig Donaldson waved. "Hey, Mrs. Callahan," he said.

I winced at hearing my married name, but let it go. "Hey, Craig. Have you seen Michael?"

"He's in the house," he said cheerfully.

Monty Croner jumped him from behind.

"Asshole!" Craig yelled. He flushed, then looked at me. "Sorry, Mrs. Callahan."

I raised my hands. "Not the language police. Where in the house?"

The boy looked chagrined as he shrugged off his friend. "He's in the basement with Coach."

My gut clenched, and my non-magicked palm began to sweat. I rubbed it on my jeans as I half-jogged to the front door with Luanne on my heels.

"How are we playing this?" Lu asked. "It's going to be hard to cover up killing him with all these witnesses."

"If he's harmed my son in any way, I'm not sure I care."

Lu widened her eyes and gave a shrug. "We'll play it by ear then."

The house was a split level, so it made finding the basement easy. Lu stopped me at the stoop and put a finger to her lips. "We have the element of surprise," she said. "Let's keep it."

I nodded, resisting the urge to run down the stairs and break down the door. Gingerly, we went step by step, listening for noises. I heard a familiar groan and a sound of pain.

Fuck surprise.

I ran the rest of the steps and burst through the basement door, which was luckily unlocked. The basement was set up as a gym, complete with several weight training areas, bench presses, a treadmill, an elliptical, a rowing machine, and a vertical climbing machine. I didn't see Michael or the coach. I heard the groan again, then a hissed, "Son of a bitch."

It had come from an open door on the other side of the treadmill. Lu was ahead of me, and she stopped as soon as she was inside the frame. Before I could barrel in, she put an arm out to hold me back.

"Lu?" Michael asked. "Mom? What are you guys doing here?"

Michael was on a padded table. He was holding an ice pack to his jaw. Coach Phil, the defensive coordinator, wrapped his ankle.

"What happened to you?" My voice hitched up an octave. "Who hurt you? Where's Jordan?"

To my son's credit, my son only looked mildly embarrassed. "I zigged when I should've zagged."

I snapped my fingers and pointed at him. "Don't get sassy. Tell me what happened."

Now he looked embarrassed. I'd feel bad about it later. "I'm okay, Mom. Sheesh. I was goofing off with the guys, jumped away from Dave to avoid getting tagged, and I hit my jaw on the pool deck then twisted my ankle."

"Hi, Iris," Phil said. "He's going to be fine. His ankle isn't swelling. I only wrapped it as a precaution after we iced it."

I saw the bucket of ice water next to the table.

"That really sucked," Michael said. "Ice hurts."

I nodded. "Let me see your face."

Michael took the ice pack from his jaw. It had a red line on the left side, but nothing horrible.

"And your ankle?"

"It feels better already." My son gave me a strange look. "What's this all about?"

"You didn't tell me you were going to coach's today."

"I did," Michael said. "I told you last week that we were reviewing films and doing the team-building stuff at his place on Sunday."

Had he? Cripes. Had I been so wrapped up with everything going on in my life that I was dropping the ball when it came to parenting?

Yep. Pretty much. Michael was seventeen, and with that came the perks of not having to mother him as much, but had I stopped mothering altogether. "I'm...I'm sorry, Michael."

"It's fine." His words were clipped. "What are you doing here?"

"You weren't answering your phone."

Phil said, "That's my fault. I had them all drop their phones in a basket when they got here. Trying to get them to focus on each other and the team, not their screens."

I felt like a big dumbass. "I'm sorry for barging in."

Lu's posture was relaxed now that she was no longer preparing to murder someone. "Hey," she asked Phil. "Where's the coach?"

"Jordan's out back grilling a hundred hamburgers." He smiled, suddenly aware of Luanne. "Forty boys are a lot to feed. The basement is a walkout," he added. "If you go around the corner, you'll see the patio doors. That's where the grill is."

Maybe Jordan was here because it was a job. A fresh start. Still, I wasn't going to be satisfied until I talked to him. "I'll go have a word with him before I go," I said.

"Mom...." Michael gave me a pleading look.

"Don't worry," I told him. "I'll behave."

The kid sighed. "Are you...okay?"

I cast a glance at Phil and then back to Michael. "Fine," I lied. "It's all good. I'll find you in a few minutes after I talk to Coach." Damn it. Had I distanced myself from Michael's life as well? I mean, I was going through the motions of parenting, but I hadn't known about the girlfriend or the team night, and I couldn't help but wonder what else I was missing.

CHAPTER 21

THE BASEMENT WALKOUT OPENED TO A PERGOLA-covered outdoor kitchen. Coach Jordan, wearing a Howlers' cap and holding a spatula, stood in front of a large grill with his back to me. Burgers sizzled, smoke wafted, and Air Supply played in the background. Jordan was alone, his hips swaying back and forth to *All Out of Love* as he flipped a patty.

My anger for the six-and-a-half-foot man replaced my self-pity. I hated that he was another threat to me and the people I loved. No matter what he said about not being in Southill Village because of me, he'd taken a job at my kid's school and was in a position of power over Michael. And frankly, I didn't trust him even a little bit.

Stone, stone, hard and cold, up, up, lock and hold. I sent out my intention to the ground beneath the demi-god and felt a small surge of triumph as his patio paving stones swallowed his feet.

"What the—" He windmilled his arms to keep himself upright as he tried to circle around.

"Hilarious," Luanne said dryly, then she arched her brow at Jordan. "You're shorter than the last time I saw you."

The demi-god twisted sideways and looked over his shoulder at Lu. His eyes glowed with power. "What are you? The comic relief?"

"I'm the hammer." She smirked. "And the nail."

Jordan gave her a brief assessment before turning his attention to me. "Did you really have to do all this?" He pointed to his feet. "It's a little overkill."

"But it makes me feel better," I told him.

"Hey, Coach," Darrell Franks said as he rounded the corner. "When are the burgers going to be ready?"

The glow disappeared from Jordan's eyes, and he dropped a hand towel over his feet. "Ten minutes." He waved his spatula at the boy. "Anyone asks again, the whole team will be doing wind sprints tomorrow at practice."

From Michael, I knew that wind sprints were leg killers where the boys had to run from the endzone to the twenty-five-yard line, back to the endzone, then down to the fifty-yard line and back, then down to the twenty-five on the other side, then back, then down to the opposite endzone and back. In other words, it was Hell.

Darrell's eyes widened. "Got it, Coach!" I could see a crooked grin on his face as he turned on his heel and jogged off. I got the impression this wasn't the first, second, or third time he'd asked Jordan about dinner.

Jordan shook his head. "They've been playing the are-we-there-yet game. Only, it's been the are-you-done-yet version. They think it's a big joke." He reached down and picked the towel up. I winced when I saw the stone that had encased his feet had crumbled to dust. "You have ten minutes before forty hungry boys round that corner."

"Nifty trick," Lu said. She sounded casual and relaxed, but I knew her well enough to know she'd be ready to fight when it was necessary. "What else you got?"

He crossed his arms over his expansive chest, his biceps bulging out of his short-sleeved polo shirt. "I'd be happy to show you."

Okay, this was verging on hostile flirting. "Why are you in Southill Village?" The tension I'd felt earlier and the despair had faded a little in Jordan's company. I forced myself to stay on high alert. "And don't give me no bullshit about it being an available job because I'm not buying the narrative."

"I've been coaching the kids for weeks now, spending a lot of time with them one-on-one because

I'm trying to what? Spend a lot of time with them one-on-one." His expression was incredulous. "Look. If I wanted to harm your son or any of the young men on the team, I've had plenty of opportunities to do it. I don't need to cook burgers for them first."

His reasoning was sound, but I still couldn't shake the ominous feeling that something terrible was coming to destroy me and the people I loved. I shook my head. "Tell me why you're here."

"Ms. Everlee, I've already told you. There was a notice on a teacher vacancy website, and I was looking for a fresh start far away from Wisconsin. If I had known I was coming to a town full of magical drama, I might've looked somewhere else, but regardless of who my father is, I'm not omnipotent."

"What do you know about the magical drama in Southill Village?" Luanne asked shrewdly. "I mean, if you aren't here for any nefarious reasons, then you should be blissfully unaware, right?"

He narrowed his gaze on her. "I haven't been blissfully unaware since my last girlfriend turned to dust in my arms." His expression pinched with something akin to grief.

Months earlier, I'd been seconds away from turning to dust because of my wild earth magic. Was it a coincidence that Jordan's girlfriend had been a tru-craft witch like me? He'd been on the Iron Grove's watch list for several years, so the two incidents didn't coincide. Maybe he'd liked the power he'd gained by absorbing her magic. Maybe he wanted to feel that again, so he was lulling me into a false sense of safety until I could die in his arms the same way.

"How did you find out about me?" I asked.

"When you stuck your bone spikes through my hand Friday night," he answered. "That was my first big clue. Tying me up with the vines was my second."

"You didn't know I existed before then?"

"I knew Michael had a mom, but, no, I didn't know that you possessed tru-craft. It's not like you're holding up a sign." He shook his head. "Though I have been feeling a pull of sorts," he admitted. "I don't know what it is, though. It's like nothing I've experienced before. It's made me want to avoid going to town."

I grimaced. Was he feeling the pixies' mating ritual signal? He was a magical creature, after all, but he was also part human. Whatever the reason, I wasn't about to give him information on Fair Konig and his troupe, especially since he didn't seem to know about them. "Avoiding town is a good plan," I said. "Frankly, avoiding Southill Village would've been your best move. You should pack up and get out while you can."

His lips thinned as he stared at me. "Yeah, not going to happen."

"You could always disappear one night." Luanne

had pulled her knife. She tapped the tip and said, "Ouch."

"Lu." I gave a quick headshake.

Jordan jumped as flames shot up from the grill. Not my doing. "Damn it." He started scooping the meat patties off the grill and onto a cookie sheet. "I hope the boys like them well-done."

Nothing about Jordan screamed killer or bad guy, but I couldn't fight this feeling of intense dread and anguish. My fear for Michael was at a ten.

Moments before my final showdown with Volres, the fire god, he'd tried to strike a bargain with me.

"Give me your body," he'd demanded, "and I'll spare your offspring. He does have it in him, you know."

"Has what in him?" I'd asked.

"The ability for magic. Although, like you, I think it will come to him late." The asshole had smiled when he'd threatened, "And then I will make him mine."

How could I trust that Jordan wasn't after the same power? My power? And if he couldn't have mine, maybe he was trying to build trust with Michael so that when my son finally sparked to tru-craft, he could take the magic from him. I'd made Volres pay for his words. He'd been an elemental creature, and as a tru-craft witch, the elements were mine to command. But Jordan wasn't an elemental creature, was he? He came from a line of immortals. He broke my magical efforts to bind him without any effort. If he wanted me, if he wanted Michael, I wasn't sure I could stop him.

"Iris," Lu said.

I heard her, but I couldn't stop the dozens of awful scenarios playing out in my head. In every single one, I lost. And as a result, I lost Michael. I lost my son.

"Iris," Lu said more sharply. "What's going on?"

"No," I muttered as I shook my head. "You can't have him."

"What are you doing to her?" Luanne demanded.

"I'm not doing anything," Jordan said.

Only, he was. He would be my destroyer, then he would kill Michael. My grimoire line would be concluded. It would be over. It would be as if we never existed.

"She's crying." Lu sounded freaked out. "If you don't stop, I'm going to slit your throat and gut you, and when you begin to heal, I'll do it again. I'll give you an eternity of torture. Stop whatever you're doing now."

Oh, Michael. My poor boy. He'd never asked for any of this. A father he couldn't rely on and an unstable mother. Maybe that's why Evan had cheated. I ruined lives. Maybe he saw that in me even before I'd sparked to tru-craft.

"Mom?" I heard Michael's voice distantly as if he were an echo.

"Michael, go back inside," Lu said.

I was a failure. My whole family thought so. I'd been useless when my mother was dying. My father was getting older, and he wasn't doing well. I hadn't even known about the fall. I was a terrible daughter. Marigold had to lie for me, keeping my secret from my other siblings. I'd made her an accomplice in the mess I'd called my life. And Keir.... I felt a sob catch in my throat. I was ruining his life as well. I'd died. I'd fucking died, and he'd been left alone. It had only been eight minutes. But the next time, it would be permanent. He said he couldn't live without me. Would he take his own life if I died? The pressure and responsibility was too much. It was all too much. Everyone would be better off if I'd never existed. Could I do that? Could I turn back time? Or better yet, could I craft a spell that would make everyone forget about me?

"There," Michael said. Then he said, "Son of a bitch. It went inside."

"Take your mom into the sunlight," Jordan said.

I felt Michael's arm wrap around my shoulders. "Come on, Mom," he said. "It's going to be all right."

The feeling of intense internal torment eased as the sun's rays kissed my skin. The physical connection to Michael helped too. The fog of shame and blame slowly lifted. "Michael?"

"I'm here," he said. His hand was a fist on my back, and his body was rigid with distress. "It's the wraith," he added. "It flew into the basement. Coach and Lu went after it. Are you...are you okay?"

I nodded, feeling anything but okay. "Better. How did the wraith find me here?"

"I don't know, but you look worse," Michael's voice was strained. "You.... You're disappearing more."

I looked down and saw that my good hand had turned to a swirling translucence. Shit. Shit. Shit.

"Your neck too," he added. "What can I do?"

I wish I knew the answer. I hated that Michael had to see this. I wanted to keep this side of my life, the dangerous parts, as far from him as possible. I couldn't, not if I wanted to protect him in the long run. I owed him the truth. What was happening to me might happen to him one day if I didn't prepare him for the spark. Good, bad, or ugly.

"I'll work a spell when I get home," I told him. "It'll slow the progress of the wild aero-craft until I can figure out how to wrangle it." Harness was what the grimoire had said. Harness the wind. As far as instructions went, it might as well have been in a foreign language. Too bad the grimoire didn't come with diagrams. "Honestly, though. I'm not sure I can stop what's happening. I don't say this to frighten you, but I want you to be prepared for...."

"No," Michael said. "You're going to figure this out. You always do."

"Always, huh?" The sun eased the deep sorrow

inside me, and I felt some of my strength return. "I wish that was true."

"It is true," he said. "You're the strongest person I know." There was a catch in his voice that made my heart break a little. "You'll find a way to beat this, Mom." His words were a demand.

I nodded. I wanted to be the person my son thought I was. Strong, brave, and able to tackle the toughest problem and make it my bitch. "All right," I told him. "I'm going to figure this shit out."

He gave me a half-smile. "Damn straight."

My head was clear again, the melancholy gone. "The wraith," I said to Michael. "Did you say it was here?"

"Yes." He shivered. "When I came outside, I saw you standing there crying, and when you didn't respond, I knew it had to be the wraith. You looked like you did when it was in your room. I saw it in the corner above the doorway, hiding in the shadows."

Keir had said he didn't know a way to defeat a wraith and that fighting it was bad. "Oh, crap. Luanne." I scrambled to my feet. "I have to help her."

"But you can't," Michael protested. "You're missing an arm."

I was technically missing two, but one was made of air magic, and the other was missing for the same reason.

I reached down and grabbed dirt from the ground with the hand that worked. I didn't have the right ingredients to cast the air spell Thomas had taught me, but I could

"*Eastern wind and binding dust, healing breath in you I trust. As the air blows, time slows, and the dirt will form a crust. Bend to my will.*" I blew on the dirt over where my arm should be and sprinkled some around my neck, adding my intention to be solid and whole once more. My arm reformed, and I made a fist pump at my hip in way of celebration. I'd managed an air spell without a chaperone and hadn't killed myself. It was a point in the win column.

"Cool," Michael said, sounding sincerely impressed.

"Yeah, it is," I agreed. "Stay out here, okay. Don't go anywhere there are shadows."

"I'm going with you," Michael told me. "You can't be around that thing without me."

Before I could argue with him, Lu exited the sliding glass doors. "He's got it." She was breathing hard and looked like she'd been in a fight with a Tasmanian devil. "Jordan captured the wraith."

CHAPTER 22

Lᴜ ᴇsᴄᴏʀᴛᴇᴅ ᴜs ᴛʜʀᴏᴜɢʜ ᴛʜᴇ ʟɪᴠɪɴɢ sᴘᴀᴄᴇ ᴛᴏ the room where Coach Phil had been wrapping Michael's foot. Going into that basement, even with all the lights on, filled me with trepidation. The hopeless way the wraith made me feel was something I was loath to experience again.

My glimpses of the shadowy creature hadn't prepared me for its appearance. It had gray, waxy skin, blue-black hair, two slits formed a nose, and its toothless mouth was wet with something that looked like crude oil. The most disturbing thing about the wraith was the depressions in the skull where the eyes should've been. Instead, there was stretched skin, a shade darker than the rest of its coloring.

Its skeletal fingers grasped at Jordan's hands as he held the creature down on his table by the throat.

"How?" I asked. "How did you capture it?"

"I let it take what it needed," Jordan said. His expression was haunted, and I felt sick to my stomach. What heartrending sorrow had the creature pulled from him?

"Are you okay?"

He nodded. "I won't be able to hold it for too long. If you have any questions, now is the time to ask. I'll destroy it after."

Someone had conjured the wraith. They'd summoned it and sent it after me. "Who is its master?"

Jordan's eyes shined silver, then the light of his eyes fanned out and covered his body until he was coated in the glow. The wraith shrank, turning its head away from his brightness.

"Whoa," Michael said.

I forgot he didn't know about his coach being a demi-god. "I'll explain later."

Jordan, who was lit up like the North star, leaned down close to the wraith. "Who sent you?"

The monster moaned, its limbs thrashing hard enough it knocked over supplies from the coach's medical cart.

"I thought wraiths were ghosts," Michael whispered.

Keir had said they weren't, but the way the thing moved through shadows and was able to disappear had made me think it didn't have a physical body. This was proof that it did.

"Tell me," Jordan commanded. "Tell me who made you."

Gray dust scattered from the wraith's parted lips on a raspy wail. "Baaaaaaaaaaaaaaahgmaaaaaaaaaaaaal-llllllll."

I looked at Lu, and her eyes had narrowed to slits under her furrowed brow. "Did that thing say what I think it said?"

She nodded, her jaw flexing as her face reddened with rage. "She's back," Luanne said. "Bogmall is back."

And she was still trying to wreck my life.

I moved closer, expecting the wraith to smell as bad as it looked, but instead, I detected hints of allspice and something slightly nutty. "That's amaranth," I said. "Bogmall must've used it to summon the wraith. She used fire magic to conjure this wretched thing. Which means she's become what she wanted. She's a sorcerer."

Luanne let out a string of curses. "I'm going to fucking kill her."

"You'll have to beat me to it," I muttered. Then louder, I added, "Why would she come after me then? For revenge? I'm the one that got away?"

"I'll track her down to the ends of the Earth if I have to," Luanne swore. "She won't get away with this. Not again."

"Who's Bogmall?" Michael asked.

Crap. One more thing I'd kept from him that I

was going to have to explain. "Later," I told him. "Promise."

My simultaneously scared and irritated son didn't argue with me.

"Whatever we're going to do, we need to do it fast," Jordan said. "I can destroy the wraith if you're done asking questions, which is preferable because, in about two minutes, there is going to be a bunch of teenagers coming in here to find out about the food situation.

"Michael and Luanne, can you two go out and head the boys off?" I asked.

Luanne's expression went from venomous to relaxed in the span of a blink. She put her hand on Michael's shoulder. "It looks like it's you and me, kid. Let's head 'em off at the pass."

Michael shook his head but didn't argue. He'd bravely faced the wraith, but I think he was more than ready to leave its presence. "Don't mess around," he said to me. "If it can be destroyed, then destroy it."

"I will," I said.

He gave me a hard stare. "Be safe." Then he left the room with Luanne.

Jordan, who was still lit up, asked, "What do you want me to do?"

"Where is Bogmall?" I moved closer. Maybe if I could find out from where the wraith had been sent, it would help Luanne and the Iron Grove find the rogue ex-druid and end her terror on me for good. "Where is your master?"

The gray shadow beast writhed and squirmed, its fingernails digging rips into the vinyl padding on the coach's treatment table. "Ennnnnnnnnd-meeeeeeeeee," it cried.

"Where is your master?" Jordan pressed his shiny, glowy hand onto the creature's chest. "Tell me, and I will end this misery of yours once and for all."

"Heeeeeeeerrrrrrre," it rasped out. "Sheeeeeeeeeeeisssssssssssheeeeeeeeeere."

The answer stunned me. "In Southill Village?"

"Yesssssssssssssssssss," the wraith hissed.

"Where in Southill?"

"Doooooonottttknowwww. Chaaaannnnnnnnged."

"What do you mean?" I asked.

The wraith wriggled more. "Ennnnnnnnnd-meeeeeeeenowwwww."

I heard laughter and joking bravado coming from the outdoor kitchen area. Luanne was badass and sexy as hell. I'm sure the boys were all trying to vie for her attention.

"Are you done?" Jordan asked. His expression was pinched as if he were in pain. "I don't know if I can hold it much longer."

I met his mercurial gaze and nodded. "Do it," I said. "Destroy the wraith."

"Avert your eyes," he said. "I don't want to blind you."

I turned away, and the entire room was bathed in concentrated white light. When the light extinguished, I pivoted back to him. The only remnant of the wraith's existence was a dark stain on the torn-up tabletop.

"It's gone for good?" I asked.

He nodded. "I've dispatched it. It won't return again."

That was a relief. Literally. With the wraith gone, I felt lighter than I had in weeks. The sense of dread had been steadily increasing since I'd come into my aero-craft. How long had the wraith been stalking me? Had its presence interfered with my ability to adapt? Maybe. Maybe not. Regardless, I'd learned two seriously important things as a result of this encounter. Bogmall hadn't moved on from me, and the bitch was somewhere in Southill calculating her next move.

"You really didn't come to Southill because of me?" I asked Jordan.

He shook his head. "I really didn't. I just want to live a quiet, normal life."

"Yeah?" I chuckled. "What's a quiet, normal life look like?"

He grinned and shook his head. "One that doesn't involve witches and wraiths."

"Hah, you moved to the wrong town, buddy."

"No kidding."

Luanne peeked her head around the door. "I could use some help out here. My training hasn't prepared me for forty football players."

Jordan asked, "What has your training prepared you for?"

"Disarm, dismemberment, death. You know the three Ds."

His eyes widened for a moment. "How about if I just go handle the burgers?"

I nodded. "Good idea."

My phone dinged. I dug it from my pocket. There was a message from Keir. *U ok?*

I texted back. *Better now. Coming home soon.*

K. C u soon.

I sent back a half dozen heart emojis and a kissy face.

Lu snapped her fingers at Jordan. "Look, Dude. I didn't sign up to be the lunch lady. I'd rather fight another Redhat and his army of leprechauns than deal with a bunch of horny teenagers, so get your ass in gear and go take over out there."

Jordan raised his hands in surrender, but I could see a glint of humor in his eyes. "Yes, ma'am."

I looked at Lu. "What about Michael?"

She shook her head. "I think he's safer here, but you're his mom."

Jordan said, "I swear on my life that no harm will

come to Michael in my care. We might not be friends, Ms. Everlee, but I hope we can be allies."

"It's Iris," I told him. "My friends...and allies call me Iris."

He nodded, then flashed a smile at Luanne as he moved past her and out of the room.

I arched my brow at the druid warrior and smirked. "You like him."

"Shut up," she said. She punched me in the arm as I crossed in front of her.

It nudged me sideways, but otherwise, I hadn't felt a thing. The air magic had taken over my upper arms. "It's getting worse," I told her.

She nodded, her face pensive with worry. "Then we better get it figured out. My brother won't be able to take it if you turn to dust in the wind."

"More like wind in the wind." I wanted to reach out to Thomas again. Whenever I talked to the old tru-craft witch, it gave me a sense of security. His instruction made me feel like I wasn't just freestyling magic and hoping for the best. "I'm going to go say goodbye to Michael," I told her. "Meet you in the car."

"I'll go get him for you." Lu gestured to my arm and neck, both of which looked far from normal. "You don't want to go out there looking like that."

There was a mirror on the wall, and I checked myself out. Cripes. The skin on my neck looked like dried mud. I absently touched it, but the ability to feel anything through my fingertips was gone. I sucked in a breath. At least my lungs were still working. If the wild magic continued, I wasn't certain how much longer that would be the case.

"It's going to be alright, Iris," Luanne said.

"How do you know?"

"Because you're a badass bitch who knows how to get shit done," she told me. "Besides, it's the only option I'm willing to entertain."

I rewarded her with a smile that didn't quite reach my eyes. I wished I saw myself the way she did. At the moment, I felt as far from badass as I could get. The wraith was gone, thanks to Jordan, but I had a bigger problem to solve. Bogmall was a power-hungry sorcerer, and I was sitting on a powder keg of magical possibilities. It was impossible to know what the wraith had reported back to its master, but chances were good that the blonde bitch knew about the pixies. I wouldn't let her have them.

I flexed my fingers made from dust.

All I had to do was figure out how to protect the pixies, take Bogmall down, and keep myself from disappearing. Easy as riding a bike...if that bike was being driven through five feet of mud in the middle of a hurricane.

I said my goodbye to Michael, and after a spirited debate, which I won, he agreed to spend the night at Doug's after the team bonding.

The ride home was quiet and contemplative as I

tried to figure out how I was going to fix things. Michael still had most of his senior year to complete, and he deserved to be able to do it safely. The only other option was to send him away to live with his dad, and neither of us wanted him to leave.

"What the hell happened here?" Luanne asked as she pulled into my driveway. The garden gate was on the ground in several pieces, and there was a crater where the gate had been.

Son of a bitch. I beat Lu out of the car when she parked, and I jumped over the wide hole and rushed into the garden. It looked as if a bomb had exploded. Pixies and gnomes worked side-by-side to repair the damage, but it was a lot.

Keir came out of the kitchen, wiping his hands on a towel. When our eyes met, he shook his head and said, "Welcome home."

CHAPTER 23

SEVERAL ROSEMARY BUSHES HAD BEEN UPROOTED, along with my peonies and a few other flowering plants. Linda, along with four other gnomes, was filling in the craters left behind by the fight. Fair Konig and his troupe were repairing my fence and gate. Keir had a cut on his cheek, a fat lip, and his soft curls were tussled. Whatever had happened here, he'd been in the thick of it.

I walked over to him and reached up to touch his cheek until I remembered my dirt-made hand and let my arm drop to my side. "Is everyone okay?" I asked him.

He put his arms around me. "No one was hurt."

"What happened?"

"A duo of bugganes burrowed in," he said. "They were on us fast."

"Yuck," Luanne remarked. "Bugganes are nasty buggers."

I'd never heard of a buggane before, so I had no idea what they were talking about. "Talk to me like I'm stupid."

Linda, who was nearby, said, "That's how I always talk to you."

I stuck my tongue out at her. There was a gnome dressed in a yellow shirt and pants, green winklepickers, and a green hat standing near my crotchety earth guardian. Its beard was longer than Linda's, and it winked at me.

Since male and female gnomes both had beards, I wasn't sure which it was, so I kept my greeting neutral. "Hi, there."

"Hello, Iris Everlee," it said formally. "I'm *Morlanshanksawsbein*."

"That's a mouthful."

"Morlan is my husband," Linda said. "He and a few others have agreed to help protect the pixies until their brood has matured."

I raised both brows. "That's mighty generous of you, Linda." Especially considering she'd been planning to pack up her donsy and leave the mountain the day before.

She beaned me with a pebble. Morlan snickered.

I tipped my head to Morlan and the other gnomes. "Thank you for your help. It's much appreciated." After, I returned my focus to Keir. "What's a buggane?"

"They're shapeshifters who are kin to ogres, and they are covered in long, thick black hair from head to toe," he replied. "And they are extremely fast."

Luanne nodded. "Think Cousin It from the Addam's Family, only a lot bigger."

I made a *yeeesh* face. "That definitely paints a picture."

"About five minutes after I got back, one came up under the gate, the other in the garden." Keir scanned the garden. "They're tough to kill because their hair acts like a shield."

I'd seen him tear up creatures that were made of stone in his pooka form. I couldn't imagine anything tougher than his claws. "Even with your black diamond nails?"

He nodded. "They have a very thick underfur. I couldn't stab or slice through it." He touched his lip. "They got in a few good licks on me."

"How did you defeat them?"

The corner of his mouth quirked up. "Zev fried them bald. It was easy work after that."

I looked around for the ifrit but didn't see him. "Where's Zev now?"

"He's getting rid of the bodies."

"We're going to owe him big time."

"Probably," Keir said. The corners of his eyes were tense as he examined me. "It has spread."

I nodded. "The wraith followed me to Jordan's house."

Zev would've told him where Lu and I had gone, so he didn't look surprised, but his voice was alarmed. "You encountered the wraith again?"

I winced. "Yeah, it was awful."

He wrapped his arms around me again, and I leaned into his embrace.

"What happened?" he asked.

"Jordan was able to destroy it."

"The sorcerer?" He leaned back so he could meet my gaze. His voice was calm, but I could hear the edge of wariness it held. "You can't trust him."

"He's a demi-god. He's not here to harm Michael or me," I said. "I'm pretty sure he is who he says he is. If it hadn't been for Jordan, I'm not sure I would've made it through the encounter. The wraith had sent me into a severe depression spiral."

"What if the reason he could destroy it is that he summoned the damn thing?" Anger simmered in Keir's gray eyes and made his words sound hard. "Did you think of that?"

"It wasn't him," Luanne said, backing me up. "He saved me when he captured the wraith. The damn thing had pinned me down. It cost him a lot to hold it. If he'd wanted to kill Iris or me, he could've let the wraith finish its work."

Keir shook his head, doubt plain in his expression. "It didn't show up in Southill and target Iris on its own."

"It was Bogmall." I put my hand on Keir's arm.

"No, I thought...." He looked at his sister. "What were you doing in Nevada if you weren't following Bogmall?"

"You weren't supposed to know about that," she said. "I was told to treat it as top secret, even from you."

"I'm not an idiot. As soon as the Iron Grove stopped giving me reports, I figured it out. So, if you followed her to Nevada, how did she end up here?"

"I followed her trail," Lu admitted. "But I came up empty. The last sighting was in the Mojave desert, and that's when it went cold. Or hot, as it turned out. The desert was a hundred and twenty degrees in the shade."

"Why would she go there only to turn around and come back to Southill Village?" he asked.

I remembered the spicy and nutty scents on the wraith. "I think she's learned fire magic," I said. "She must've found an ignis-craft witch to sacrifice the way she'd tried to do with me."

"What makes you think that?" Lu asked.

"The wraith. She'd used ingredients that are specific to fire magic to conjure it. I could smell it on the creature. Allspice and amaranth." I stepped out of Keir's arms. "Unless that's what a wraith normally smells like."

"I haven't heard of them having any particular aroma." Keir looked at Lu. "Did any witches go missing in Nevada?"

She shook her head. "I met with a coven who lived in the Mojave. They had nothing suspicious to report. I didn't have any more leads. If you hadn't called me back here, I would have started my journey back here the next day."

I felt sick as I thought about the poor witch Bogmall had stolen power from. The ex-druid was single-minded in her grab for power. "She's back in Southill. She's not going to stop. And if the wraith has been following me for a few weeks, which I'm pretty sure it has, then Bogmall knows about the pixies. They're in as much danger as the rest of us."

"Was Thomas able to help you craft a spell to put up a barrier?" Keir asked.

"No, but he gave me another idea that I think might work even better."

Luanne leaned in. "Well, let's hear it."

"I can possibly use an air spell he taught me that prevents sound from escaping a space."

"That sounds like it could work, *Kleinkind*." Linda had popped up between us. I looked down at her. "We should get started right away."

"There's one little problem," I said.

"Just one?" Keir asked.

"Well, six to be exact." I sighed. "I need a coven

to pull off the spell. At least six others aside from me."

"Of tru-craft witches?" Lu scoffed. "There's no way we can make that happen."

"What if we call the Grove. They have a directory of tru-crafters. If there are any close by...."

"Thomas said it had to be people I had a bond with. They don't necessarily have to be witches."

"My donsy and I will stand with you, *Liebling*," Linda said.

"That's really sweet," I told her. "But I don't have a bond with them. Only you. It has to be six people I love. With you, Keir, and Lu, I would still need three more."

"What about Zev?"

I shook my head and frowned. "I'm super fond of him, but I don't know if I'd go as far as love. And while he's been great in a pinch, I'm not sure I trust him. It feels like he has an agenda most of the time."

Lu glanced around us. "Zev is solid," she said. "But he's a djinn. His loyalty is always going to be to himself first."

"As I suspected. Which means Zev is out. Any other ideas?" I looked at Keir, then Lu, then down to Linda. The gnome was frozen in place. I looked at the other gnomes in her donsy, and they'd stopped moving as well.

"What the heck happened here?" Marigold said as she came into the garden. "Did another satyr attack?"

She saw the gnomes in various positions. She picked up the nearest one wearing yellow clothes with a green hat. I groaned when she said, "Oh, how cute. You got Linda some friends."

I was totally paying for this. "That's her husband, Mar. Put him down. He's not a toy."

"Ooops, sorry." She carefully set the gnome down. "My bad. So, what did I miss?"

Luanne gave me a look I couldn't decipher, and when I didn't pick up what she was laying down, she held up her four fingers. "Marigold makes four."

"Uhm, nope." I glanced down at Linda. "If Marigold is in the fold, then Linda is out."

"Oh, yeah, right," Lu said. "Well, damn."

"Out of what?" Marigold asked.

I wasn't thrilled to yank my sister deeper into my world, but I had promised to make an effort for honesty. "I need a coven. It doesn't have to be witches. Just people I have a bond with. People I can trust."

"How many?" she asked.

"A minimum of six. No matter how I slice it, though, I only come up with three."

Marigold shook her head as she dug her phone out of her bag purse.

"Who are you calling?"

She held up a finger as she put the phone to her ear. "Hey, Rose," she said. "Yeah, I'm over at Iris's now. I need you to call Dahlia and Rowan, and the three of you need to get your butts over here as soon as possible."

"No," I said. But Marigold put her finger over my lips to shush me. I knocked her hand away and tried to take the phone.

She danced back a few feet, nodded a few times, and then said, "Great. See you in ten minutes." My sister disconnected the call and then met my gaze. "One coven on the way."

Luanne let out a yip of triumph, then she high-fived Marigold. She frowned. "Wait, Rose and everyone knows about your magic?"

I nodded. "I told them this morning. Even so, it's a bad idea to bring in non-magical peeps. This won't work," I said.

"I think it will," Lu disagreed. "And with your other three siblings, you won't need Linda."

I cast a horrified look at my gnome. "I'll always need Linda."

Lu rolled her eyes. "You know what I mean."

I turned to Keir. "This could work, couldn't it?"

He nodded. "I think so."

"They could get hurt if we get attacked."

"We'll protect them," Luanne said. "Zev will be back soon. He'll help as well."

Marigold shuffled from foot to foot, her excitement palpable.

"This isn't going to be fun," I told her.

She arched a brow at me and smirked. "Says you. What could go wrong?"

This was a bad idea. My family had just found out about me this morning. I wasn't even sure they believed me, even with proof. What could go wrong?

Everything.

CHAPTER 24

I GRABBED THE GRIMOIRE, WENT TO THE bathroom, threw some baby powder in the air and said, "Soundproof the bitch while I scratch an itch. Bend to my will."

As the dust stirred around me, blocking sound from leaving the four walls around me, I screamed as loud as I could for about thirty seconds. After, I sat on the throne, grim in my lap. If there was ever a time that I needed guidance from this book, it was now.

"Okay, give it to me straight." I pressed my palm against the book, unable to feel embossed symbols because my hands were made of magical glue. "I need your guidance, and I need you to be a lot clearer about how to fix my shit."

I held my breath as I flipped the book open.

Where the prior message had been, a new one appeared.

Blood of my blood, daughter of bright and fade.

Heart of my heart, there is a price to be paid.

Bone to earth, blood to fire, with every element the price is higher.

Only fools refuse to use their tools.

Overcome your fear, or you will disappear.

Goddess, help you.

Well, that was a bust. "Thanks, Grimoire." For nothing. If I wanted to be called a fool, I'd talk to Linda. All that was missing was having a rock thrown at my head. On top of that, the book hadn't told me a single thing I didn't already know.

I got up and splashed water on my face, combed my hair, and prepared myself for when my brother and my other sisters arrived. If I wanted this to work, I had to project confidence. I had to be confident. I'd learned quickly that part of spellcraft was believing. I had to find a way to believe I could do this.

"I *will* protect the pixies. I *will* defeat Bogmall. I *will* master aero-craft." I repeated the three sentences like a mantra. But first, I had to turn my family into my very own coven. Joy.

A soft knock startled me. "Iris, they're here," Keir said.

I opened the bathroom door, breaking the silence spell. "I'm ready."

"You can do this." He placed his hands on my shoulders. "I have faith in you."

"That wasn't the tune you were singing this morning."

"This morning, I was mad at you for dying."

"And now?"

"And now, I just want to support you however you need me. That's my purpose. I don't determine the outcome of your life. Your tru-craft is your journey. I'm just happily along for the ride."

"I don't want this to be my journey. I want it to be ours. Doing this alone would suck."

"I am and will always be by your side. But today, I let my fear of losing you override what you needed from me."

I peered up at him. "Did you rob a Xanax factory? You're being awfully chill." He'd left earlier without saying anything to me. "Where did you go today?"

He smiled. "I have an altar at the top of the mountain. I went up to ask the goddess for clarity."

"And did she give you the answers you wanted?"

His gray eyes softened as he met my gaze. "She's never actually spoken to me, but the meditation helped center me. I was so focused on the possibility of a future without you that I forgot what was important."

"And what's that?"

"It's the here and now. The present. And I'm determined to be present with you, Iris."

I smiled at him as some of the tension I'd been holding released. I hadn't realized how much his anger had affected me. "Then let's be present together."

He kissed me. "Do you know what you need for the spell?"

"I think so. But I'm not sure I have everything I need." It was going on six o'clock. "What we can't get from the store, the gnomes and the pixies might be able to help with."

I went into the living room. Dahlia, looking decidedly nervous and uncomfortable, sat on a chair with her knees pressed together. Rowan and Rose were on the sofa, and Marigold was pacing back and forth. Luanne leaned against the wall taking in the scene with the interest of a painter studying a muse. She had a slight smirk on her face that told me she was enjoying this way too much. The woman did love a little chaos. I wondered if Rose and she had gotten a chance to have a private word. From the way Rose was avoiding looking at Lu, I was guessing the answer was no.

"What's this about, Iris?" Dahlia asked. "Rose said you needed us here right away." Her gaze drifted to my neck and arms, and she blanched. "Is that normal? I mean, for your condition?"

Leave it to my oldest sister to try and give my wild magic a diagnosis. "Being a witch isn't a condition," I said. "But, no, this isn't normal."

Rowan got to his feet. "Let me take a look," he said. He grasped my arm gingerly, moving it around. Flecks of dust clouded around the appendage.

"You can't diagnose me either," I told him. "I wish there was a physical or psychological reason this was happening to me, but there's not. This is metaphysical, and it's something I'm going to have to figure out." I took my arm back.

"Then why did you call us?" Rose asked. "I mean if you don't need us." She sounded angry and hurt. I guess she'd had time to digest that I'd been keeping secrets from her, and she had decided she was going to be butt-hurt about it. Which was totally fair, but I needed her over it for a moment.

"Rose, I understand you feel a bit blindsided—"

"A bit? You've been lying to me, Iris. For months! Marigold told us what you've been going through, and I can't believe you didn't trust us enough to let us in."

Was she hurt that I kept tru-craft a secret from her? No doubt. However, I think it hurt her more that Marigold knew before her. Great. Our baby sister was jealous.

"I'm sorry," I told her. "Everything has been a complete mess since my tru-craft sparked. I've had magic and multiple magical creatures trying to kill me, and I've struggled to accept that this is my world now. I'm constantly worried about Michael and you all becoming collateral damage in my shitshow of a life. I thought keeping it from you would somehow keep you guys safe. Honestly, I'm still not sure if telling you was the right thing."

"But Marigold was allowed to know."

"Marigold was in the wrong place at the right time." I crossed the living room and sat down on the far side of the couch. "If it's any consolation, she didn't take it well."

"When your sister turns her hands into flamethrowers, it's a little unsettling," Marigold said in her defense.

"The point is, I had planned to tell all of you after I told Michael."

"Michael knows." Rose's eyes were big as saucers.

"Yes, because he's my kid, so this can affect him. He needs to be more prepared than I was." Holy emotional blackmail. Rose was really sticking it to me. "He needed to know," I implored her. "Can you just let it go? I love you, and I need your help, but if you can't get on board, then I'll have to find someone else to take your place."

Dahlia stood up. "We all agreed we'd support Iris."

Rose sniffled, then nodded. "I'm in," she said grudgingly.

Rowan said, "Me too."

Marigold nodded as well. "I was the one who called all of you, so you know where I stand."

"Great, with you four, along with Keir and

Luanne, I have the six I need to make this spell work."

"And what spell are we making work?" Dahlia asked. I was beginning to think my sister was actually getting into the idea that I could be a real witch.

"I need to cast a spell to protect a troupe of pixies." Bob came into the living room and rubbed his face against my leg. I picked him up. Even with numb arms, holding Bob soothed me. "I'll need the six of you to act as compass points, lending me your strength while I craft the silence barrier."

"You know that every time you say pixies, it sounds ridiculous," Rowan said. "It makes it harder to buy into all this magical mumbo-jumbo."

Luanne snorted a laugh. "Then maybe you should meet them."

"They're real," Marigold said emphatically. "They're cute but aggressive."

That sounded about right. "You guys give me a minute to talk to Linda, then come out to the garden." I needed Linda to know that none of this was possible without her, even if she couldn't be part of my coven. I loved and trusted her as much as I did my siblings.

Keir walked with me to the door. "Give me a signal. I'll bring your family out."

I pressed my forehead to his. "Thanks."

Linda and Morlan were out by the bench, and Fair Konig was standing next to them. The donsy of gnomes had made the garden almost good as new, and the pixie troupe had finished mending the fence. I whistled. "You guys do good work together."

"We are at peace," Linda said. "Your burden is my burden. I am sorry for threatening to leave you."

"Nope," I told her. "No need to apologize. Childhood trauma can really mess with your head. We're all okay then?"

Fair Konig fluttered his wings. "We are once again friends to the *Lupesabeinfeltchner* donsy, and we look forward to many years of kinship."

"Excellent." I rubbed my hands together. "Linda, you know I love you, right?"

"Stupid, Kleinkind," she muttered as her cheeks turned red, but I could tell she was pleased. "Don't try to butter me up, as they say. Just come out with it."

"You can't be a part of the spell that I have to cast. I need my brother and sisters, and if they are in the mix...."

She raised a hand. "I understand."

I gave her a smile. "You'll always be a part of my coven, though. You're my family, Linda. Just like everyone in that house."

I saw Zev out by the gate, patrolling the perimeter. He gave me a quick wave. He wasn't family yet, but he had definitely moved into the friend category. "I do need some help, though. I don't have the ingredients I need, and I think you guys might be able to find them for me."

"I will do what I can," Linda said stoically.

"I need amber. It's an air stone. From what I've read, it has amplifying properties, and it's good for protection and clarification."

Linda turned to her husband. "Our donsy can find the amber. How much do you need?"

"I'd like at least seven good chunks of it. A big one is fine as long as it can be broken up."

"I will get you what you need," she said. "Anything else?"

"The rest I need the pixies' help for."

She and Morlan dove into the grass and disappeared.

Great, one ingredient down. I turned my attention back to the pixie king. "I also need mint for protection and luck." Because we were going to need all the luck we could get. "I can get that on a grocery run. And finally, I will use a fine powder. Something that will easily hang in the air. This is where you and your troupe can help out. Whatever dust I use, can you and your troupe keep it stirred up once the spell begins? When the powder stops circulating, the spell will end."

"Yes, we will take shifts agitating the dust to keep the spell active." His wings hummed with excitement. "Mica powder," Fair Konig said. "It has strong air properties, and it's extremely lightweight."

"Awesome. Do you know where I can find some?"

"I don't," he said. "But it's a common mineral, shiny and flaky. It just needs to be ground into a fine powder."

I gave him a quick smile. "No worries. I'll figure it out. My family is going to be acting as my coven for this spell. Can I bring them out to meet you and your troupe?"

"Yes, of course." He bowed deeply. "It would be my honor."

"Great." I turned to the window and signaled to Keir to send out the siblings.

It seemed my haphazard plan was coming together haphazardly. I looked at my hands. One translucent, the other like clay, and I tried to force the doubt from my mind.

As I walked back to the house, I repeated my mantra. "I will protect the pixies. I will defeat Bogmall. I will master aero-craft."

I had to. The only other options were failure and death.

CHAPTER 25

WITH NON-MAGICALS ENTERING THE GARDEN, MOST of the pixies scattered to hide in the various bushes and plants.

"Fair Konig," I gestured to each one of my siblings. "This is Dahlia, Rose, Rowan, and you've met Marigold."

"A fierce warrior queen," Fair Konig acknowledged. "I will never forget your bravery and valiance when you came to the aid of my Annibish and myself."

Marigold gave a little flourish with her hand. "Glad to help."

No, she wasn't. Killing that satyr had freaked the hell out of her. It had freaked the hell out of me. But it didn't take away from the fact that she had been both brave and heroic. She hadn't just saved the king and queen of the pixies, she'd also saved my ass.

Annibish flew out of a barbary bush and did a quick circle around Marigold. My sister smiled nervously and gave a pageant queen wave when several other pixies followed Annibish's lead.

"All hail the conquering hero," I said to Marigold out of the side of my mouth.

"I feel a little sick," Marigold whispered back. "I don't even want to think about that hooved and horny asshole."

"This is a story I want to hear," Rose said.

"No, you don't," Marigold told her. "It ends with decapitation."

It actually ended with pixies having sex in my stomach region, but potatoes-po-tah-toes.

"Who got decapitated?" Rowan asked as he pushed his glasses up his nose. His gaze followed the pixies' movement, and I could tell he was trying to decide if he'd been drugged.

"You're not hallucinating," I told him. "Pixies are real."

Dahlia said, "I see them too, Ro. We all do. Unless this is some kind of mass hysteria, this is as real as real gets."

"I know," Rowan replied uncertainly. "And they're all having babies."

"The females," I said for clarification. But then I shrugged. "I'm assuming." I addressed Fair Konig. "Do the male pixies carry the offspring?"

"Occasionally, but it's rare."

"I'm pregnant," Rose blurted out. She put her hands to her mouth as if she couldn't believe she'd just said that to a yard full of pixies.

Annibish zoomed up to hover at eye level with my younger sister. "Can I see your baby?"

"Uhm...."

I laughed. "It doesn't work like that with humans," I told the eager pixie. "Our pouches are on the inside, and they stay sealed for nine months while our babies cook."

"Humans are so strange," Annibish said.

Zev wandered over. "I think we need to do the spell sooner than later. I have a bad feeling."

"What kind of feeling?" I asked him. The ifrit wasn't omniscient, but he was powerful, so I took him seriously.

"It feels like something dangerous is heading our way."

"Who is your friend, Iris?" Dahlia asked.

"Oh." Once again, only Marigold knew who and what Zev was. I raised my brows at the djinn to get permission to tell my other siblings that he was a djinn. "May I?"

He smiled, then dropped his sunglasses down his nose. His eyes flashed with fire. "Allow me." He held out his hand to Dahlia. "I am Zevian Diabreesa Ma'ham. I am a fire djinn. An ifrit."

"Cool, like the video game," Rowan said.

Zev shook his head. "It seems you're not the only one who plays Final Fantasy, *Sahira*."

When the games first came out, Rowan would come over, and we would play for hours. That was years before Michael was born. We hadn't played in over two decades, so the fact that he remembered made me smile. If I survived the next few days, I would see if Rowan wanted to restart our game nights.

Marigold said, "Zev isn't like the video game. He doesn't turn into a giant horned red monster."

His lip curled up in a sultry smile. "For you, I would make the effort."

My sister rolled her eyes, but her smile was pleased. I'd have to nip that in the bud. Marigold was playing with fire. And according to Luanne, she couldn't be with Zev unless she wanted to get burned. Literally.

"Okay, we still need some spelling supplies," I said to redirect the energy. "Linda and her donsy are finding me some amber, but I need some mint leaves or oil. And I need powdered mica."

"I have fresh mint at home," Rowan said. When I raised my brows, he added, "I like a mojito on the weekend. Sue me."

"Awesome. Rowan has the mint. Anyone know where we can get powdered mica?"

"I do," Rose said. "I'm sure you have it right here at the house."

"I think I'd know if I did."

Rose smiled. "Do you have that translucent face powder I bought you for your birthday last year?"

I blinked a couple of times because I was struggling to remember, but then it came to me. "Yes. It's under the sink in the bathroom."

"It's made with mica. It's great on aging skin because it doesn't cake."

I frowned at the aging skin remark.

She softened the blow by saying, "I use it religiously."

"Then we have our mica." I stared at the garden as I considered the layout. "Rowan, go get the mint. Dahl and Rose, you two can map out a five-point star in the center of the garden, then enclose it in a circle." I looked to Fair Konig. "I think it will be easier for your troupe to control the dust if I put up the silence barrier in a small section of the garden. Where do you want to spend the next day or so?"

"One moment." He flew over to Annibish, and the two of them zipped around the garden from one section to another before returning. "There is honeysuckle growing up the north fence. Between it and the bee pollen you procured, it will make a good place for our children to draw their first breaths."

"The honeysuckle it is." I gestured to my oldest and youngest sisters. "That's where we will map out the star. I need it to be about fifteen feet in diameter." There were hundreds of pixies, so I adjusted my number. "Let's make it twenty feet. I have garden string and stakes in the shed."

"What can I do?" Marigold asked.

"You can help me figure out my rhymes." Marigold was a good writer, and I had to have every word right. "It doesn't have to be a long spell. It just has to describe function and intention."

Keir said, "Lu, Zev, and I will keep watch for any intruders."

I thanked him with a noisy kiss. "That's why I love you."

"I thought you loved me for the giant bunny ears and razor-sharp teeth," he joked.

"Those are a close second."

I FOUND the face powder Rose had given me after digging in a bag of unused makeup under the sink. I took it out of its wrapper, so Rose would never find out that I hadn't even opened it. In a way, it was as if the universe knew I was going to need it one day, so it had nudged me to put it away for a rainy day. If Rose ever asked, that's exactly what I was going to tell her.

Marigold had helped me write the spell, and while it wouldn't win any literary awards, it would do the trick. It was a little after seven by the time Rowan got back with the mint. Rose and Dahlia had made quick work of staking out the pentagram. I'd been impressed by how they'd been able to set the lines through the bushes and the flower beds without ruining the plants. The pixies had assisted them with an aerial view. Even the amber stones made it.

Linda had burrowed up through the bathroom floor while I was alone having a wee break. When I complained about her intrusion, she'd said it was the only way she could get the amber delivered to me since my house and yard were teeming with ordinary humans. She wasn't wrong. My four siblings were all over the place. I took the amber, then made her leave so I could finish up. I hadn't had to pee with an audience since Michael was young, and I liked it that way.

I gathered my thoughts and my courage, pulled up my big girl panties, washed my hands because I wasn't a neanderthal, and said, "I will protect the pixies. I will defeat Bogmall. I will master aero-craft."

Marigold was in the kitchen when I came in from the hallway. "You ready, sis?"

"Yep. Where's the rest of the crew?"

"Your coven is waiting for you outside," she told me.

My coven. It sounded ridiculous to my ears. It also sounded lovely. I hadn't been alone, not with Keir and Lu fighting by my side, but having my family act as my coven made me feel like I could face any obstacle the universe threw at me. Of course, whether I survived the spell or not remained to be seen.

I looped my arm in Marigold's, and we walked out the kitchen door into the garden. "Okay, people. It's go time." I waved at Fair Konig. "Get your people, all of them, into the circle. Anyone with pixie dust will have to stay inside the magic barrier until after the rites are concluded, and you guys are safe."

The bearded pixie king set about ordering his troupe to the task. After a minute, he came back. "They are all within the perimeter of the star."

I gave him a reassuring smile that I didn't necessarily feel. "You have to get in there too, Fair Konig. You maybe most of all. You're the creator of the dust and need to be protected as much as anyone else in your troupe."

"But it is my responsibility to keep them safe."

"And the only way to do that is to stop attracting bad guys. If you get in that circle and stay there, the bad guys won't be able to find you."

Annibish flew over and tugged on the pixie king's arm. "We have sworn to put our trust in Iris," she said. "Now we must honor that trust."

He scowled his distaste at hiding, but he didn't argue as Annibish dragged him inside the star.

"Are we ready to do this?" I asked my family, which included Luanne and Keir.

"We're ready when you are," Dahlia, who was used to being in charge, answered.

"Where do you want us?" Keir asked.

I had the stones in a bag, the powder in my

pocket, and the mint leaves in another pocket. I placed Keir on the northern star, as he was my guiding light. Then I had Luanne, Marigold, Rowan, Rose, then Dahlia space out in equal distances around the circle.

"Do we need brooms?" Rose asked.

I shook my head and smiled. Another *Practical Magic* reference. "Not this time." I took the powder and the mint from my pockets. I gave each one of my coven a couple tablespoons of the face powder to hold in their right hands and a chunk of amber and a sprig of crushed mint to hold in their left. "Just hang on to those for now. Concentrate on the ingredients. Think about the reason we use them, protection, clarity, luck, and silence. After the incantation, when I give you the word, I want you to toss the powder into the air."

"Then what happens?" Rowan asked.

"The spells should block all signals and noise from this part of the garden. The pixies will take shifts keeping it stirred up so that the spell lasts. As long as the powder is circulating in this area, it should keep them undetected until their babies are mature enough to leave their mothers' pouches."

There was a series of excited cheers, squeaks, and clicks from the pixies.

I went to the center of the star with my own set of ingredients. "I'm ready to begin." I held my hands up. Instinctually, my coven copied my actions. "I'll say the incantation once, then you guys can join in, okay?"

They agreed.

"In this circle, there is trust that binds. Energy shared from hearts and minds." I centered my thoughts on the people I loved who were in this circle. They'd all shown up for me with barely any questions asked. I'd lied to them for months, and yet, they still supported me. Dahlia was a rod of strength. Rowan was the reed that bends but does not break. Rose was the web that kept us together. Marigold brought the joy of new experiences. Luanne was unwaveringly loyal, and Keir.... Keir was my other half. He was the heart and the soul. With these six by my side, anything was possible. Anything. Including this spell. *"Northwind blows, no sound or signal to hear. Inside this barrier, our path is clear. If danger comes, remain hidden in plain sight, protecting this troupe day and night."*

I repeated the spell as I focused on the silence outside the pentagram. My intention crystallized in my mind. The signal was unchanged, but the spell would act to bounce the signal around inside the area without letting it out into the world.

I said it again, *"In this circle, there is trust that binds. Energy shared from hearts and minds. Northwind blows. No sound or signal to hear. Inside this barrier, our path is clear. If danger comes, remain hidden in plain sight, protecting this troupe day and night."* This time, my coven said it with me, and I could feel their intention as their energy filled me, and I sent it back out in return. After speaking the incantation one more time, I said. "Release the powder."

I threw my handful into the air. The rest of my coven did the same. "Bend to my will," I demanded. The powder shimmered as it circulated in the air.

As several dozen pixies flew in circles inside the pentagram to keep the powder floating, Dahlia began to laugh, then I laughed, and the others all joined in. Even Keir was laughing. The spell had made us all feel....good. Happy, even. So weird and wonderful. Of course, I was still a mess, but I felt like we'd gotten the spell right.

"Did it work?" Rose asked.

"Let's find out." I smiled at her. "Step outside the barrier and see if you can hear us."

Rose set the mint and amber down and walked about ten feet away. "Can you hear me?"

"Yes, I can hear you. I'm supposed to hear you. Can you hear me?" I asked her.

"Holy crap," Rose said. "Are you messing with me?"

Could she hear us? That would mean it hadn't worked. My stomach sank. "Messing with you how?"

"Wow. It's like watching a silent movie." She clapped her hands. "It worked! I can't hear a thing."

Dahlia hugged Rowan. Marigold hugged Lu. I wrapped my arms around Keir and kissed him. "We did it," I said. "We shouldn't have any more unexpected guests."

"Zat is amazing," Linda said from outside the circle. "The spellcraft is magnificent, *Dummer Liebling*."

"Oh, my gosh!" Marigold squealed. "Linda really does talk."

CHAPTER 26

"How is this possible?" I turned to Dahlia. "Can you see and hear Linda?"

"Yes." She blinked several times. "Wow, the gnome is actually alive. Marigold had said she came to life when non-magicals were around, but it's hard to imagine until you see it for yourself."

"She's real, all right. I have the bruises to prove it."

Rowan asked, "How does being around the gnome leave bruises?"

"Because she likes to throw things at me to get my attention."

On that revelation, Linda beaned me with a pebble. "Come outside the barrier, *Kleinkind*. I can't hear what you're saying in there."

I gave Dahlia and Rowan a see-what-I-mean look.

Dahlia actually smiled. "I used to want to throw stuff at you all the time when you were little."

I gave her a flat stare. "All the time, huh?"

She giggled. "Sometimes I still do."

I gave her a sly smile. "One bossy bitch throwing shit at me is plenty."

Another rock hit me in the ear. "Ouch." I whipped around and faced down the gnome. "Stop it."

"I can't hear you," she said. "If you want me to stop, then come out from the barrier."

"Give me a minute. Sheesh." I held up a finger. The middle one.

Linda let out a string of Germanic expletives, but she stopped throwing crap at me.

I turned to the pixies. "If you leave the protection of this spell, I'm not sure if you'll be able to get back in without it rippling the edges. If that happens, your signal may get out again. You have to stay in here. Do you understand?"

Fair Konig nodded. "We will not leave this space."

"Good." I turned to my makeshift coven. "Let's go out one at a time, stepping back from the circle. Try not to take too much powder with you as you go."

"How will we know if the signal is blocked?" Luanne asked.

Good question. It wasn't like we had bad guys to test the success of the spell out with. Then I remembered that both Keir and Zev had said they'd felt the pull of the pixie dust. "Keir and Zev can tell us. If they don't sense the signal outside the circle, then huzzah, success."

One-by-one, my sisters, my brother, my friend, and my soul's companion moved out of the circle's perimeter.

As I prepared to leave, Fair Konig flew over to me. "Iris, your aero-craft is very strong, but I can sense your tenuous hold on the magic."

"You mean the fact that I'm disappearing didn't clue you in?"

His tiny face was serious. "Yes. I apologize for not seeing it sooner. When your magic revived Annibish, I thought it had been on purpose, but now I can see that you are struggling."

Observational skills aside, I could tell Fair Konig was trying to go somewhere with this conversation. "It's okay. Saving Annibish is the one side-effect I can live with. Did you want to tell me something else? This will be our last chance until your children are mature."

"Air is the one element that balances all elements. It's invisible, yet it moves mountains, it feeds flames, it can become liquid, and it makes the spirits soar. You cannot cage the wind. You have to learn to move with it. To direct it." He beat his wings, then drifted for a moment as the currents he created moved him back and up. "Only then can you harness the wind."

I tried to take in everything he was telling me, but

I wasn't sure how I could apply his wisdom to the wild magic taking over my body. "I will try," was the best I could manage.

"Find balance, Iris Everlee," he said. "It doesn't have to be a fight."

Not according to the grimoire, I thought. It had said I had to fight what wasn't there. And it also told me that every element takes a high price from me. I wasn't sure there was a lot of balance to be found in either of those things. "Thank you, Fair Konig, for your counsel." The words sounded formal, but right as I said them.

The pixie bowed deep, a pleased look on his face. "I am ever at your service."

I carefully extracted myself from the pentagram. When I got outside the circle, the concentrated buzzing of the hundreds of pixies was gone. It hadn't faded or died down. It was just....nothing. "Wow."

Keir and Zev had been waiting for me when I exited. "We can't feel the tug of the pixie dust anymore," Keir said. "It worked. You did it."

"I don't know why you're so surprised," I said jokingly. "I bring it every time."

Keir chuckled. "You do indeed."

Luanne had gone inside the house. Rowan, Marigold, Dahlia, and Rose were over by the bench chatting with Linda and her husband, Morlan. I wasn't sure what it meant that the gnome could animate in front of them now. "Have I turned my entire family into tru-craft witches?" I asked Keir.

He shook his head. "No, but you infused us all with a bit of magic." He touched his chest. "I felt it as the spell took shape. You took some of our energy and gave us back some of your power." His voice was filled with astonishment. "It was like nothing I've ever experienced."

"So they aren't going to start disintegrating with wild magic?"

He laughed. "No. Nothing so dramatic. You've made us a true coven. They are part of the magic world now, so Linda can appear to them."

"That's amazing."

He grinned. "You're amazing."

"Not enough." I held up my arms. "I'm still dealing with this wild magic crap."

Zev held out his hand toward my stomach. "May I?" he asked. The first time we'd met, he'd tested my fire by placing his hand on my stomach. Only now, my stomach was a mixture of air glued together with magic.

I'd been reluctant. When he'd searched for my ignis-craft, I'd pulled a Wolverine, and I'd turned my rib bones into weapons and shot his hand full of holes, similar to what I'd done with Jordan.

But now, I trusted Zev not to hurt me. "Go ahead."

He pressed his palm against the air magic that

made up my abdomen and closed his eyes. After a few seconds, he said, "It's still there. I can feel the ignis spark in your stomach."

"What does that mean?"

"It means that beneath all this chaos, you are still there."

I was getting all kinds of sage words from the elementals in my life. "Good to know. Does that mean if it takes me completely over, I'll still be, you know, me?"

"I can't be certain," the ifrit said. "But I think I can feel your fire fighting for you."

It struck me as odd in that moment that I had three active elements. After each one, Linda, Zev, and Fair Konig had come into my life. Earth, fire, and air. All elementals. Linda had introduced herself as my earth guardian to Thomas. Even Keir had called her that when he'd first entered my garden a few months back. Did that mean....?

"Zev, are you my fire guardian?"

His expression transformed into an emotion I hadn't seen on him before. Surprise. He frowned as he thought about my question. Then finally, he nodded. "I think I might be, *Sahira*. That makes the most sense."

"Of what?"

"Of why I feel protective over you and why I haven't required any favors to come to your aid. It is a question I've been pondering for several weeks."

Keir gazed at me curiously. "You think Fair Konig is your air guardian."

"I do. It can't be a coincidence that when an element is sparked that an elemental arrives as sort of a guide."

"What did the pixie king tell you after I left the circle?" he asked.

"He said that air brings balance to every other element and that I couldn't cage it but that it could be directed."

"Like choreography?" Zev inquired.

"More like a conductor," I replied. "Air is the orchestra."

Unlike with the wild earth magic, I wasn't in pain. The aero-craft destroyed by taking away, not adding. I worried that I would turn into nothing if I couldn't find a way to make peace with the chaos. Suddenly, the weight of the past couple of weeks, including the harrowing last few days, settled on me.

"I'm exhausted," I told Keir. "I think I need to lay down for a bit."

"Are you okay?"

"I'm tired, is all. I think the adrenaline of constant danger has worn off. The pixies should be safe for now. There's nothing going on that a few hours of sleep won't cure."

"I'll stay in the garden and keep watch. Just in case anything arrives that might have caught the signal before we suppressed it."

I said my goodbyes to my siblings and thanked them for their help. They'd come through for me like they always had. Once again, I was reminded that blood didn't make family. The Everlees were proof positive.

When they left, I kissed Keir with all the enthusiasm I could muster, which, I admit, wasn't much.

"What does my future look like?" I asked him.

"The possibilities are endless," he told me. He gave my bottom a playful squeeze. "Get some rest. We'll talk more when you get up."

"Hold you to it."

I kissed him again, then went into the house, down the hall, and fell into bed without even taking off my shoes. Within seconds, I was blissfully out.

A ding-dong noise startled me awake. I groaned as I rolled onto my side. It was the doorbell. It sounded again. I waited to see if Keir or Luanne would answer. But nope. At least, I thought, a bad guy wouldn't ring. They'd simply break down the door. I got up and staggered to the bathroom.

The bell went off again. "Just a minute!" I shouted. I peered at my reflection in the mirror. I looked like hammered shit. I wrapped an oversized robe around me. It covered most of the magical chaos.

I hustled to the door as it rang again. Cripes. Whoever it was, he or she was persistent.

I peeked out the living room window. Yolanda

Carver and her daughter Maddie stood at the door. Why were they here?

I opened the door. "Uhm, hi. Can I help you?"

"Oh, I'm sorry, Ms. Everlee. Did we wake you up?"

It was just starting to get dark, which meant I hadn't been asleep for more than an hour.

"I've had a long day," I explained. "Made it an early night."

Maddie looked confused. "Michael texted and asked me to come over."

Yolanda, her dark hair pulled back into a ponytail, was smiling as she stood behind her daughter. "I think he thought it was time for us all to meet properly. I know I've been itching to get to know you."

"That's nice." Why would Michael invite them over here? One, he wasn't home, and two, he knew there was a bunch of shit going down right now. I can't believe he'd be irresponsible enough to ask them to come to the house. Maybe he'd planned this earlier in the week and had forgotten about it. That seemed the most plausible explanation. "I'm afraid our plans have changed. Michael isn't home tonight. I'll call you next week, and we can make a plan."

"Absolutely," Yolanda said. She winced and added, "Can I use your bathroom? We live outside of town, and it's a long drive home for this old bladder."

"Mom," Maddie complained. "That's so embarrassing."

I'd been in the situation myself before, so I wasn't taken aback. "Nope. Not embarrassing at all. Believe me, I completely understand," I said. "Come on in. I hope you don't mind using a teenage boy's bathroom." While I sympathized, I wasn't going to share my own bathroom with a stranger. "It's right up the hall."

"At this point, I'd take a bedpan," Yolanda said.

I laughed. She was funny. Maddie hung back in the living room while I walked her mom through the kitchen to the hall. I played out scenarios where Michael got serious with Maddie. Eventually, after college and a decent job, they'd get married, then Yolanda would be my in-law. I could do worse. I mean, my son could end up with someone like Carla for a monster-in-law.

"It's the first door on the left," I said.

Yolanda wiggled the handle. "It's locked."

I frowned. "It shouldn't be." She moved as I approached the door. I turned the knob, and it opened right up for me. "That's weird. It's unlocked now."

Before I could turn back to the young cheerleader's mom, she pushed me inside Michael's bathroom and incanted the words, "*Outside this house, no sound, no light. Keep all outside from joining this fight.*"

I felt a surge of energy.

"What the hell?" I narrowed my gaze on her, readying myself for a fight. "Why did you shove me?"

My bathrobe had fallen open when she shoved me, exposing the wild magic at play.

"Well, well," she said. "It looks like I've shown up just in time to drink you up, and your tru-craft is doing all the work for me." The woman's churlish snarl turned into a devilish grin. "You won't escape me this time, Iris. No one is coming to your rescue."

Her black hair changed to blonde, and she grew two inches. Her face and eyes transformed as well. I recognized the bitch immediately.

"Bogmall." I pursed my lips as I called to my fire. "I was wondering when you would show up."

CHAPTER 27

"I SEE MY WRAITH HAS DONE ITS JOB WELL." SHE sounded amused. Bogmall stepped into the bathroom like an ex-druid hexenmeister with a death wish. "You've almost destroyed yourself."

I called to the fire in my blood, but I couldn't get my hands to flame on. Flippin' air magic! Zev had said he could still feel it in me, but the aero-craft had replaced my body parts, so there was no blood to borrow heat from. I stepped backward, kicking my shoes off and praying I still had feet. I looked around the bathroom for a weapon or something I could use for a defensive spell. Other than a dirty towel on the floor and hair in the shower drain, it was looking like slim pickings. I wished my grimoire was in there because it was heavy enough that it would hurt the sorcerer if I threw it really hard.

"Don't try to run away. You'll only make me hurt you more."

"Do you practice your evil villain speech in the mirror?"

She laughed maniacally as if to punctuate my point.

"Laugh at this." I called upon the fire in my blood, at least I had some left in my legs, and kicked my foot up and shouted, "Eat fire, bitch." Flames sputtered from my toes. I was trying to torch my nemesis, not light a scented candle. "More fire," I said, shaking my foot. "More freaking flames!" Two feet of orange flames burst from my big toe. *Note to self: If I survive this, practice flaming toes maneuver.*

Bogmall's eyes widened, but she didn't stop smiling. She wiggled her fingers in a way that made me uneasy and recited, "Fire of my foe, my enemy, I command you to come to me."

The flames twisted around on my toes as if yanked. I windmilled backward into the tub and hit my head on the shower tile.

My traitorous fire flew across the bathroom to land in Bogmall's palm. "Interesting," she said as she studied the flames. "You have ignis-craft." She shook her head and smirked. "The rumors are true. You do have more than one element. No wonder you're such a hot commodity, and no wonder so many want you dead."

Her body shimmered, and she changed again to

Yolanda, then just as quickly back to herself. Did tru-craft magic act differently in sorcerers, or was Bogmall in league with someone or something else?

"I'm adorable," I jibed. "No one wants to kill me."

"There's a reason your kind have been hunted to extinction, Iris. Those who can hold more than one element are the most powerful witches. There are many creatures beyond sorcerers who would happily kill you in order to absorb your magic. Including other tru-craft witches."

I frowned as I struggled to get up. The space where my abdomen had been was getting weaker, and it was harder to support myself. Still, I managed to get up to the edge of the tub. "You'll find I'm hard to kill."

"Oh, honey. I find that difficult to believe. You're not that talented. You're just extremely lucky. And judging by the way your magic is wasting you away, I'd say your luck has just about run out."

Luck. Mint was for luck, and I had several crushed leaves in my pocket, still, along with a chunk of amber left over from the sound barrier spell. Damn it, I'd had spell ingredients with me the whole time.

"Mom?" I heard Maddie in the hallway. "Everything okay?"

The girl. I'd forgotten about her. Was she one of Bogmall's cabal of crazy? She seemed awfully young, but that was usually when indoctrination began.

Had she been groomed to seduce my son to get to me?

"Wait in the living room, Maddie. I'll be right there," Bogmall said.

Maddie didn't listen. She rounded the corner and saw the blonde sorcerer holding fire in her hands. Bogmall glared at her. "I told you to wait in the damn living room."

"Who...who are you?" Maddie's voice quivered. "Where's my mom?"

Okay, maybe the girl wasn't in on it. "Run, Maddie," I ordered the girl. "Go to the garden and get help now." I concentrated on the amber and mint. Keep it simple, I reminded myself. "Northwind blows, the door to close."

The door slammed shut.

"Three elements," Bogmall said. "More and more interesting." She conjured a curved knife with a fancy jeweled blade. "It's going to be hard for you to cast spells when I slit your throat."

"You should be afraid of me," I said. "It's dangerous to underestimate me."

"Nothing you conjure can harm me, witch." Her image flickered again. "I'm not actually here. I'm just borrowing the fire witch." She touched the tip of the blade and pricked a finger on her flaming hand. It began to bleed. "If you damage this body, then you'll be harming sweet, innocent Yolanda. If you kill me, you kill her."

The woman was a diabolical psychopath. If Yolanda was an innocent, could I sacrifice her to get rid of Bogmall? I thought of Michael and what would happen to him if I died. If Yolanda was ignis-craft, then Maddie would eventually spark, and she would be left, like me, without a mother to guide her. I couldn't allow that to happen. I had to find another way.

"How are you doing this?" I asked. "Are you possessing her?"

"Like I'm going to tell you," she scoffed. "You're not James Bond, and I'm not Goldfinger, spilling my evil plan so you can foil it."

"At least you admit you're evil," I muttered.

Her eyes flashed with anger for the first time. "You think you are invulnerable, Iris. But you're not. You have too much power and too little will to use it. I'm going to enjoy taking everything away from you. I'm going to delight in it."

"If you don't want to be accused of being evil, you should stop acting evil."

There was a pounding at the door. "Iris!" It was Keir, and the strange way his voice sounded, told me he'd transformed into a gigantic tarry-eyed and fanged bunny-lope. "Let me in!"

Why wasn't he busting down the door? "Keir! It's Bogmall. She's...She's found a way to jump into someone else's body."

His roar shook the walls.

"By the time the forcefield spell wears off, you'll be long dead," Bogmall said, "And I'll be long gone."

I wanted to punch the smirk off her face.

So, I did.

With a lunging left hook, I caught Bogmall with a fist to the side of her mouth. I felt bad for whatever that did to Yolanda, but it wasn't a killing blow. I'd apologize later.

There was a lot of scraping, snarling, and howling going on in the hallway. The forcefield spell was strong if a pooka and an ifrit couldn't get through.

Bogmall jabbed upward with her knife, and it caught me in the stomach. It penetrated the air magic as if it were my body, but I didn't feel anything. Small miracles. Bogmall screamed and dropped the knife as I grabbed her hair and bashed her in the face a couple more times with my dirt-made elbow. "Eat dust, bitch." I smashed her head against the tiled floor, then remembered there was an innocent person in real jeopardy beneath me.

Bogmall thrust her flaming hand at the place where she punctured me, and there was a loud *Boom!* as my midsection exploded, throwing me back and over the toilet seat.

"Iris!" Keir shouted again. "Iris!"

"I'm alive!" Barely, though. Cripes. I couldn't sit up. She'd detonated the wild magic in my midsection as if it had been a powder keg.

Bogmall wiped the side of her mouth as she got

up from the floor. There was a satisfied, smug glint in her eyes as she stalked toward me.

"Not this time, Iris. Nothing and no one can save you now."

What was it that the grimoire had said?

To fight what is not there, first, you must harness the air.

Was Bogmall the thing that was not there? But how could I harness the air? Fair Konig had told me that the wind can't be caged. Maybe I'd been thinking about harness in the wrong way. What else had the grimoire told me?

Bone to earth, blood to fire, with every element the price is higher.

I'd used bone and minerals to bind my terra-craft to me. I'd called on my blood to control fire. With every element, the price is higher.... Could it mean location and not cost? Was it possible that the solution was that simple? But if I tried to tap aero-craft without spelling ingredients, the magic would take its toll on me. The last time, I'd ended up dead for eight minutes. Then I remembered the rest of the grimoires note.

Only fools refuse to use their tools.

Overcome your fear, or you will disappear.

Screw it. If I didn't do this, I would be dead anyway.

I took in a breath and concentrated on my lungs expanding and contracting.

"No," Bogmall seethed. "Not this time." She

bellowed and picked up the knife as she charged me, knocking me back, wedging me in the crevice between the toilet and the vanity.

The move knocked the breath from me. I barely managed to get my arm up as she thrust the knife down in a move that would've sent the blade into my chest. I sucked in another breath, calling the air in my lungs, lungs that were made of aero-craft magic, and I blew it out in Bogmalls direction. The wind, much like the tornado I'd created, was strong and unstoppable. It threw Bogmall across the room and pinned her against the wall. I could feel the magic bolstering my strength as I rose from where I was wedged and floated like Storm from the X-men across the small bathroom to where the woman writhed.

I couldn't kill her. Not without killing Yolanda, but something Fair Konig said gave me an idea. "Air balances all elements," I said. "It moves mountains, it feeds the flames, it creates the rain because it is the storm." I hovered close, my face inches from hers. "And it...it makes the spirit soar." Her cheeks rippled as the wind hit her full in the face. "When I see you next, Bogmall, I will end you." I took another deep breath as I reached out and forced her mouth wide. Into the opening, I breathed out the words, *"Back to your master, soar, spirit, soar. I bind you to her body, your traveling days no more."* I grabbed her by the throat, as fear and rage helped her fight against my spell, until I screamed, *"Bend to my will!"*

Bogmall's eyes rolled back until all I saw were the whites, and her body once again became the dark-haired Yolanda.

I dropped to the floor as I eased Yolanda down. She started to cry.

"I'm sorry," she said. "I'm so sorry. She took me from my coven. I'm from Nevada."

"The Mojave?" That had been where Lu had lost track of her.

"I tried to stop the sorcerer, but I couldn't. She's powerful. So much power. Oh, goddess. What she made me do...I can't...," she sobbed. "I couldn't fight her. She...she threatened Maddie. She would've killed my child." Yolanda shook her head. "Forgive me. Please."

"It's okay," I told her. I knew the lengths I would go to if Michael's life was on the line. "Maddie's safe. And so are you."

The door splintered into thousands of tiny pieces as my giant pooka tore through the frame with his antlers. He looked like the beast of nightmares because he was.

Yolanda screamed, and I put my hand over her mouth to quiet her. I smiled at Keir to reassure him that I was okay and to keep him from killing the ignis-craft witch who had been an unwilling partici-pant in Bogmall's plan.

He shifted down to mostly human, but his black

eyes swirled and bubbled like hot tar pits. "Where's Bogmall?"

I snatched the dirty towel from the floor so he could wrap it around his waist. "Gone," I told him. "She possessed Yolanda and was controlling her."

"How did you get her out?" he asked.

I looked up at him and said, "I finally found my balance."

Zev and Lu came in after him.

"We couldn't get inside," Zev said. "I couldn't break the barrier spell."

Lu, whose hair was flying wild, and her clothes dirty and disheveled, looked as if she had gone to war. "Linda tried to take me in through the ground up, but that failed too." Her eyes widened. "Hey, your arms are back."

I nodded. "I think aero-craft and I are good."

I heard weeping from somewhere down the hall. I took my hand from Yolanda's mouth. "Go to your daughter, Yolanda. She needs you."

The bruised and battered woman scrambled to her feet and fled past Keir, Zev, and Lu to find Maddie.

Keir tugged me up into his arms. "I was so afraid," he said as he nuzzled my ear.

"So was I," I replied. "Until I wasn't." I flattened my palm against his cheek. "I'm all right, Keir." And I knew that it was true. I'd managed to balance earth, air, and fire. And for the first time, I finally began to understand what it was to control the elements. I leaned my head back and went up on my toes. I kissed Keir until my body hummed with energy. Embracing who I was, what I was, felt as if our connection had gone even deeper. When the kiss ended, I smiled at him. "I'm more than all right. I'm really fucking good."

He pressed his forehead to mine. He grinned, his gray eyes crinkled at the corners. "Yeah, you are."

Like me, Keir wasn't afraid anymore. Whatever came next, we would get through it. Together.

CHAPTER 28

Two days later...

"The babies are here!" Rose shouted from the garden. "It's happening!"

I grabbed Keir's arm and dragged him out of the kitchen. One by one, the piskys with their pixie parents began to exit the pentagram area. Annibish chased after a tiny thing, her laughter making my heart burst with joy. "Iverlee," she shouted. "Get back here."

"That girl is going to be a handful," Dahlia muttered. "Much like her godmother."

I didn't care if it was a little dig. I beamed with pride. I might not have hatched the girl or whatever happened in those pouches, but I'd done everything but die to protect them and get them safely into the world.

Linda and her donsy had shown up for the event

as well. Luckily, Michael was at school, so it didn't affect the gnome's ability to animate and enjoy the spectacular finale to the fruit baskets rites. I smiled. I knew what it was called, but in my head, it would always be the time of fruit baskets. I glanced at my oldest sister.

"You know, this won't happen again for a thousand years."

"Really?" she asked.

"Yep. What you're witnessing is a rare phenomenon."

She smiled. "It feels like it." Dahlia slipped her hand into mine. "Thank you, Iris."

"For what?"

"For sharing your life with us." She gave my hand a squeeze before letting go and joining Rose near the circle.

Marigold came over. "Did you know there are children in that group named for all of us? There is a pixie with my name in there." She was wonderstruck.

Frankly, so was I. I can't believe I ever thought of pixies as anything but amazing. I was sad Lu had to miss the extraordinary miracle. She'd taken Yolanda and Maddie back to their coven in Nevada. I knew her swift action had more to do with trying to find Bogmall than transporting the ignis-craft witch and her daughter, but I was glad they had Lu to protect them until they were home safely. Michael had been a little heartbroken, but he and Maddie were going to keep in touch. Yolanda invited me to meet her coven if I was ever in the area. I had a lot to do before that could happen.

I was no longer going to be at the mercy of my magic.

Rowan was laughing and joking with Keir. Even Zev seemed happy. The only thing missing was my dad. I wanted him to see this part of my life. To be a part of it. But like with Michael, his presence would've made it impossible for the gnomes to be here. Linda and her donsy had earned the right to see the pixies' rites to the end, and I wasn't going to take it from them.

I'd made a promise to myself that I would make sure Dad got to experience so many wonders. I wouldn't distance myself from him or any of my family again. Not ever.

How the worst weekend had turned into the best week was beyond me, but I was going to take it. In a week, I would go to the Iron Grove. I'd visit Thomas and meet the archdruid, Keir's grandmother. It was the only cost the aero-craft witch had asked for when he'd offered me his wisdom and his advice. I agreed to stay for one week. After all we'd been through the past few months, it seemed like a small price to pay.

Fair Konig flew over to me. He held out a small silky pouch. "This is for you, Iris Everlee."

"What is it?"

"It's my part of the bargain. It is the ritual

payment for those who protect us when we are unable to protect ourselves."

I took the tiny pouch and examined it. "It's cute."

"It's *feenstaub*," he said.

I blanched. "Pixie dust?" Aka magic stem cells. "I can't accept this."

"Yes, you can." He stroked his beard. "I will be offended if you don't."

"But won't it bring all the monsters to my yard?"

"No. There isn't enough there to put off a signal, as you call it. It's just enough for a small miracle if you need it."

My voice was hoarse with emotion. "Thank you, Fair Konig. I accept."

His wings hummed loudly as he flushed with pleasure. Annibish yelled, "Iverlee!"

Fair Konig grinned. "I better go help."

"Good idea." I walked the garden path to my kitchen and went inside. I didn't want to lose or misplace the pixie dust, so I took it back to my room and put the dust in my closet safe. It would be my rainy day stash. Hopefully, I would never need it, but it was nice to know it was there.

My grimoire was on my bed where I'd left it. I was no longer afraid of the book. I wrote all the air spells I had crafted over the past few days. The book, if a book could have feelings, seemed much happier with me as well. Bob was on his back next to it, licking his chest as he wiggled back and forth in an effort to groom himself.

I sat down and picked up the grimoire. It had three symbols, earth, fire, and air. It stood to reason that I had the potential for five elements. The next one, the one that had been calling to me, was nero-craft. I glanced over at Bob and gave his belly a rub to steel my nerves.

Then I licked my thumb and wiped a trail of spit over the leather-bound cover. "Water," I said. My heart fluttered as an inverted triangle began to glow as it joined the other three symbols. "Yes," I hissed.

"What are you up to?" Keir stood in the doorway, and for a moment, I felt like a kid caught stealing candy from the store.

"I sparked nero-craft," I told him.

He shook his head, a smile tugging at his lips, then said, "Well, shit."

THE END...UNTIL *Spell Over Troubled Water*

NOTE FROM RENEE:

Hi, Readers!

If you enjoyed **When The Spell Blows**, I would love for you to help me get the word out to other readers. There are a couple of easy ways to make this happen:

- Tell your friends and family who read fantasy, paranormal, and romance books about the series. **Word of mouth** is a great way for other readers to learn about books they wouldn't otherwise find!
- And, if you have a moment, please **leave a review** at your favorite book retailer!

It goes without saying, but I'll say it anyways, readers and fans of my books are the #1 reason I love my job. So **thank you so much** for your enthusiasm for my worlds, and thank you for buying this book!

Hugs and gratitude,

Renee George

PARANORMAL MYSTERIES & ROMANCES
BY RENEE GEORGE

Grimoires of a Middle-aged Witch
https://www.renee-george.com/GMW
Earth Spells Are Easy
Spell On Fire
When the Spells Blows
Spell Over Troubled Water
Ghost in the Spell

Nora Black Midlife Psychic Mysteries
www.norablackmysteries.com
Sense & Scent Ability (Book 1)
For Whom the Smell Tolls (Book 2)
War of the Noses (Book 3)
Aroma With A View (Book 4)

Peculiar Mysteries
www.peculiarmysteries.com

You've Got Tail (Book 1)

My Furry Valentine (Book 2)

Thank You For Not Shifting (Book 3)

My Hairy Halloween (Book 4)

In the Midnight Howl (Book 5)

My Peculiar Road Trip (Magic & Mayhem) (Book 6)

Furred Lines (Book7)

My Wolfy Wedding (Book 8)

Who Let The Wolves Out? (Book 9)

My Thanksgiving Faux Paw (Book 10)

Witchin' Impossible Cozy Mysteries

https://www.renee-george.com/WitchinMysteries

Witchin' Impossible (Book 1)

Rogue Coven (Book 2)

Familiar Protocol (Booke 3)

Mr & Mrs. Shift (Book 4)

Barkside of the Moon Mysteries

www.barksideofthemoonmysteries.com

Pit Perfect Murder (Book 1)

Murder & The Money Pit (Book 2)

The Pit List Murders (Book 3)

Pit & Miss Murder (Book 4)

The Prune Pit Murder (Book 5)

Two Pits and A Little Murder (Book 6)

Pits and Pieces of Murder (Book 7)

Madder Than Hell

https://www.renee-george.com/MadderThanHell

Gone With The Minion (Book 1)

Devil On A Hot Tin Roof (Book 2)

A Street Car Named Demonic (Book 3)

Hex Drive

https://www.renee-george.com/hex-drive-series

Hex Me, Baby, One More Time (Book 1)

Oops, I Hexed It Again (Book 2)

I Want Your Hex (Book 3)

Hex Me With Your Best Shot (Book 4)

Hex Me All Night Long (Book 5)

ABOUT THE AUTHOR

I am a USA Today Bestselling author who writes paranormal mysteries and romances because I love all things whodunit, Otherworldly, and weird. Also, I wish my pittie, the adorable Kona Princess Warrior, and my beagle, Josie the Incontinent Princess, could talk. Or at least be more like Scooby-Doo and help me unmask villains at the haunted house up the street.

When I'm not writing about mystery-solving werecougars or the adventures of a hapless psychic living among shapeshifters, I am preyed upon by stray kittens who end up living in my house because I can't say no to those sweet, furry faces. (Someone stop telling them where I live!)

I live in Mid-Missouri with my family and I spend my non-writing time doing really cool stuff...like watching TV and cleaning up dog poop

Follow Renee!
Bookbub
Renee's Rebel Readers FB Group
Newsletter